ECHOES OF THE PAST

ASHLEY FARLEY

ALSO BY ASHLEY FARLEY

Marsh Point

Long Journey Home

Songbird's Second Chance

Heart of Lowcountry

After the Storm

Scent of Magnolia

Virginia Vineyards

Love Child

Blind Love

Forbidden Love

Love and War

Palmetto Island

Muddy Bottom

Change of Tides

Lowcountry on My Mind

Sail Away

Hope Springs Series

Dream Big, Stella!

Show Me the Way

Mistletoe and Wedding Bells

Matters of the Heart

Road to New Beginnings

Stand Alone

On My Terms

Tangled in Ivy

Lies that Bind

Life on Loan

Only One Life

Home for Wounded Hearts

Nell and Lady

Sweet Tea Tuesdays

Saving Ben

Sweeney Sisters Series

Saturdays at Sweeney's

Tangle of Strings

Boots and Bedlam

Lowcountry Stranger

Her Sister's Shoes

Magnolia Series

Beyond the Garden

Magnolia Nights

Scottie's Adventures

Breaking the Story

Merry Mary

ONE
WILL

I don't understand women. Females are as foreign to me as green Martians from out of space. With three older sisters, I should have insider knowledge of menstrual cycles and fashion and friendship drama. But my sisters are six, eight, and ten years older than me. I've never had a normal sibling relationship with them. There was certainly nothing ordinary about our family.

I considered my wife a real girly girl. Although Tracy didn't wear her femininity like a badge, as though she had something to prove. She was the quintessential Southern girl—pretty and sweet on the inside and out. She owned a boutique specializing in women's fashions, never left home without her face on, and paid a stylist four hundred dollars every eight weeks to dye her hair the perfect shade of blonde.

Tracy insisted I help with our young daughters, but I almost always screwed things up. I got shampoo in their eyes at bath time and chose the wrong color combinations for their clothes. And now, in getting my two-year-old ready for her first day of preschool, I've gotten the round hairbrush stuck in her unruly mass of sandy waves. I twist the brush, trying to untangle it, but it becomes even more embedded in the rat's nest.

"Ouch, Daddy! That hurts," screeches Sophie.

Caroline, my four-year-old, stands patiently next to me with hairbands in hand, waiting for her turn with the brush. "This isn't good, Daddy. What're you gonna do?"

"I'm not sure. Do you have any ideas?"

Caroline looks up at me with blue eyes so like my own. "You could try the detangle spray."

"Detangle spray? I've never heard of such a thing."

"It sometimes works. Except . . . " She furrows her brow. "I forgot. We ran out."

The toaster pops up, and I glance over at the charred pieces of bread. "Great," I mutter under my breath.

Caroline follows my gaze. "Dad! You burned the toast again."

"I'm sorry, honey. I don't have time to make more. You'll have to eat a Pop-Tart."

"But you got the wrong kind," Caroline whines. "Mama always buys the ones with frosting."

It's been six weeks since Tracy died, yet the girls still referred to their mama in the present.

When I twist the brush again, Sophie lets out a scream that echoes throughout the house, making my ears ring and my heart pound against my rib cage. Opening the utensil drawer, I remove a pair of kitchen scissors and cut the brush out of her hair.

Caroline gasps, her eyes wide at the sight of the gaping hole in the back of her sister's hair.

The ringing of the doorbell is followed by a loud knocking.

"Who's that?" Sophie asks, completely unaware of the havoc I've wreaked on her hair.

"Probably Miss Ellie," I say. "She's picking you up for school."

Caroline pouts. "Can't you drive us? Mommy always takes me on the first day."

"Not today, sweetheart. Miss Ellie was kind enough to offer, and we don't want to hurt her feelings."

The clicking of heels on hardwood precedes Ellie's appearance in the kitchen doorway. "Is everything all right in here? I thought I heard someone scream."

Caroline blurts, "Dad got the brush stuck in Sophie's hair. He cut it out with the scissors."

Sophie's eyes dart from me to the brush in my hand. Her tiny hand reaches behind her head, feeling for the hair that's no longer there. She whimpers and big tears fill her pale eyes. I feel like crying too. It hurts how much she reminds me of her mama.

Ellie teeters on her heels as she enters the room. "Here, honey. We can fix that right up." She takes a hair band from Caroline and smooths what's left of Sophie's messy waves into a ponytail. "There. Now. All set. Are you going by Sophie now, not Sophia?"

"Caroline started that," I explain. "It fits her personality."

Caroline hands Ellie the other hairband. "Will you please do mine? I don't want Daddy touching my hair."

"Sure, sweetheart." Ellie fastens Caroline's hair back in a ponytail. "Where's Kayla?" she asks about our most recent nanny.

Caroline doesn't give me a chance to answer. "Daddy made her quit."

I give my daughter a scolding glare. "I didn't make her quit, Caroline. She and I had a little misunderstanding."

Ellie cups my cheek in her hand. "You poor, dear man. You have so much on your plate."

"We're fine," I say, brushing her hand away. I drop the hairbrush in the trash can and open the pantry in search of Pop-Tarts. I tear open the silver package and hand strawberry Pop-Tarts to each of the girls. With a curled lip, Caroline bites off a corner while Sophie gobbles hers down, her hair seemingly forgotten.

Leaning back against the counter, I notice Ellie's attire—a flowery summer frock with gold-heeled sandals and blonde hair piled high on top of her head. Tracy always wore yoga clothes when driving car pool. "Why are you so dressed up?"

The faint blush that creeps across her cheeks tells me her effort was for my benefit. "Is it a crime for a girl to wanna look pretty?" she asks, a seductive smile playing on her lips.

I shrug. "I thought maybe there was an opening ceremony at school I'm supposed to attend."

Her smile disappears. "No, parents' night is next week."

The small town of Water's Edge has a surprising number of divorcees, most of whom have shamelessly let me know they're interested in dating me when the time comes. I've made myself clear that time is way off in the future. If ever.

I pop a pod into the coffeemaker. "Why are the kids starting school today anyway? Wouldn't it make sense to wait until after Labor Day?"

"I agree." Ellie giggles. "They should've asked us for our opinions."

"I know why they didn't ask me," I grumbled. I'm not an authority on anything relating to kids. "Since I no longer have a nanny, I guess I'll be picking them up. What time does school get out?"

"At noon. I have nothing urgent on my calendar today, and I'm happy to drive both ways. If you'd like, I can arrange an appointment for Sophie with my hairstylist."

"That would be great. Better your hairstylist than my barber. Does the preschool have an after-school program?"

"They do. But space is limited, and demand is high. Although, in your case, they may make an exception. It's worth giving them a call. Ask for the headmistress, Betty Bleaker."

The name brings about a glimmer of hope. "I know Betty well. I've done work for her over the years, most recently a kitchen renovation several years back."

Ellie winks at me. "Always helps to know someone in charge." She shepherds the girls towards the door. "We need to get going. Poor Zoe is waiting in the car." Over her shoulder, she calls to me, "Too-da-loo."

I wait until I hear the front door close before dropping to a chair at the breakfast table. Setting my phone down in front of me, I call the nanny service on speaker and ask the operator to connect me to the director. When Susan Steele comes on the line, I can tell by her abrupt tone she's not happy to hear from me.

I cut right to the chase. "I'm calling about a replacement. I assume you heard what happened with Kayla."

Susan clears her throat. "I heard Kayla's side of the story, Mr. Darby. I'd like to hear yours."

"Of course." I fall back in my chair with my coffee. "I came home late from work and found my girls watching television at nine o'clock."

"And . . ."

"And that's well past their bedtime. Their mother kept our girls on a strict schedule."

"I agree schedules are important, Mr. Darby. But Kayla claims they were watching a special program, and the girls really wanted to finish it. She says you overreacted, that your anger scared her."

"Humph. Maybe she shouldn't be so sensitive."

"You said the same about Kellie when you reprimanded her for making a mess in your kitchen."

"A mess? A tornado would've caused less damage to my kitchen. My wife was a fanatic about cleanliness. I'm accustomed to having a tidy home."

"They were making cookies, Mr. Darby. Baking creates messes. She cleaned up afterward, did she not?"

"That's beside the point." I draw circles on the table with my finger. "The girls are cranky during the day when they don't get a proper night's sleep. And today was the first day of school. Forgive me for wanting them to be well rested."

"The crime isn't the issue, Mr. Darby. Your response to the offense was inappropriate."

I sense my frustration mounting. I need to get off the phone before I lose it with this woman. "Whatever, Mrs. Steele. You're right. I'm an awful person. Just send me someone new."

"You've been through three nannies in six weeks. *If* I had a replacement to send you, I'm not sure I would. Unfortunately, I'm fresh out."

"Fine. I'll find a new nanny service."

"The problem isn't with my service or my nannies. The problem, Mr. Darby, is you," she says and hangs up on me before I can argue.

The second call to Betty Bleaker goes better. She's sympathetic when I explain I'm in a bind and need to enroll my girls in the after-school program. "I understand your situation, Mr. Darby. I adored your wife, and I'd like to help. As of now, our program is filled. But that is liable to change next week. Give me a few days, and I'll call you back."

"Thanks, Betty. Anything you can do would be great, even if it's only a couple of days a week."

Pushing back from the table, I pace the kitchen floor while I finish my coffee. Getting the girls into the after-school program would take care of our immediate needs. I'll be home with them at night, and I don't work on weekends. I'm not a fan of having young nannies in the house anyway. They leave their long hairs in the shower drain and talk to their friends on the phone late at night. And despite what Susan Steele says, they are so overly sensitive. I refuse to turn my girls into snowflakes. I will toughen them up, so they don't cry every time someone looks at them wrong.

The girls and I are better off going it alone for now. Unfortunately, I suspect that going alone means more disasters like the hairbrush incident.

TWO
JULIA

My husband's trial is a bona fide media circus. Many believe Judge Guzman's decision to allow cameras in the court-room is a strategic move to draw attention to the escalating human trafficking crisis in our country. But after watching her preside over the trial for weeks, I think she's grandstanding, enjoying her moment in the limelight. Immediately following the jury's guilty verdict yesterday, the judge announced the sentencing hearing for this morning. Delaying the sentencing would cause the thousands of reporters camped out in front of the courthouse to lose interest in the case.

I'm watching her closing remarks on television from the dingy apartment that has been my home for four months. She's been going on for over two hours about the atrocities of human trafficking. I hold my breath as she announces Grady's sentence—two hundred and forty years in prison. My emotions are mixed as she slams down her gavel and declares the court dismissed. I'm not surprised. I fully expected him to get the maximum. I'm bewildered, even though I've had months to come to terms with my husband's crimes. And devastated that our beautiful life together has ended.

Eleanor comes to stand beside me with the TV remote in hand. She powers off the television. "It's over. He's going to prison for life."

"It's not fair that I got the same life sentence as him when I've done nothing wrong."

"It may feel that way now, Julia, but once you get where you're going, you will have more freedom. This chapter of your life is ending, but another one is just beginning."

"Yeah, right." I'm sick of her psychobabble. She's a nice person, and she means well, but she doesn't know what it's like to walk in my shoes.

Eleanor sets the remote down on the coffee table. "Have you finished packing? We need to leave soon. We have a long trip ahead of us."

"I'm ready, but I have to help Conrad get his things together." I don't bother asking her where we're going. She won't tell me.

Getting up from the sofa, I cross the living room into the adjacent kitchen where my four-year-old son is seated at the small Formica table eating a bowl of Froot Loops. I've lost weight these past months. My slim figure is now borderline anorexic. But the pounds I've lost, Conrad has gained from eating junk food and greasy takeout and not getting enough exercise. Once a week, I give Eleanor my grocery list of fresh fruits and vegetables. But she never returns from the store with any of the items I've requested. I don't blame her. She does the best she can on her strict budget.

I don't recognize my son without his mess of curls. Any more than I recognize my reflection in the mirror. With my hair now boy short and dyed the same mahogany hue as his, I could be Conrad's much older brother.

I sit down opposite him and reach across the table for his small hand. "Are you ready to take off on our adventure?"

"Is Daddy coming with us?" His big brown eyes fill with tears. He knows the answer. But it doesn't stop him from asking the question.

"No, son. We've talked about this. Daddy has to go away for a very long time."

Conrad wrenches his hand free of mine and stuffs it in the baseball glove on the table beside him. He covets the cheap glove and wooden bat, both gifts from his father on his fourth birthday six months ago, the only items Eleanor allowed him to bring with him from our former lives. My husband was the star pitcher in high school. When his parents were killed in a car accident, he gave up his chance of playing in college to take over the family business. He often spoke about our son fulfilling his abandoned dream.

Looking past my son, I stare out the grime-smeared window at the city of Austin. Aside from my visit to the courthouse, I haven't left this apartment since I turned my husband into the police, and we entered Witness Protection at the beginning of May. Because of the sensitive nature of the case, the prosecution pressured the judge for a speedy trial. Eager for her moment of fame, Judge Guzman eagerly complied.

Conrad strokes his baseball bat. "I don't wanna go to Adventure, Mommy. Why can't we go back to the farm?"

"I wish we could, sweetheart. But the farm belongs to someone else now." I haven't asked, and no one has told me what will become of the small farm Grady inherited from his parents. I assume someone will sell the property on Grady's behalf and the money will go into a trust for him.

I long for the farming life, rising with the roosters and going to bed before dark. But Grady ruined everything for all of us.

"Will Adventure be cold?" Conrad asks.

I smile softly at his use of the word *Adventure*, as though it is a destination and not an exciting trip. "Not necessarily. Adventure may be warm year-round so we can play outside every single day."

Conrad's eyes get big. "Do you think so really?"

"There's a chance. We'll find out when we get there."

I've never known a life outside of Austin. I was raised here, and when I married my high school sweetheart, I moved from my daddy's house to my husband's farm. To think I can never go home again both saddens and terrifies me. I will never again see my parents or my two sisters or any of my nieces and nephews. Our future is out of my control. But one thing is for certain: I will always look over my shoulder for the men I saw that godforsaken night, the night that changed our lives forever.

With a heavy heart, I push back from the table and take my son's empty cereal bowl to the sink. "Come on, son. Let's gather your things."

Conrad traipses through the apartment to the room we share. We take less than ten minutes to pack his belongings—a toothbrush, the articles of clothing Eleanor has purchased for him, and his small collection of activity books and toys.

Before exiting the apartment, Eleanor hands me a small envelope. "If for any reason we get separated, you'll need your new identification documents."

I zip the envelope into my purse. "Have you found out anything about my royalties?"

Eleanor gives her head a solemn shake. "I'm still working on it. I should know more in a day or two."

"You promised, Eleanor." My loss of income is a source of contention between us. I'm an indie author of over twenty cozy mysteries that earn me several thousand dollars a month. For me to continue receiving my royalties, the government needs to determine a way to pay taxes owed and safely transfer the rest into a trust for me.

"I'm aware, Julia. And I'm making good on that promise. I'm hopeful we will have our answers soon." She scoops Conrad into her arms. "Here we go. Stay close to me."

U.S. Marshals carefully execute our departure from the building by holding elevator doors, sweeping us through the lobby, and escorting us to a waiting caravan of three black Suburbans. We're directed to the middle of the three, where another marshal occupies the front passenger seat. I smile at him and he nods at me, but he doesn't speak.

Eleanor buckles herself into the driver's seat and speeds away from the curb. Tears stream down my cheeks as we drive through the streets of my hometown one last time.

A tiny voice in the seat beside me asks, "Why are you crying, Mommy? I thought you were excited to go to Adventure."

I force a smile. "I am, sweetheart. Just a little sad to be leaving Austin. But don't worry. I'll be fine." I pull my tablet out of my purse and hand it to him.

I never had to restrict his screen time when we lived on the farm. We rarely watched television or played video games. Since entering Witness Protection, however, all he's done is play video games. Eleanor promises *freedom,* but our lives will never be normal.

I wait until we've left the city limits of Austin before dumping the contents of the envelope Eleanor gave me into my lap—new Social Security cards and birth certificates for both of us, and a government identification card for me. Also included is a prepaid credit card worth several hundred dollars."

I run my finger across the names on the birth certificates. Julia and Conrad Becker. Casey and Levi Bishop have ceased to exist. Mother and son have vanished into thin air.

THREE
WILL

I'm at the construction site for a multimillion-dollar home on Sandy Island when a patrol car pulls up, and the young officer I've been spending too much time with lately gets out.

Cody tips his hat at me. "Afternoon, Will."

I give him a curt nod. "Cody. I assume this isn't a social call."

Cody's cheeks blush as he shakes his head. "Sorry, sir. Detective Marlowe needs to see you at the station. Do you need a ride?"

"Nah. I'm heading back to town now anyway. Tell Marlowe I'll be there in a few minutes." I roll up the blueprints for the house and slide them into a cardboard tube.

Maurice appears at my side. "Is everything all right, boss?"

"Marlowe wants to see me again. I don't know why the police can't let Tracy rest in peace." I clap Maurice's shoulder. "You're doing an excellent job here, as usual. Keep up the good work."

"You can always count on me, boss. If you need anything, you let me know."

"I will. And I appreciate your support." I feel Maurice's hazel eyes on me as I make my way to my pickup truck. Maurice has worked for Darby Custom Homes since my father first started the company fifty years ago. At the time, Maurice was a teenager, right out of high school, and while he's pushing seventy now, he's still going strong. Not only is he my most valuable foreman, he's one of my best friends, more of a father figure to me than my dad. He's worried, as am I, about the continued harassment by the police into my wife's accidental death.

I leave Sandy Island and cross back over the Merriweather Bridge into town. The bridge is named after my ancestor, one of the town's founding fathers. Prestigious men and women, senators and lawyers and renowned community volunteers make up the branches of my family tree. At least on the branches above my immediate family. My mom, Eileen Merriweather Darby, was the last to carry the family name and the first to tarnish it by being a drunk.

Coming off the bridge, I take a left onto Main Street. I admire the attractive buildings, a mixture of old and new, that house businesses like gourmet shops, boutiques, and flower stores. Coastal Hardware, one of the few establishments I frequent, takes up an entire city block on Main Street.

While my achievements may not match the grandeur of my forefathers', my specialized knowledge in historic preservation plays a crucial role in safeguarding the charming character of our small southern town.

I park my truck in front of the police station and enter the building, asking at the front desk for Detective Marlowe. The rookie officer shows me to the now-familiar interview room.

"Detective Marlowe will be right with you," he says on his way out.

I thumb my nose at whoever is watching me from the other side of the two-way mirror before taking a seat at the table.

I wait ten minutes before Marlowe enters the room. "Afternoon, Will. How are you?" he asks, his tall frame looming over me.

"I've been better. My patience is wearing thin, Detective. I don't know what else I could possibly tell you about my wife's accident."

Marlowe glances at the two-way mirror. "Let's take a walk. I need some fresh air."

I follow him out of the interview room and down a long hallway. I wait outside the break room as he darts inside and retrieves two bottled waters. He hands me a water, and we exit the building through the back door.

I stop walking when we reach the parking lot. "Are we going somewhere, Detective?"

"We can if you want. My car's right over there." He sweeps an arm at the parking lot of patrol cars and nondescript sedans. "Or we can talk here. Either way, I thought it best to have this conversation in private."

I frown. "Why? What's wrong? Has there been a new development in my wife's case?"

The detective takes a long pull from his water bottle. "I'll be straight with you, Will. While the evidence is consistent with your story, your wife's head injury is a gray area."

Dread knots my gut. "What do you mean?"

"Because there was no water in her lungs, we can confirm that she died from a blow to the head. However, since you and Tracy were the only ones on the boat, there are no witnesses to corroborate your story. I'm getting pressure to file homicide charges against you, predicated on the allegation that you struck your wife with a blunt instrument."

"Damn it!" I hurl the half-full water bottle across the parking lot.

Two police officers on the far side of the parking lot look our way.

Marlowe places a hand on my shoulder. "Shh, Will! I realize you're upset, but you need to calm down."

Shrugging off his hand, I collapse against the side of a patrol car. "You have no idea how upset I am. I loved Tracy. I did not kill her. Who is pressuring you?"

Marlowe lowers his voice. "Chief Dorsey for starters. Although

I have a hunch someone higher up is putting the squeeze on him." Marlowe leans against the car beside me. "This feels personal to me, Will. Are you aware of anyone who may have a vendetta against you?"

I give my head a grave shake. "Not anyone who would send me to prison for a crime I didn't commit."

"This is my case and my reputation at stake. Regardless of how much they pressure me, I refuse to arrest you without rock-solid evidence."

My shoulders sag as a wave of relief washes over me. "Thanks."

Marlowe pushes off the car. "I can't guarantee you won't be arrested in the future, but it won't be me bringing the charges."

The back door to the police station swings open and Cody sticks out his head. "Detective! Come quick! Reporters have mobbed the front of the station. Someone leaked to the press about Will's arrest."

Marlowe's face tightens. "That's odd. Even more reason to believe someone with a lot of authority is pulling strings."

"What do we do?"

"I'm going to make a statement to the press. I want you to stick close to me," the detective says and leads me back through the station.

Reporters with camera crews swarm the front steps of the police station. Silence spreads throughout the crowd when we appear at the top of the stairs. In a loud and clear voice, Detective Marlowe says, "Thank you for your interest in this case, but I'm sorry to say someone has given you incorrect information. There is no evidence Will Darby is responsible in any way for his wife's death. A storm came up while they were out in their boat. Tracy was driving at the time. She turned into a giant wave and lost her balance. We believe she hit her head on the side of the boat when she went overboard. As far as I'm concerned, the case is closed. I'm ruling Tracy Darby's death accidental."

The reporters all talk at once, calling out questions the detective refuses to answer.

"I'll walk with you to your truck." The detective takes hold of my elbow and guides me through the mob.

We're nearing the bottom step when a young man with a mop of curly brown hair holds his phone in my face, presumably using the phone's video recorder. "Why did you kill your wife, Will? Is it true she was planning to leave you? Were you having an affair with another woman?"

Anger surges through me. Smacking his phone away, I grab a fistful of his shirt and rear back my fist.

Marlowe grabs my hand, preventing me from punching the reporter.

"Let it go, Will. This little punk is not worth the trouble." Marlowe clamps a hand onto my arm and drags me out to my truck. "You need to control your anger, man. I've been watching you these past few weeks. You're a rumbling volcano. If you don't get a hold of your emotions, you could lose everything. That little scene you just caused will end up all over social media. I understand your in-laws are suing for custody of your daughters. If that's true, this is the last thing you want them to see. I'm willing to help you, but not if you're gonna act like that."

"I don't need your help." I wrench my arm free of his grip and get in my truck. As I speed away from the station, I punch the roof of my truck. The truth is, I do need Marlowe's help. Without it, I could go to prison for a crime I didn't commit.

FOUR
JULIA

I fall into a deep sleep a few miles outside of El Paso. When I wake several hours later, we're passing through Lubbock. I suspected we would be traveling north. Winter apparel—stocking caps, scarves, and parkas—will make hiding our identities easier. But I'm disappointed just the same. I was foolishly hoping for a balmy climate, someplace tropical with palm trees and ocean breezes.

I glance over at my son, who is snoring softly in the seat beside me. Our escorts, the Suburbans in front and behind us, are now gone, and Eleanor is having a quiet but heated political discussion with the nameless marshal in the passenger seat.

I remove my computer from my bag and open it on my lap. Eleanor confiscated all my Apple devices and exchanged them for a cheap Dell computer and an Android phone and tablet. I look down at the blank document in my writing app. I haven't written a word in four months. To connect with my characters, I need a peaceful setting, which the dingy apartment in Austin failed to provide. I miss the farm more than I ever thought possible. The rolling hills and grasslands, the bluebonnets that blanket the area in the spring, offered the tranquility I needed to write my first twenty cozy mysteries.

"Mommy, I have to go potty," my son says, his face flushed from sleep.

"Okay, sweetheart." I tap Eleanor on the shoulder. "Le—" I stop myself from calling my son by his real name. "Conrad needs to use the restroom."

"Here." The marshal tosses me an empty Styrofoam cup. "Tell him to use this!"

I throw the cup back at him. "Forget it. Besides, I need to pee too. Who are you anyway?"

"U.S. Marshal Roderick Painter. You can call me Rod. I'll be taking over your case when we get to Denver."

My mouth falls open. Eleanor is abandoning us? I've trusted her with my life for four months, and she's turning us over to this arrogant jerk. "Is Denver our final destination?"

"Not hardly," he says with a huff of sarcasm. "Austin to Denver is the first leg of our very long journey. But it's the end of the road for Eleanor. She'll return to Austin tomorrow morning, and I'll continue with you to your destination."

My throat swells. I always assumed Eleanor would stay with us until . . . Until when? Until forever. She's too professional to talk about herself, and I've been too self-absorbed to ask about her personal life. I'm sure she has a spouse and children. She would never dessert her family for us. We're just another case for her. She will return to her ordinary life and soon forget about us.

Rod shifts in his seat to face me, his beady black eyes creeping me out. "We're on a tight schedule, which means you need to suck it up and pee in the cup," he says, tossing the cup back to me.

I crush the Styrofoam cup and drop it on the floor. "I assume tight schedule means you're getting a bonus if you deliver us to our destination early."

His cheeks redden, letting me know I'd hit on the truth.

We pass a road sign announcing multiple convenience stores at the next exit. I tap Eleanor's shoulder. "Look! There are several options for restrooms at the next exit."

"I'm on it. We need gas anyway," she says and speeds across two lanes of traffic to the exit.

"Whatever. But make it quick," Rod says, turning back to face the front.

I glare at the back of his head, my dislike for this guy swelling inside of me.

Eleanor drives to the convenience store farthest from the highway, pulls up to a gas pump, and hands Rod a credit card. "Fill her up."

Inside the store, she leads us to the restrooms at the back, making certain the ladies' room is empty and locking the door behind us. I search for Eleanor's reflection in the mirror as I'm washing my hands. "Why didn't you tell me you were leaving us?"

She looks at me over the top of her blue eyeglass frames. "By now, you should be fully aware that I operate on a strict need-to-know basis."

"I'm aware." I dig a wet thumb into my chest. "But *I* need to know if Mr. Personality is capable of protecting us."

"Of course. Rod worked for the Secret Service for ten years, the last three on the vice president's detail."

I snatch a brown paper towel out of the dispenser. "So he's new to WITSEC?"

She flaps her hand in the so-so gesture. "Fairly. But he's capable."

"He's on-the-job training at our expense," I mumble, balling up the paper towel and tossing it into the trash can.

"Calm down, Julia. Your safety is our priority."

"How high is that priority, Eleanor?"

Her blank expression tells me everything I need to know.

"That's what I thought." I help Conrad wash his hands, and we exit the restroom.

Conrad chooses a package of Fig Newtons and a bottle of

apple juice, which I pay for with the prepaid credit card Eleanor gave me. This is the first purchase I've made in four months. One of many simple daily acts that have now become anomalies. While I'll never get my old life back, I'd be satisfied with some semblance of normalcy. I have a hunch that what Witness Protection has in store for me is nothing of the sort.

I've never left the state of Texas, and as we travel deeper into Colorado, I glue my eyes to the mountainous scenery passing outside my car window. Growing up, our vacations were limited to annual trips to Rockport Beach during the summers. On the farm, leaving our crops and animals unattended wasn't an option. I wonder for the millionth time what has become of our horses, goats, and chickens. Having to leave behind our border collie, Lucy, nearly broke my heart. Once we get settled, I'll get us a new dog.

I think back six months to the first night I heard the murmured voices in my kitchen. Sneaking out of my bedroom, I crouched down at the top of the stairs, but I couldn't make out what they were saying. I suspected they were involved in something illegal. I feared my husband was dealing arms or drugs. Why else would they be meeting in a remote farmhouse in the middle of the night? Then about a month later, when I got up during the night to pee, I spotted headlights in the driveway. I followed the sound of their rumbling engines a quarter mile to our barn and watched in horror as the men from my kitchen transported the anguished-faced women and children from a passenger van into our root cellar.

Smuggling guns and drugs is one thing, but I could not tolerate human trafficking. As much as I loved Grady, I didn't think twice about turning him in to the police. The image of the uniformed officers hauling Grady off in handcuffs will forever be etched in my brain. I'll never forgive him for what he did to me. For ruining our lives. For playing me for a fool in thinking he could run his human trafficking operation right under my nose.

The nature of the crime made Grady's a federal case. The men I heard in my kitchen and saw at my barn belong to a cartel. They are thugs who do the dirty work for an organization known as The Six, the modern-day mafia, an elite club of six men whose identities remain a secret even from our government.

The justice department offered Grady a plea deal to turn state's evidence against the members of the cartel. But he refused. I assume out of fear. I've studied tens of thousands of mug shots, but I've been unable to identify the cartel members. Eleanor thinks they are undocumented immigrants, and she's probably right. They know who I am, but I don't know who they are, which puts my son and me in grave danger. The program protected me at all costs before and during the trial. Judge Guzman couldn't afford to lose her star witness. But now that Grady is in prison for life, I'm no longer of use to them. While they are obligated to take care of me, I'm not high on their priority list, as evidenced by them assigning a rookie to my case.

The closer we get to Denver, the more my doubt about the program grows. WITSEC will hide us in a remote cabin in the mountains of Montana where protecting us will be easier. What quality of life will we have in the wilderness?

I don't sleep a wink that night in our roadside motel on the outskirts of Denver. And when Eleanor taps on the door connecting our adjoining rooms early the following morning, I tell her we need to talk.

Eleanor's shoulders sag. "I know that look. It would be a mistake for you to consider leaving the program."

"I'm no longer considering it, Eleanor. I've made up my mind."

She glances over at the bed where my son is beginning to stir. Grabbing my wrist, she pulls me into her room, out of earshot. "You won't survive, Julia. You've never been on your own. You went from your daddy's house to your husband's."

"Then it's time I start taking care of myself," I say, my jaw set in determination.

"You don't know how to do that on a good day, let alone with The Six hunting you down and a four-year-old in tow. Do you even have a plan?"

I hunch a shoulder. "Not really. We'll get on a bus and head east. We'll figure it out as we go."

Eleanor looks at me as though I've lost my mind. "You'll be dead within a few days."

Her certainty makes me more determined than ever to prove her wrong. "I agree the thought of being on my own scares the hell out of me. But the sacrifices my son will have to make if we stay in the program scares me even more. Admit it, Eleanor. The justice department no longer needs me. My happiness is of little concern to WITSEC."

Her expression softens. She knows I'm right. "I won't give you my blessing, but I can at least help you on your way," she says, gathering up her wallet and glasses and stuffing them in her purse.

I follow her to the door. "Where are you going?"

"Shopping. Be packed and ready to leave when I get back."

I stare open-mouthed at Eleanor. She hasn't left me alone since I entered the program. Am I sure I'm ready to be out on my own? "What should I tell Rod?"

"Don't tell him anything. If he asks, pretend you haven't seen me this morning," she says and disappears into the foggy morning.

Returning to my room, I take a long hot shower, give Conrad a bath in the grimy tub, and pack up all our belongings.

An hour later, Conrad and I are seated on the edge of the bed, waiting for Eleanor, when Rod knocks on the door. "I'm gonna grab some breakfast. I'll be back in a few minutes," he says, and to my relief, he doesn't ask about Eleanor.

He's no sooner left when Eleanor returns. "I saw Rod on his way out for food. He won't be gone long. We need to get you out of here."

I gesture at our suitcases waiting beside the door. "We're ready."

"Good. Here." She hands me five prepaid credit cards like the one she gave me yesterday. "There's a few hundred dollars on each. That's the best I could do on short notice. If you spend wisely, it should be enough to give you a solid head start."

I place the cards in my wallet. "You're very generous. Thank you, Eleanor."

She hands me a Colorado driver's license with my name on it.

I give her a quizzical look. "What's this for?"

"For this." She hands me a car key and opens the door to reveal a silver Honda Civic parked in front of our room. "The title is in the glove box. The license is a fake, so don't get pulled and don't get in a wreck. When you land at your final destination, you'll need to register the vehicle with the state and get a car insurance policy. None of this is legal, and I'll probably get fired, but it's the best I can do. You'll be safer traveling by car than public transportation."

I throw my arms around her. "I don't know how to thank you."

"You can thank me by staying safe." Pushing away from me, she presses a business card into my hand. "Rick Harvey is the attorney working on your trust. Call him when you get settled. He should have everything set up within a few days." She inhales an unsteady breath. "All right. Time to hit the road."

We each grab a suitcase and wheel them out to the trunk of the car. I open the back door to reveal a new car seat for Conrad. His old one is with Rod in the Suburban. "I don't believe this," I say as I buckle Conrad into the seat. "How'd you do all this in an hour?"

"I pulled mega strings. Now get going." When I hesitate a fraction of a second, she adds, "It's not too late for you to change your mind and stay in the program."

"No way. I'm scared to death, but this is something I have to do. For myself, and for my son."

Hugging Eleanor one last time, I get in the car, start the

engine, and turn left out of the parking lot. I have no idea which way is east. I just want to get as far away as possible before Rod returns.

FIVE

WILL

I'm burning toast again on Friday when my sister barges in unannounced.

"There you are!" Ashton says, dropping her purse onto the counter. "I've been calling you. Why aren't you answering your phone?"

"I turned it off."

Before Ashton can interrogate me, the girls rush over from the breakfast table to greet our visitor. Sophie hugs my sister's legs while Caroline announces, "Dad burned the toast again."

Ashton looks down at the blackened toast in my hands. "I see that."

I drop the toast in the garbage can. "Add cooking to the list of survival skills a single parent must learn."

"Where's your nanny?" Ashton asks.

"She quit," I say, and Caroline chimes in, "Because you made her quit."

I give my sister a look, pleading with her not to ask questions. "Nannies are too much trouble anyway. They're always asking for days off and staring at their phones. We're gonna try things on our own for a change. Right, girls?"

Sophie nods, her curls dancing around on her head. Ellie's hairstylist shorn her long crazy waves into springy corkscrews.

Ashton smiles down at her. "Look at you. You cut your hair."

Sophie smooths her hair back. "I look like a boy."

Ashton kneels in front of her. "With your pretty face, you could never look like a boy." She spins Sophie around as she inspects the haircut. "It's spunky, just like you."

Caroline glares at me, an evil glint in her eyes. "Daddy got the brush caught in Sophie's hair. He had to cut it out with the scissors. Miss Ellie took Sophie to the hair salon after school yesterday so a stylist could fix it."

Ashton's slate-blue eyes go wide, but before she can respond, Caroline begins begging for blueberry pancakes. "Puh-lease, Aunt Ashton. Will you make them for us?"

"Sorry, girls. We don't have time for pancakes. Miss Ellie will be here soon to drive you to school." I remove a box of Pop-Tarts from the pantry. "You'll have to settle for these."

Caroline stomps her foot. "Not Pop-Tarts again."

"I'll scramble you some eggs. They won't take but a minute." Ashton retrieves the eggs and milk from the refrigerator. "You're about to get your first cooking lesson." She shows me how to break an egg into a bowl and slides the bowl in front of me. "Now crack three more eggs, add a splash of milk, and beat them with this," she says, handing me a fork.

Ashton melts a paddy of butter in a skillet, and I pour in the scrambled eggs. She grabs a plastic spatula out of the utensil drawer and slaps me in the gut with it. "Now stir them with this until they're done."

When Ashton deems the eggs ready, I transfer them from the skillet onto two plates. We settle the girls at the table with their food and go out to the porch to talk.

I let out an audible sigh. "I have to watch everything I say in front of Caroline. She doesn't miss a beat."

"What did you do to make the nanny quit? I thought you liked her."

"She kept the girls up after their bedtime after I repeatedly instructed her to stick to their schedule." I run my hand down my face. "I probably shouldn't have gotten so angry."

A smirk appears on my sister's lips. "Mm-hmm. Like you shouldn't have gone off on that reporter yesterday."

I drop down to a rocking chair. "You don't need to scold me. I already heard an earful from Detective Marlowe yesterday."

She sits down beside me. "I'm worried about you, Will. This isn't the first time your anger management problem has gotten you into trouble."

I cut my eyes at her. "Who says I have an anger management problem?"

"You've had one since you were a boy." Ashton rests a hand on my forearm. "You're not to blame after what we went through. But our dysfunctional family and alcoholic mother left permanent scars on you. The truth is, Will, with so much going on in your life, your emotional instability is causing problems for you, and you need to get help."

I jerk my arm away. "What I need is for everyone to get off my back."

"I heard Detective Marlowe's statement yesterday. Sounds like *he's* getting off your back," Ashton says in an encouraging tone.

I let out a grunt. "For now."

"What's that supposed to mean?"

"Marlowe is being pressured to bring murder charges against me. I—" The sound of a car horn brings me to my feet. "There's Ellie."

"I'll help you get the girls ready," Ashton says following me into the kitchen.

We collect the girls' belongings, steer them out to Ellie's waiting minivan, and watch them drive away.

Turning back towards the house, I say, "Thanks for stopping by, but I need to get to work."

Ashton grabs me by the arm. "Not so fast. Who is pressuring Marlowe to charge you with Tracy's murder?"

"Chief Dorsey. But Marlowe thinks someone higher up is pressuring him."

"But there's no evidence against you, is there?" When a pained expression crosses my face, Ashton says, "You're holding something back."

"What did you tell Detective Marlowe when he questioned you?"

Ashton lets her hand drop from my arm. "As little as possible. If you're asking whether I told him you and Tracy were in a fight at the time of her accident, the answer is definitely no."

"Because you know that would implicate me in her death. Do you think I killed my wife, Ashton?" I ask and watch closely for her reaction.

She jerks back her head in surprise. "No way! I was on the rescue boat that day. I witnessed you hanging over the side of your boat, searching the water for Tracy. And I saw how devastated you were when you boarded the rescue boat." She tilts my chin. "Do I think you have some anger issues? Yes. But I don't think you're a murderer."

"If only Tracy had let me drive, this never would've happened."

"But she refused. She caused her own accident. Tracy was responsible, Will. Not you. But these angry outbursts are not helping. You need to get your anger under control before something really bad happens."

Her words echo Marlowe's from yesterday. *If you don't get a hold of your emotions, you could lose everything.*

"I'm dealing with a lot right now, Ashton. Just give me some space."

"I'm trying to help, little brother. Do you want me to keep the girls this weekend?"

The idea appeals to me. But I can't keep dumping my children on other people. We need to figure out how to move on with our lives together. "Thanks. But we're fine. Maybe we'll come out to Marsh Point on Sunday for a boat ride."

Ashton presses her hands together. "Perfect. I'll plan a Labor Day cookout."

I manage a smile, even though a cookout is the last thing I want to attend. When the time comes, I'll create a legitimate excuse to bail.

———

A PROBLEM at a project site causes me to be late in picking up the girls from school at noon. My girls seem unfazed by my tardiness, but Ellie's daughter cries hysterically all the way home.

Ellie is waiting for us in her driveway when we arrive. She throws open the back door, unbuckles Zoe from the car seat, and hugs her trembling daughter tight.

I roll down my window. "I'm sorry, Ellie. I had a crisis at work and lost track of time."

"It happens." Her snippy tone tells me it is not okay for me to be late in picking up her daughter. "Have you found a new nanny yet?"

"Nope. I've decided not to get a new nanny."

Ellie's eyebrows shoot up above her designer sunglasses. "You're making a terrible mistake. You won't last long alone. You know the saying. Behind every good man is a good woman."

I put my truck in reverse. "And I lost *my* good woman six weeks ago."

Zoe cries into her mother's neck. "I was so scared, Mommy. He just left us there. I didn't think anyone was coming to get me."

Ellie jiggles her daughter. "Shh. It's okay, honey. Mommy

won't let it happen again." She shifts her daughter to the opposite hip. "I'm sorry, Will, but this situation isn't working out for me. I'll have to make other arrangements. I need to be in a car pool with someone I trust to pick up my daughter on time."

"I think that's best for both of us." I back out of the driveway and peel off down the street.

From the back seat, Caroline says, "It's okay, Daddy. Zoe is a crybaby. No one at school likes her."

If Tracy were here, she'd use this opportunity to teach Caroline about being kind to others when they are going through difficult times. But since I'm fresh out of profound advice, I ask what the girls would like for lunch instead.

"Grilled cheeses!" they call out in unison.

"Grilled cheeses it is," I say with little enthusiasm. And none of us are surprised when I burn them.

"I'm starving. What're we gonna eat, Daddy?" Caroline asks, watching me stuff the ruined sandwiches down the disposal.

The sight of three ripe bananas in a basket on the counter brings an idea to mind. "We'll have my specialty sandwich. I lived off them when I was in college."

Caroline gives me a skeptical look. "What's so special about it? And why haven't you ever made them for us?"

"Because you never asked me to." I walk the girls to the table. "Now sit here while I make them."

Five minutes later, I join them at the table with three sandwiches on plates.

Caroline peels back the top layer of bread. "What is this?"

"Banana and mayonnaise," I say, sinking my teeth into my sandwich.

Caroline turns up her nose. "Seriously, Daddy? That's gross."

"How do you know when you haven't tried it? Aunt Ashton used to make me banana and mayonnaise sandwiches all the time."

"Really?" Caroline's admiration for Ashton is nothing short of hero worship. When she takes a bite of the sandwich, her face lights up. "This is actually good. Try it, Sophie."

Sophie takes a nibble. "Yummy!" she says and gobbles down the sandwich half.

Caroline asks, "Daddy will you play with us after lunch."

I have no idea what playing entails, but if I'm going to be a single parent, I need to find out. "Sure. But we should clean up the kitchen first."

Sophie sticks out her lower lip, and Caroline says, "Aww. Can't it wait?"

Their eager faces make me smile. "I guess so. Just this once."

We clean our plates and add them to the growing collection of dirty ones in the sink. For the next three hours, we play games and puzzles and dress up. My daughters think I'm the funniest-looking daddy ever in a pink tutu. We don't bother putting anything away after we're finished with it, and by the time four o'clock rolls around, the inside of our house looks like a tornado blew through.

I use the excuse of making a business call to plant them in front of a movie. Taking my phone outside to the porch, I spend a few minutes with each of my foremen, making certain their projects are in good shape before taking off for the long holiday weekend. While I'm on the phone, I notice our yard, in Tracy's absence, has grown into a jungle. Like I need one more thing to tend to.

The girls fall asleep during the movie and wake grumpy and hungry around five.

Caroline refuses to take a bath with Sophie, which sends Sophie into a temper tantrum. It takes me two hours to bathe them, locate clean pajamas, and comb through the tangles in their hair. I must remember to buy some magic detangler next time I go to the store.

They argue over what to have for dinner. Caroline wants chicken, Sophie a pizza, and I have a hankering for a burger.

"Let's order takeout from The Nest," I suggest. "Then everyone can get what they want."

The girls usually go wild at the mention of our town's most iconic restaurant. But tonight, they could care less.

After placing the order online, I grab my keys and head for the door. "I'll be back in a few minutes."

My daughters race after me with Caroline calling, "Wait for us, Dad! You can't leave us here alone."

"Of course not," I say, even though I was totally going to leave my children home alone. While I feel like the worst father ever, I'm not yet ready to give up and hire a nanny. If a woman can do this, so can I.

SIX

WILL

The girls shake me awake as they climb into bed with me early Saturday morning. "Get up! Get up!" they chant as they clamber to their feet and begin jumping up and down on the bed.

I groan. Why are they here? Tracy lets me sleep in on Saturdays. I roll over and reach for my wife, but the feel of her cold pillow brings reality crashing back.

Sophie dives on top of me, knocking the air out of my lungs. "Can we go to the pool today, Daddy?"

I consider the effort necessary to prepare for a pool outing—slathering on sunscreen and gathering all their pool gear, including towels and goggles and toys. But the vision of me dressed in a pink tutu and the thought of being stuck inside the house with them all day makes the decision easy.

I prop myself up on my elbows. "On one condition. When we come home from the pool, you'll have quiet time while I clean up the house."

"Deal!" Caroline says, and Sophie bobs her head.

I throw back the comforter and swing my legs over the side of the bed. "But we need to eat breakfast first. And since there's no more bread in the house for me to burn, what say we go to Main Street Diner for pancakes?"

Caroline victory dances on the bed. "Yippee!"

And Sophie hugs my neck from behind. "Can we go now?"

Caroline adds, "In our pajamas?"

I chuckle. "I don't see why not. As long as you wear shoes." But the stares we receive when we enter the diner twenty minutes later tells me this wasn't such a good idea.

I glance around the crowded restaurant. All the tables appear to be occupied. I spot Ellie, who is seated with Zoe in a large booth on the far side of the diner. Before I can back out the door, Ellie waves us over.

"Yoo-hoo! Will!" She calls out. "Come sit with us. We have plenty of room."

"This woman must have a tracking device connected to me," I mutter under my breath.

Caroline looks up at me. "Did you say something, Daddy?"

"No, sweetheart," I say and steer my children through the maze of tables.

Ellie motions my girls to Zoe's side of the booth and moves over to make room for me on the bench next to her. The waitress arrives right away, and I order blueberry pancakes for all three of us.

Ellie waits until the three girls are engrossed in their own conversation before whispering to me, "Tracy would not approve of them wearing their pajamas in public."

The smell of her coffee breath makes me want to gag. "In case you haven't noticed, Ellie, Tracy's not here."

"These are impressionable years for your children. You must teach them to always present their best selves in public." She rests a hand on my forearm. "For your children's sake, you should find yourself a wife."

I inch away from her on the bench. "The only wife I need is Tracy."

Ellie walks her fingers up my arm. "I know, dear man. You're not ready yet. But when you are, I'm available."

Her audacious flirtation repulses me, and I move even farther away from her on the bench.

"We're going to the pool later," Zoe brags.

Caroline sticks her tongue out at Zoe. "Yeah? So are we."

My head begins to throb. This is going to be a long weekend. When the waitress arrives with our food, I focus my attention on eating my pancakes. I'd rather spend the day dressing up like princesses and fairies and ballerinas than be around this insufferable mother and her boastful daughter. But I promised the girls, and so when we arrive at the pool two hours later, I attach myself to my next-door neighbor to avoid getting stuck with Ellie. Bob's daughters are several years older than my girls, and I trust them to help keep an eye on the younger ones.

"So, Bob, I've been meaning to ask who takes care of your lawn?"

Bob lets out a roar of laughter. "I noticed you have a jungle in progress next door." He sips his Bloody Mary through a straw. "We've tried every lawn service in town. None of them are great. You have to stay on top of them. In their defense, they can't keep up in the summer when everything grows at such a rapid rate. Our current crew is the best we've had. I'll get Sherry to forward you the contact info."

"That'd be great." Watching him slurp his Bloody Mary makes me yearn for a beer, but I would never dare drink alcohol and drive with my daughters in the car.

"What happened to your nanny? I enjoyed seeing her around, if you know what I mean," he says, his eyebrows dancing across his forehead.

I laugh. "She was a looker, for sure. Unfortunately, things didn't work out."

Sophie appears at my side. "Daddy, I have to go potty."

"Already? You just went before we left home. I'll take you in a few minutes. Go back to the pool," I say, giving her a gentle shove.

Bob shakes the ice in his drink. "I don't know why they don't just pee in the pool like we did."

I laugh, even though I don't think he's funny. I never peed in the pool when I was growing up. Then again, we seldom went to the pool. We lived on Catawba Sound. We had a natural saltwater pool in our backyard. "Sophie was barely potty trained when Tracy died," I tell Bob. "She regressed after the accident. Most of the time, she thinks she needs to go when she doesn't. I don't like taking her into the men's room with me. And she's too young to go to the ladies' room alone."

Bob's face goes serious. "I see your point. If you want, Alicia can take her for you."

His eleven-year-old has started babysitting on a small scale. Tracy hired Alicia a few times to entertain Caroline and Sophie while she was working around the house.

"I may let her if Sophie asks to go potty again."

The lifeguard blows his whistle and hollers, "Code Brown! Clear the pool."

Bob hangs his head. "Aw, man. There goes my day at the pool. Now, Sherry's gonna make me tackle her honey-do list."

"I don't understand. What's Code Brown?"

"Someone pooped in the pool. They'll close it for the rest of the day for cleaning."

My gaze follows Bob's to the turd floating near Sophie. *Ugh. This can't be happening.*

I rush over to the pool and scoop my crying child out of the water. "It's okay, sweetheart. This is my fault. I should've taken you to the potty when you asked." I motion for Caroline to get out. "Come on, Caroline. Time to go home."

"But Dad. We just got here."

"Don't argue, Caroline. Let's go."

Tears sting my eyes as I hurry my children out to the car. I haven't cried since Tracy's funeral, and I feel an ugly one coming on. I'd planned to make an excuse not to go to Ashton's cookout, but an hour later, when I receive a text from her with the details, I immediately respond, offering to come early and take everyone for a boat ride. I'm feeling less confident in my ability to take care of my daughters with each passing moment.

———

I HAD reservations when Ashton hired my firm to renovate Marsh Point, our family's antebellum waterfront home. Ever since I left for college, the traumatic memories from my youth have made it difficult for me to be in the house for any length of time. But stripping the walls down to the studs exorcized the ghosts. And with the demons gone, I can appreciate the elegance of the architecture and the majesty of the setting.

Ashton and Sully are waiting for us on the dock when the girls and I arrive. I buckle Caroline and Sophie into life jackets, lower the boat, and start the engine. With the girls snuggled in Sully's lap on the bench seat in front of the console, and Ashton perched next to me on the leaning post, we head out towards the ocean.

"I'm glad to see you so happy," I say to Ashton. "After everything Owen put you through, you deserve it. And Sully seems like a great guy."

Ashton's lips part in a soft smile. "He is. The girls have certainly taken to him."

"Tell me again why you two never dated in high school." Sully was one of Ashton's closest friends in high school. They were so much older than me, I never got a chance to know him well.

"I was too busy taking care of my siblings to date anyone," she says with a twinkle in her slate-blue eyes.

I reel away from her in shock. "Really? You mean you never had a boyfriend?"

"Nope. Not a single one."

"I'm sorry, Ashton. I never realized the extent of your sacrifice." I tap on the throttle, adjusting our speed as we approach some waves. "Women are wired differently than men. You're meant to take care of children. Men are definitely not."

She gives me a gentle shove. "You're a chauvinist. You'd better be careful who you say that to." A somber expression slides behind her smile. "Truth be told, my maternal instincts were more about survival than an inherent tendency to nurture. Someone had to take care of us. As the oldest, that job fell on me."

I hang my head. "I'm still waiting for my survival instincts to kick in. I'm not sure I'm cut out for single parenting."

"You've only been at it a few days, Will. You're learning a lot of new skills. Naturally, everything will seem difficult in the beginning."

"You're missing the point. I wasn't a great dad when Tracy was alive. I don't think I have it in me. Maybe I inherited the sucky parent gene from Mom."

"She would've been a fine mom if not for the alcoholism."

I roll my eyes. "Why do you always defend her?"

Ashton ignores my question. The subject of our mother is a point of contention between us. "Have you considered getting another nanny?"

"That's not an option. The nanny service fired me. Besides, I don't like having a stranger living in the house."

"Give yourself a break, Will. You'll eventually figure things out."

"I'm not so sure about that." My girls would be better off living with someone else. I just don't know who that someone else is.

Ashton drapes an arm around my shoulders. "These past couple of months have been brutal. You need a break. Why don't you let the girls stay with me tonight?"

"What about Sully? I'd hate to cramp your style with your new lover boy."

"Ha ha. Sully is leaving for Charleston after dinner. He has an important meeting early tomorrow morning. And I would love to have the girls. I have their new rooms all ready for them. They will be my first official guests." During the renovations, Ashton reconfigured the upstairs floor plan to create more bedrooms. With no children of her own to dote on, she's become something of a surrogate mother to my daughters since Tracy died. She insisted Caroline and Sophie have their own rooms and has extended an open-door invitation to spend the night anytime.

"In that case, I accept. Sophie and Caroline will be thrilled."

I relish the idea of sitting around in my boxer shorts and watching football. But when I return home after the cookout, the house feels lonely without my children. I resist the temptation to drive back to Marsh Point. The girls will benefit from having their favorite aunt to themselves. I wander around the house, not sure what to do with myself. Moving to Mariner's Landing was Tracy's idea. I much prefer the older homes in the town's historic area. I don't belong in this house. Come to think of it, I don't belong in my own skin. I've been a misfit all my life. In my dysfunctional family with sisters so much older than me. I was as close to Tracy as I've ever been with anyone in my life, but I held something of myself back, even from her. I'm a broken man. And I can't see myself ever being whole.

SEVEN
JULIA

Conrad and I set out on the twenty-two-hour trip with Columbia, South Carolina the destination entered in my Maps app. The drive is exhausting for both of us. I drink enough caffeine to stay awake without having to pee every hour. Conrad has multiple temper tantrums, screaming and kicking his car seat and crying himself to sleep. I feel like the worst mother ever for torturing him like this, but the sooner we get where we're going, the less danger we'll be in. When we stop for food and restroom breaks, I choose restaurants in congested areas. We pull our baseball caps low to hide our faces and try our best to blend in with the crowds. When I get a flat tire near Kansas City, a kind service station attendant helps me plug it. Later, failing to check the gas gauge, we coast on fumes to a St. Louis convenience store. After filling up with gas, we drive to a nearby motel where we spend our first night.

The long hours on the lonely highway give me too much time to obsess about our predicament. But it's too late to turn back now. Grady destroyed our lives, and I'm doing the best I can to make the best of what's left.

I breathe a loud sigh of relief when we pull into the parking lot of a seedy motel on the outskirts of Columbia.

"How long until we get to Adventure, Mommy?" Conrad asks as I unbuckle him from his car seat.

"We're getting close. We have a two-hour drive to get to the coast in the morning, and then we'll start searching for Adventure. What do you think about living near the ocean?"

"I've never been to the ocean. Why can't we live on our farm?"

"You know why, son." The farm and his father will eventually fade from his memory. I'm sad he won't remember our good times at the farm as a family, but forgetting the past is in Conrad's best interests.

The shady-looking man at the front desk in the motel's office gives me the creeps. I'm reaching for the door, preparing to bolt, when he asks, "Are you interested in a room, miss?"

Dropping my hand, I approach the check-in desk. "Yes, please."

He looks past me at the parking lot. "Is it just the two of you? No husband?"

Without thinking, a *yes* slips from my lips. Why didn't I tell him my husband was at the burger place next door ordering take-out? I'm not used to lying. I need to think faster on my feet.

He strokes his straggly beard with one hand as he studies the computer screen. "Kings are all I have left."

"That's fine. We can share a bed."

I feel his steely gaze on me as I rummage in my purse for my wallet, like a predator eyeing its prey. I slip out one of the prepaid cards Eleanor gave me, but I feel certain he saw the others lined up in the wallet.

Once the registration is complete, the desk clerk hands me a folder with two key cards, and I hurry out of the office. We order dinner from the Burger Shack next door, and I drive around to our room at the back of the building. We appear to be the only guests booked in this remote section of the hotel. The seclusion is a good thing when you're hiding. But I have a sick feeling the desk clerk put us here for a reason. I tell myself I'm being paranoid and unload our meager belongings from the car.

We eat our dinner at the small table beside the window with the heavy curtains open and the sheers pulled tight. Conrad plants his elbow on the table with his head resting in his hand, staring down at his food without taking a bite.

"What's wrong, sweetheart? I know you're tired. This has been a difficult trip. But I promise we're close to finding our new home. Then you can start school and make new friends."

Conrad drags a french fry through a puddle of ketchup. "Do my new friends have to call me Conrad?"

"Yes, son. That's your name now," I say, biting into my cheeseburger.

He sticks out his lower lip. "But I don't like that name. I want to be Levi again."

I'm running out of patience. We have this same argument nearly every day. "What if we think of a nickname for you? Conny has a nice ring to it."

"Yuck. That sounds stupid. What about Buddy?"

I stare up at the water-stained ceiling as I consider the name. "That could work. But why Buddy?"

"That's what Daddy always called me."

I tap my chin. "Come to think of it, I call you Buddy sometimes too. But when people ask for your name, you tell them Conrad, but you prefer to go by your nickname, Buddy. Deal?"

"Deal," he says and stuffs the ketchup-soaked fry into his mouth.

After dinner, I help Conrad brush his teeth and change into his pajamas. He selects two books from his small library, and I tuck him into bed. Most kids sleep with a stuffed animal. My son sleeps with the beloved baseball bat and glove his father gave him. We only make it through one bedtime story before he falls fast asleep.

After putting the books away, I pause to peek out the window.

Street lights illuminate the deserted parking lot. It's almost ten o'clock, and we are the only guests staying at the back of the motel. I have an uneasy feeling in the pit of my stomach that something is very wrong. I close the heavy drapes and turn my back on the window.

I stretch out, fully clothed, on the bed beside my son. Although I'm exhausted, I need to stay awake to protect Conrad. But my eyelids soon grow heavy, and I doze off. I wake with a start to the sound of the door clicking open.

Clamping a hand over Conrad's mouth, I roll with him off the opposite side of the bed. I whisper for him to remain quiet and shove him under the bed. On my knees, I pat the bed covers for the baseball bat. I hear the intruder prowling around near the foot of the bed where I left my purse, and when I turn on the bedside table lamp, the desk clerk jumps to attention with my wallet in his hand. I go after him with the bat, cracking him on the back of the head with one swift hit. The desk clerk drops my wallet as he crumples to the floor.

My mind races. What do I do? Does he need medical attention? I kneel beside him and check for a pulse. He's still alive, and there's no blood gushing from his head. Calling the police would bring unwanted attention to myself, and I highly doubt the desk clerk would implicate himself by reporting the incident. My best option is for us to get as far away from this motel as possible.

Conrad appears in the bathroom doorway. "What happened, Mommy? Is that one of the bogeymen," he asks, his nickname for the cartel members.

"The guy who works here tried to steal my wallet, and I knocked him out with your baseball bat. We need to leave. Here!" I toss his suitcase on the bed. "Help me pack your stuff."

Five minutes later, when we flee the room with our belongings, the desk clerk has begun to stir.

"Where are we going now, Mommy?" Conrad asks as I peel out of the parking lot.

"I'm not sure." I glance down at the dashboard clock. "It's three o'clock in the morning. No sense in going to another motel now. We might as well continue to the coast. Close your little eyes and try to get some more sleep."

"What about you? Aren't you tired?"

"No, honey. I'm wide awake now."

Conrad folds his arms over his chest. "So am I," he says, but a few minutes later, when I glance back at him, he's fallen back asleep.

Sitting ramrod straight, I grip the steering wheel as I navigate the deserted downtown streets of Columbia. The close call has set me on edge. Although I'm sure the desk clerk's act was random and not tied to my husband's criminal dealings, it's a stark reminder of the dangerous world we inhabit. I should've insisted the desk clerk move us to a room at the front of the hotel. I've led a sheltered life, and I'm in over my head. I've always counted on my father and husband to protect me.

I reach for my phone, my thumb hovering over Eleanor's contact information. My life is not the only one I'm risking. I've placed my child, my innocent four-year-old son, in harm's way. I drop the phone back in the cupholder. While Witness Protection may offer us a better chance of survival, I will never be happy without my freedom. I sneak another peek at Conrad. And he'll have a better chance at a more fulfilled life on our own. I'll be more careful from now on. I'll buy a handgun and learn how to shoot it. I'll do whatever it takes to keep my son safe.

EIGHT
WILL

Just after lunch on Monday, I'm on my way out of the house to pick up my children from Marsh Point, when a stranger approaches me on the sidewalk out front. He's an attractive young man dressed casually for the holiday in khaki slacks and a striped polo shirt.

He stops in front of me. "Are you Will Darby?"

"I am. Who are you?"

"An independent process server delivering official documents."

I glance down at the manila envelope in his hand and back up at him. "Seriously? On a holiday?"

"Happy Labor Day." He shoves the envelope at me and hurries back to his black sedan parked on the curb.

I watch him drive off before opening the envelope and scanning the top page of the sheaf of documents. Tracy's parents are following through on their threat to sue me for custody of my children. Everything suddenly becomes crystal clear. Loretta and Clarence Beaumont are the ones pressuring the police chief to charge me with their daughter's murder. They hold me responsible for Tracy's death, and they will stop at nothing until they get their revenge.

I avoid the speed limit as I race through town to the historic district. Why is everything in my life so difficult? I'm constantly wading through quicksand, but I can never reach the other side. Tracy was the perfect wife. Beautiful and charming and capable. But even our life together was less than ideal. Am I feeling sorry for myself? Heck, yes. After everything I've experienced, I deserve to. I consider putting an end to my misery by ramming my truck into one of the moss-draped live oaks lining Pelican's Way. But upon my death, Loretta and Clarence would get custody. And the only thing worse than me being a single parent to my daughters would be Tracy's parents raising them.

At Marsh Point, I enter the house and call out for my sister as I pass through the center hallway to the veranda. Spotting them on the beach, I cross the lawn towards them. The girls are splashing in the edge of the water while Ashton watches them from a nearby beach chair.

"Will! What're you doing here? I didn't expect you until later." She shields her eyes from the sun as she looks up at me. Seeing my tormented face, she says, "Uh-oh. What's wrong?"

I drop down to the beach beside her. "Tracy's parents are suing me for custody of Caroline and Sophie."

Ashton's face tightens. "No judge in their right mind would give an elderly couple custody."

"Loretta and Clarence are hardly elderly. They're in their late sixties, a young late sixties."

"Still, they'll be pushing ninety when the girls go to college."

"They don't care. The only thing that matters to them is getting their grandchildren away from me. I think the Beaumonts are the ones putting pressure on the police to charge me. And I played right into their hands by going off on that reporter."

"The Beaumonts certainly have the money and the power," Ashton says, her expression pensive.

"Yep. The judge will readily give them custody if I'm in prison. Unless . . ."

"Unless what, Will?"

I cut my eyes at her. "Unless you raise them."

My sister smacks her chest. "Me?"

"Yes, you. Now's your chance to have the family you've always wanted."

"What're you talking about? You know I decided a long time ago not to have children."

I angle my body towards her. "And you recently admitted that was your biggest regret in life. Now's your chance to remedy that. I'll still be their father, and I'll offer full financial support. As much as I can from prison."

"This discussion is pointless, Will. You haven't been, and probably won't be, charged with a crime. But I will help you find a child custody lawyer. And I'll help you fight Tracy's parents."

I didn't expect my sister to take the bait right away. She's starting over after an unhappy marriage. I don't blame her for not wanting to be burdened with two young children at age fifty. But if I work on her, she'll eventually change her mind.

Sophie runs over to my sister. "Aunt Ashton! I don't feel good," she says without so much as a glance in my direction.

I'm invisible to my children. They know I'm useless when it comes to taking care of them. "What hurts, sweetheart?" I ask.

Sophie pats her belly. "My tummy," she says to Ashton, as though my sister had asked the question.

Ashton presses her palm against Sophie's forehead and then the backs of her hands to her cheeks. "I don't think you have a fever."

"It's probably something she ate," I speculate. "What did you have for breakfast, Sophie?"

"Um . . ." Sophie lowers her eyes as she bites down on her lower lip.

"I made blueberry pancakes, but she didn't want any," Ashton explains.

"She would never willingly pass up your blueberry pancakes.

I'd better take her home." Getting to my feet, I brush sand off the back of my shorts. "Come on, Caroline. We need to go home. Sophie doesn't feel well."

Caroline stomps her foot on the hard sand. "Aww. Do we have to? Can't I stay here with Aunt Ashton?"

"It's fine with me," Ashton says. "I'll bring her home later this afternoon."

"All right. If you're sure?" I lift Sophie into my arms and carry her to the car. We've no sooner left the driveway when I hear my daughter retch and smell the stench of vomit.

I slam my foot on the gas and drive as fast as I dare back through town. My entire back seat is covered in vomit, and I nearly gag at the odor as I remove Sophie from her car seat. We make it to the bathroom, but as soon as I set her down, she throws up all over me, the wall, and the floor.

She looks up at me with a pitiful expression that breaks my heart. "Daddy, I need to go poop," she says, but before I can lift her onto the toilet, diarrhea runs down her leg.

The pooping and vomiting go on for hours. When the virus appears to have run its course, I clean Sophie up as best I can and carry her to her room. Stripping off her soiled clothes, I slip a clean nightgown over her head and tuck her into bed with a plastic wastebasket on the floor beside her.

Smoothing back her hair, I kiss her forehead. "Try to get some sleep," I say and wait until I'm certain she's asleep before beginning the arduous process of cleaning up.

I'm outside scrubbing the back seat of my truck around six o'clock when Ashton's convertible pulls into the driveway.

The top is down, and Caroline waves at me from the back seat. "What're you doing, Daddy?"

"Cleaning my truck."

Ashton gets out of the car and peers over my shoulder at the back seat. Pinching her nose against the stench, she says, "I'm guessing Sophie didn't make it home. How's she feeling?"

"She was violently sick earlier, but she's been sleeping for a while. I should check on her," I say, gathering up my cleaning supplies.

Inside the house, the three of us part ways in the foyer. I head to the laundry room with my load, Caroline takes off for her room, and Ashton goes to see about Sophie. I'm putting away the cleaning supplies a minute later when my sister's voice echoes throughout the house. "Hurry, Will! Come quick!"

I drop the bucket and dash down the hall to Sophie's room. "What's wrong?"

"She's burning up with fever," my sister's fearful expression sends a jolt up my spine.

Sophie's face is flushed, and when I press the back of my hand to her forehead like I saw Ashton do earlier on the beach, my daughter's skin is hot to the touch. "What do we do?"

"We need to get her to the emergency room right away," Ashton says.

I gently pick up my daughter and cradle her in my arms. "Her little body is on fire. We need to hurry."

My sister and I dash through the house, all thoughts eclipsed by the urgency of getting help for Sophie.

Ashton stops me in the driveway. "What about Caroline? Do you want to take her with us? Or do you want me to stay here with her?"

"I need you with me." I notice Bob in his front yard and yell to him, "Hey, Bob! I need a favor. Sophie's sick. I'm taking her to the emergency room. Can Caroline stay with you?"

He drops his rake and strides towards me. "Of course. We'll feed her dinner. She can spend the night if necessary. Is there anything else I can do?"

"Say a prayer."

"Sure thing, man. Let me know how it goes."

"You drive," I say to my sister and get in the back seat of her convertible with my daughter.

I coo encouraging words to Sophie during the drive, but she's unresponsive, a limp rag doll in my arms. This is all my fault. My incompetence as a parent may have cost my daughter her life. I close my eyes and pray to God and Tracy and everyone who will listen to please save my child.

The hospital is only a few miles away, and Ashton makes it there in record time. The emergency room is crowded with patients who suffered injuries during their Labor Day festivities.

"My daughter is burning up with fever," I tell the woman at the reception desk.

She takes one look at Sophie and summons an orderly with a gurney, who whisks Sophie away. I understand their concern when I see the isolation sign on the examining room door. They're worried Sophie has contracted an infectious disease. I fully expect the doctor to appear in a hazmat suit, and I'm relieved when he shows up in blue scrubs with a white coat.

"I'm Dr. Mitchell," he says, listening to Sophie's chest with a stethoscope. "What symptoms does she have?"

My voice is tight as I explain, "She's been throwing up with diarrhea most of the afternoon. When it finally stopped, I put her in the bed and went to clean up. When we checked on her a little while later, she was burning up with fever."

The doctor shines a pin light in my daughter's ears. "Has she had any liquids?"

"I tried to get her to drink some water, but she didn't want any."

"Did you call her pediatrician?"

"I . . . um . . . I figured it was the stomach flu and would eventually run its course."

The doctor looks at me like I'm an idiot. "That's usually the case for adults. But it doesn't take much to dehydrate a child. Who is her pediatrician?"

When I shrug, the doctor looks over at Ashton. "Mom?"

"I'm not her mother. I'm her aunt." Ashton places a hand on

my back. "Will's sister. The child's mother died in early July. As you can imagine, this has been a difficult time for him and his girls."

"Is it bad, Doctor?" I ask. "Is my daughter gonna die?"

The doctor softens a little. "I certainly hope not. We'll get her started on some IV fluids and take some blood work to rule out the possibility of something more serious. But I think it's probably rotavirus. We've had a lot of it lately."

"Wouldn't she have gotten a vaccination for that?" Ashton asks.

"Yes. But what's been going around appears to be a new strain."

The doctor leaves the room, and a young blonde nurse immediately appears. The dehydration makes finding a vein in Sophie's arm difficult. I feel pain, as though it were my own arm, as she jabs Sophie several times with the needle. Once the IV is in place, the nurse draws three tubes of blood and starts the flow of clear fluids.

I wait until the nurse has left the room before speaking. "This is bad, Ashton. What if I broke my child? What if she doesn't recover? I can't do this. I suck at parenting. The girls are better off with Tracy's parents."

Ashton takes hold of my arms and gives me a firm shake. "Hush! Don't you dare say that. We're not turning those children over to Loretta and Clarence Beaumont." She draws me into her arms. "Let me help you, Will."

I collapse against her. "Help me how?"

"I think you and the girls should come stay with me at Marsh Point for a while."

I hold my head back so I can see her. "A while? As in a couple of weeks?"

"Longer than that. At least through the holidays. You're welcome to stay a year. However long it takes for you to get back on your feet."

I frown. "But what about you and Sully? Your relationship is so new."

"Sully's a father. He'll understand. Besides, we're not serious like that. We're just having fun."

"I don't know, Ashton. That seems like too big of an imposition."

She palms my face. "Mama left the house to me for this very reason, Will. To bring our family back together. I have plenty of room. Too much room, actually. I would love to have you and the girls. We'll figure this parenting thing out together."

A year ago, I would never have considered living at Marsh Point. But the renovations have wiped the slate clean. The house is ready for new memories. "Your offer is incredibly generous. My house is part of my problem. Tracy's presence is everywhere. I feel like she's watching over me, but not in a good way. I sense her judging me, waiting for me to do something wrong."

"Your imagination is getting the best of you. I think a change of scenery is definitely warranted." A smile tugs at the corner of my sister's lips. "Who knows? Maybe you'll end up selling that house and finding a historic waterfront home to renovate."

"Maybe. That would be my dream."

Hope blossoms inside of me. I haven't felt optimism in so long, I almost don't recognize it. Unfortunately, it's short-lived, replaced immediately by the looming sense of dread that has been hanging over my head for as long as I can remember.

NINE
JULIA

I spend the morning navigating the quaint streets of South Carolina's Lowcountry, passing through its charming small towns. The sight of moss-draped trees and the serene marshy shorelines captivate me, each bend in the road revealing a picturesque new vista. I fall instantly in love with Charleston, but a quick Zillow search tells me what I already suspected: I can't afford to live here. We explore John's Island, Kiawah Island, and the tiny town of Rockville on Wadmalaw Island but pass on all three for various reasons. I earmark Edisto Beach and Beaufort as possibilities, although neither quite feels like home.

We're making our way south towards Hilton Head when Conrad kicks the back of my seat. "Mommy, I'm hungry."

I glance at the clock. "Wow! It's two o'clock already. I guess you are hungry. And so am I, come to think of it."

A passing sign alerts me to Water's Edge five miles ahead. Although I'd noticed the town on the map, I'd written it off as being too small. But I'm pleasantly surprised by the attractive buildings that greet us on Main Street. Coffee and flower shops. A large hardware store, gourmet grocery, and the Velvet Spoon. I'm a sucker for gelato. Turning the corner, I drive a block east where we discover a row of restaurants, most of which offer outdoor seating overlooking Catawba Sound.

I locate a space in the parking lot shared by the waterfront businesses, and we get out of the car. Strolling along the boardwalk, I ask, "Where would you like to eat?"

He stops in front of a tavern. "What about here?" He reads the wooden sign above the door. "The Turtle's Nest."

I'm not surprised. One of his favorite books is about sea turtles. But I am impressed at the rate at which he's learning to read. "Works for me."

The restaurant's interior is a warm cocoon with worn wooden floors and mounted turtles adorning the ship-lapped walls. Lunchtime has passed, and at this late hour, only a handful of tables are occupied.

"Where do you wanna sit?" I ask Conrad. "Table or booth?"

"Let's sit there," he says, pointing at the wooden bar occupying the far wall.

"Fine by me."

Making our way over to the bar, I give him a lift onto a stool and sit down beside him.

The yellow specks in Conrad's brown eyes glisten as he takes in the restaurant's decor. "Is this Adventure, Mommy?"

"I'm not sure. It certainly feels like an adventure. The town has a good vibe, and the downtown area is just what I'd imagined. Should we explore further after lunch?"

He gives me an eager nod.

The waitress, a pretty blonde with a curvaceous figure, brings us menus and tall glasses of ice water. "I'm Amber. Welcome to Water's Edge."

I furrow my brow. "How do you know we're not from here?"

"I've never seen you folks around. And I pretty much know everyone in town. Are you passing through? Or are you new to town?"

"Both," I say. "We're in the market for a new home. We may decide to stay if we like it. Have you lived here long?"

"All my life. I wouldn't live anywhere else. Some people think our town is boring, but the relaxed pace suits me just fine." She looks over at Conrad. "What's your name, kiddo?"

Conrad gives me a tentative look, and I nod for him to answer. "Conrad. But my friends call me Buddy."

"Buddy. I like that. My son, Jackson, is about your age. How old are you?"

Conrad holds up four fingers, his thumb folded onto his palm.

"Four would've been my guess. If you're looking for a preschool, First Presbyterian Church has a wonderful program. Best in town." Amber chuckles. "The only one in town, actually. They may be full. But it's worth giving the administrator, Betty Bleaker, a call."

"Thanks for the tip," I say, making a mental note of the woman's name.

"Can I get you something to drink?"

"I'm fine with just water," I say, and Conrad orders a lemonade.

"I'll give you a minute to look over the menu," Amber says and moseys off to check on another customer at the other end of the bar.

I point out the kid's section on the menu. "Can you read any of your choices?"

"Hot dog. French fries. Chicken tenders. What's that word?" he asks tapping on the menu.

"Macaroni. Would you like some macaroni and cheese?"

"No thanks. I'll have chicken tenders," he says, dropping the menu onto the bar.

When Amber returns a few minutes later, I order the chicken for Conrad and a cheeseburger with grilled onions for me.

"Excellent choices." She jots down our order on her pad and

looks up at me. "I'm not sure what line of work you're in, but if you're looking for a job, we're hiring here at The Nest."

"Thanks, but I already have a job. I'm a thriller writer," I say and realize my mistake right away.

"Cool. I love to read. What are some of your titles?"

"I . . . um . . . I haven't actually released anything yet."

"I see," she says in a disappointed tone. She either doesn't believe I'm a writer, or she's disappointed I'm not famous.

She tears our order from her pad and slips the pad into her apron pocket. "Well, if you need some money to tide you over, we have positions open for bartenders and servers."

"I'll keep that in mind."

Thoughts of my career weigh heavily on me while we wait for our food. A thriller writer sounds foreign to me. A continuous stream of cozy mystery plot ideas flows through my brain at all times, but the only thriller idea I've come up with so far is the one based on my own life. And writing that novel would mean exposing myself. If I don't come up with an idea for a novel soon, I may very well be applying for a job here.

Our food arrives, and we attack our plates as though we haven't eaten in a week. My burger is cooked medium rare, the way I like it, and the meat is flavorful.

"Mommy, can we please live at The Nest?" Conrad asks, stuffing a french fry in his mouth.

I laugh. "We can't live in the restaurant, sweetheart. But we'll look around more when we leave here. Maybe we'll even spend the night."

"Is there an affordable motel nearby?" I ask Amber when she comes back to check on us.

Amber shakes her head. "Sorry. The absence of hotels and resorts has kept our quiet town from turning into a resort destination." She props herself against the bar. "You could try Myrtle's Bed and Breakfast though. Take a right onto Main Street and go about a half mile. Her house is on the left, just as you enter the historic section. It's real pretty with wraparound porches." She lowers her voice. "FYI, the rooms in the main house need updating. The cottages out back are newer."

"Good to know. Is it expensive?" I say, popping the last bite of my burger into my mouth.

"I have no idea what her rates are. Since summer is officially over today, she may be lowering them." Amber pushes herself off the bar and sashays away.

We finish our lunch and pay for the meal. As we're exiting the parking lot, I ask Conrad in the rearview mirror, "Which way, Buddy?"

He grins at the use of his nickname. "That way." He points out the far window. "Across the bridge."

We cross the sound and drive south for about a mile on Beach Drive. Locating a public access, we walk down the boardwalk, take off our shoes, and dig our feet in the sand. Conrad spreads his arms wide like wings and zooms around the beach, mimicking the seagulls. My heart sings as I watch him. After months of being cooped up, he can be a rambunctious little boy again.

We spend hours splashing in the surf, building sandcastles, and searching for shells. Our clothes are wet and sandy, our cheeks pink from the sun, but I haven't felt this alive since our ordeal started last May. While my intuition tells me Water's Edge is a good fit for us, we must overcome several major hurdles before I can make the final decision.

Myrtle, a tiny woman with a neat silver-streaked bob, greets us in the foyer when we arrive at her bed and breakfast. "Welcome to Myrtle's. Are you interested in a room for the night?"

"We would love to stay here, although I'm not sure I can afford your rates."

Her smile reaches her warm brown eyes. "You're in luck. Most of my guests checked out today, and I have several cottage rooms available. I can offer you our offseason rate."

Even with the discount, the room is more than I want to spend on accommodations. But it's late in the day, and we have nowhere else to go. "Thank you, Myrtle. We'd like a room for three nights."

The prepaid credit cards Eleanor gave me didn't last long, and I'm down to my last six hundred dollars. Water's Edge is the remote, small town I was hoping for, and I'm putting all my eggs in one basket. I have until Thursday to figure out my life.

Myrtle leads us past a sweeping staircase, out the back door, and down a garden path to a wood-framed cottage. Located on the first floor, our room features two queen beds and a sitting room that opens onto a small brick patio. After showing me the idiosyncrasies of the room, she hands me a key and invites us to join her for breakfast in the morning on the porch.

"That sounds lovely," I say. *One less meal I have to pay for.*

I wait until she's gone before placing a call to the attorney working on my trust. When Rick Harvey doesn't answer, I leave a detailed message. I didn't expect him to be working on Labor Day, but when he hasn't returned my call by noon on Tuesday, I call again, leaving a more urgent message.

As Amber predicted, the preschool has no openings for the fall semester. "But since we're very early into the school year, there's always a chance one of our students will drop out," Betty Bleaker says.

"Do you have anyone else on the waiting list?" I ask.

"Not at the moment," Betty says. "I need to meet your son before I can place him on the list. Are you available tomorrow morning for a tour?"

In other words, she wants to make certain Conrad is a suitable candidate for their program. "I can make that work."

Conrad and I spend the afternoon looking for somewhere suitable to live. Available housing is limited in Water's Edge. There are no apartment buildings offering modern conveniences and outdoor heated pools. A carriage house on the estate of a historic home has potential. But it's only one bedroom and unfurnished. And I'm fresh out of furniture.

I also don't have the money for the deposit and first month's rent. I can't even open a checking account with no money to fund it. I reach out to Rick Harvey three more times, pleading with him to call me back.

I'm near tears over breakfast at Myrtle's on Wednesday morning. In twenty-four hours, we'll be homeless. I don't have the gas money to leave town, even if we had somewhere else to go. I could apply for the server job at The Nest, but who would watch Conrad while I'm at work? And where would we live until I earn the money for an apartment?

Our visit to the preschool goes well. Conrad engages the teacher and interacts with the other children. Betty Bleaker appears impressed with his advanced development. "I will add him to the waitlist for now, although I can't guarantee anything will open for the fall. However, one of our families is relocating to Atlanta over the holidays, and I can offer him that spot for the spring term."

January is only four months away. It's not ideal, but I can make do. "That would be wonderful. Thank you so much."

"I'll need a deposit to hold the space. We can go to my office and do the paperwork."

The bottom drops out of my stomach. I have no money for a deposit. "Can I take the paperwork home with me? I'm new to town, and I haven't had a chance to open a checking account. I can drop the forms off later in the week."

"Yes, dear. Of course," Betty says and walks us to the school's main entrance.

Conrad skips along beside me on the way to the car. "I like this school, Mommy. Can I go here?"

"Yes, son. As soon as a space opens up. But you may have to wait until after Christmas." I don't have the heart to tell him we may have to leave town.

We pick up premade sandwiches from a convenience store on our way over to Sandy Island. After we have our picnic, we go for a long walk on the beach. I have enough money for this last night at Myrtle's, and then we're on our own. I'm wondering how safe it would be to sleep on the beach when I spot a sign advertising a house for rent for the winter. We trudge through the thick sand to the little yellow cottage. Finding the screen door unlocked, we sneak onto the porch and peek through the window at the living room, which features attractive furnishings in neutral colors. Beyond the living room is a small dining area and adjacent kitchen.

Conrad tugs on my hand. "Are we gonna live here, Mommy?"

"I don't know, son. Would you like to live at the beach instead of in town?"

"Duh. I can go swimming every day and play in the sand with my dump trucks," he says, forgetting that he'd left them at the farm.

"I doubt we can afford it. But I can call about the price."

"May I help you, sir?" The voice startles me, and I turn around to face an older gentleman with snow-white hair.

"Oops. I'm sorry, *ma'am*. I saw your short hair and mistook you for a young man."

I run my hand across the top of my head. "No need to apologize. I noticed your sign. Are you the owner?"

"I am. Would you like a tour?"

"Sure! Why not?" I extend my hand. "I'm Julia Becker, and this is my son, Conrad."

Conrad chimes in. "But my friends call me Buddy."

The man smiles, revealing a mouthful of teeth too white and perfect to be real.

"I'm Godfry Phillips. My friends call me Fry."

Conrad scrunches up his nose. "Why? Because you like french fries?"

I gently knee my son in the back. "Don't be rude, Conrad."

The old man chuckles. "No worries. The second part of my name is spelled f-r-y but pronounced f-r-e-e. From the time I was a young boy like you, my friends have been calling me Fry."

Conrad appears confused but lets it slide.

As we follow Fry inside, I notice he's surprisingly fit for someone who must be at least seventy years old.

In addition to the rooms we've already viewed through the window, there are two bedrooms sharing a single bath. The cottage is clean and quaint and will more than adequately fulfill our needs while we get our feet on the ground.

When we return to the porch, Conrad asks if he can swing on the hammock in the small backyard. "Sure, Buddy. I'll be right here if you need me." I turn to Fry. "What are the terms of your lease?"

"I can only offer a nine-month lease. The house is already booked solid for next summer." Fry tells me the monthly rental rate, which I could easily afford if I had access to my money.

"The cottage is perfect for us, but I'm new to town and haven't opened a bank account yet. Any chance you could hold it for me until tomorrow? I'll be an ideal tenant. I'm neat and clean and promise not to throw any wild parties."

Fry furrows his bushy white brow. "I'm not too keen on renting to outsiders. You're not in any kinda trouble, are you?"

I keep a straight face despite my racing heart. "No, sir. I'm a writer. I like to move around to picturesque settings for inspiration."

His eyes travel to Conrad, who is stretched out in the hammock staring up at the sky with his hands propped behind his head. "What about the boy's father?"

"He's deceased." It's not a total lie. Grady is dead to me.

Fry looks at me with uncertainty. "I have a feeling you're holding out on me. But I like you, and I'm willing to give you a chance. I'll give you until tomorrow at five. But I can't hold it any longer than that. Call me when you make up your mind," he says and recites his number while I enter it into my phone.

I want to hug him, but something tells me he's not the

hugging type. "Thank you, Fry. I'll let you know one way or another by tomorrow afternoon."

Conrad and I walk hand in hand back to the beach. As soon as we're out of Fry's sight, I place another unanswered call to Rick Harvey. If I don't hear back from him in twenty-four hours, I'll have to wave the white surrender flag and call Eleanor. And something tells me WITSEC won't be thrilled to have me back in the program.

TEN
WILL

Caroline and Sophie are thrilled about the prospect of living full-time at Marsh Point. Even though we're not moving until the weekend, they eagerly stuff all their belongings into whatever tote bags and suitcases they can find.

Sophie appears to feel fine, but I insist she stay home from school on Tuesday to make certain she's fully recovered from rotavirus. She's bursting with energy, and I can't hold her back on Wednesday morning. After dropping the girls at school, I make the rounds to my job sites, explaining to each of my project managers that I'll be taking the rest of the week off to tend to personal business.

"Good for you," Maurice says when I tell him I'm moving in with my sister. "Miss Ashton will take good care of you and the young'uns. I hope you'll talk to your sister about your problems. She's a good listener. Let her help you."

I grumble, "You, of all people, know how much I like having help."

"Keeping your worries bottled up inside ain't good for your soul, Will. Your wife left a big hole in your life. If you don't fill that hole with good stuff, the bad stuff will get inside you and eat you alive."

"That's excellent advice. I'll keep that in mind." I slap his back. "You're a good friend, my man. I don't know what I'd do without you."

"God willing, you won't find out anytime soon," Maurice says with a chuckle.

The girls and I grab sandwiches from Custom Crust on the way home from school. After we eat, I turn on a movie for them while I wander aimlessly around the house, attempting to wrap my mind around the daunting process of moving. I understand the logic in not making major decisions after the death of a loved one. And while my initial plan was to rent the house while we're living at Marsh Point, I don't ever want to come back here. This was Tracy's house. She made her mark on every room. To move on without her, I need a fresh start.

I call the best real estate agent in town, who happens to be my sister's old high school friend. I catch Sadie between appointments, and she arrives at my door in less than ten minutes.

"I would be thrilled to list your house, Will. But are you sure it's a good idea so soon after Tracy's death?"

"I'm positive." I tell her my reasons for wanting to sell the house and explain that I'm moving in with Ashton so she can help me take care of the girls.

Sadie claps her hands. "In that case, give me the tour," she says and follows me from room to room with blonde curls bouncing around her shoulders and high heels clickety-clacking on the hardwood floors.

I end the tour in the primary bedroom.

Sadie runs a hand along a row of hanging dresses in Tracy's walk-in closet. "Your wife had excellent taste. Who's running the boutique for you?"

"Her assistant, Mollie. She's doing a great job. I'm hoping she'll eventually offer to buy it."

Sadie fingers the sleeve of a faux fur jacket. "What will you do with all these clothes?"

"I'm not sure. They'll be out of style by the time my girls are old enough to wear them. I guess I'll donate them to charity." I give Sadie the once-over. "Unless you want them. You're about her size."

Sadie retracts her hand from the faux fur jacket. "No way! I couldn't take her clothes."

"Why not? You'd save me from having to donate them to charity. Besides, Tracy would love for someone as fashionable as you to have them."

She hesitates. "How about if I share them with my friends? Do you think Tracy would be okay with that?"

I smile. "She would love that."

We leave the primary bedroom and head back towards the foyer. "So, when were you thinking of putting it on the market?"

"As soon as possible. We're moving to Marsh Point this weekend."

"That'll work in your favor. You won't have to worry about keeping it clean for showings. Leave the furniture if you can. Houses show better furnished." She retrieves her purse and opens the front door. "I'll gather some comps, and we'll set a price. Mariner's Landing is hot right now. You should do well. Yours is one of the nicest homes."

"I built all the houses in the development, Sadie. This one is *the* nicest."

Sadie's face lights up. "Right. I forgot. You being the builder is an excellent selling point. I'll be in touch soon," she says and hurries out to her SUV.

She's no sooner left than I receive a call from my sister. Ashton doesn't give me a chance to say hello before she blurts, "I found you a child custody attorney. Or I should say, Sully found you one. Her name is Vanessa Longhorn, and she lives in Charleston. I've set up a Zoom call for you at five o'clock today. The link should be in your inbox. Vanessa has a long waiting list of clients. She's doing Sully a favor by talking to you. He designed the cabinets in her gazillion-dollar home on Kiawah Island. She's interviewing you, Will. You'll have to convince her to represent you."

"I'm not sure I want someone so exclusive representing me."

"You do if you want to keep the girls. I did some research. Good custody attorneys are hard to find. She can pick and choose her clients."

"All right. I guess there's no harm in talking to her."

A few minutes before five, I set the girls up at the kitchen table with their paper dolls and promise to cook them hamburgers on the grill if they're quiet while I'm on the call. Sitting down at my desk in my study, I click on the link for the conference and wait ten minutes for the attorney to appear. Vanessa has black hair pulled in a tight bun and stark features that give her face a hard edge.

I expect her to get right down to business, but Vanessa surprises me when she says, "I'm so sorry for your loss, Mr. Darby. I frequently shopped at her boutique on my way to visit my parents in Florida, and I was saddened to hear about her accident."

"Thank you," I croak out past the unexpected lump in my throat. I've heard countless stories like this since Tracy's death. She touched the lives of many. I wait until I trust my voice again before continuing. "And please, call me Will."

She gives me a curt nod. "And I'm Vanessa. Now, down to business. I've spoken with opposing counsel. They are building their case against you based on your anger management issues."

Heat flushes through my body. "Tracy's parents are making that up. I don't have any anger management issues."

Vanessa arches a manicured brow. "Really? Because I've seen the video with the reporter outside the police station. It's all over the Internet."

"That reporter accused me of killing my wife. What was I supposed to do?"

"Walking away would've been a better choice." Vanessa rifles through some papers on her desk. "And speaking of your wife's accident. Tracy confided in her parents. According to them, she was terrified of you and planning to leave you."

I fall back in my chair. "Sounds like you've already decided I'm guilty."

"I'm playing devil's advocate. Only you and Tracy know what happened on that boat."

My gut hardens. "My mother passed away in May. So, I haven't been in a good place these past few months. Is a guy not allowed to grieve?"

"Were you close to your mother, Will?"

"If you're suggesting I was pretending to grieve—"

Vanessa folds her hands on her desk. "I'm not suggesting anything, but I can tell you're harboring a lot of emotions." She hesitates, as though deciding whether to continue. "You shouldn't have custody of young children if you're struggling with anger issues."

Her words strike a nerve, leaving me speechless and uncertain of how to reply.

Vanessa rants on, "The Beaumonts' attorney was practically gloating about your short temper. She'll use it to their advantage, and when she's done, you'll be painted as a villain. They are pushing for a speedy trial based on the potential danger for their grandchildren. I can convince the judge to delay, but only if you're willing to seek help. At some point, you'll need to have an extensive psychiatric evaluation. It's the only way, Will. Otherwise, you're going to lose your daughters."

I look down as I swallow back tears.

"And there's the matter of Bert."

My head shoots up. "How do you know about Bert?"

"From the Beaumonts' attorney. They plan to dredge up every bad thing you've done in your life, and they will drag your name through the mud. I'm one of the top custody attorneys in the Southeast. I didn't get that reputation by losing cases. If you want to win, you have to do as I say. Take a couple of days to think it over. But don't wait too long. Your in-laws mean business."

ELEVEN
JULIA

Conrad and I load up our plates from the offerings on Myrtle's breakfast buffet. Scrambled eggs, sausage links, and hash browns. Ham biscuits and toast slathered with fig preserves and mini muffins in fall flavors such as cranberry and pumpkin spice.

"My, you two sure are hungry this morning," Myrtle says when she stops by our table.

"Yes, ma'am. You're such a talented cook, we can't help ourselves." I don't tell her this may be our last meal for a while. After three days of leaving Rick Harvey long-winded voice messages, he still hasn't returned my call. At this point, I'm doubtful he ever will.

When we finish eating, we return to our room for our luggage and say a tearful goodbye to our new friend. I don't have enough gas to leave town. What is left in my tank will run out soon, and we'll be stranded wherever we land. The beach is as good a place as any. If we get desperate, I'll break into one of the beach houses, now abandoned by owners who have returned to their everyday lives in other parts of the state.

I'm watching my son chase seagulls when I receive a call from

Betty Bleaker at the preschool. "I have great news for you! One of our students has dropped out of the program. If you're still interested, the spot is yours."

Without thinking, I blurt out, "Thank you so much. When can he start?"

"On Monday, provided you get me the paperwork and fall tuition payment by the end of business today."

I grip my phone, wondering what I'm getting myself into. "Of course. I have some things to take care of this morning. How late will you be there this afternoon?"

"Until four o'clock. I'll see you soon," Betty says and hangs up.

I call Rick Harvey again, leaving yet another desperate message.

I get to my feet and begin pacing up and down the beach. I consider reaching out to Eleanor, and asking if she could wire me the money for tuition. With Conrad in school, I could work mornings at The Nest until I can save enough money for rent. I hear stories about people living in their cars. It's not ideal, but it wouldn't be forever.

As I'm searching my phone for Eleanor's contact information, Rick Harvey's number flashes on my screen with an incoming call. "Mr. Harvey! I'm sorry to blow up your phone, but I'm desperate to talk to you."

"I understand. I apologize for the delay in getting back to you. Your case is unusual. Truthfully, I was worried I wouldn't be able to make it work. But this morning everything has fallen into place."

I let out a sigh of relief. "Thank goodness."

"I've learned a lot about indie publishing these past few days. Your royalties are healthy now, but because your situation prohibits you from advertising and promoting your backlist, those royalties will eventually dwindle."

"I realize that, and I plan to start working on a new novel soon. Under a pen name of course. I'm in a bit of a bind, Mr. Harvey. I'm flat broke. When can I have access to my money?"

"Well . . ."

He hesitates so long my heart begins pounding against my rib cage. "Is there a problem?"

"Yes and no. I've established your trust, but I'm waiting for the funds to be transferred. I'd say no later than Wednesday of next week."

My mind races. Wednesday is seven whole days away. "Isn't there anything you can do to expedite it? If I don't pay my son's preschool tuition by four o'clock, he'll lose his spot. And I've found a cottage for lease, but the deposit and first month's rent are also due today."

"I see. You *are* in a bind. Let me think for a minute," he says, and silence fills the line.

I hold my breath, waiting for his answer. I'm about to give up hope when he says, "I may be able to work a little magic. Would five thousand dollars be enough to hold you over until next week?"

After paying the rent and tuition, I would only have a small amount leftover. But we'll have a roof over our heads, and Conrad will be in school. Who cares if we have to eat cheese sandwiches for a few days? "That would be great! Thank you so much. I've been holding off opening a checking account until I have money to fund it. Can you help me with that?"

"Of course. Go to the bank now and fill out the paperwork. Let me know once that's done, and I'll send the wire."

"I'm hesitant to let you off the phone for fear you'll ignore me when I call," I say in a teasing tone, even though I'm completely serious.

He chuckles. "I promise that won't happen again. If I don't answer right away, I'll call you back within a couple of minutes."

"Great. I'm headed to the bank now."

Pocketing my phone, I call out to my son. "Guess what, Buddy? I worked it out so we can rent the cottage. And you can go to your new school starting on Monday."

"Yay!" Conrad runs over to me and skips alongside me back to the car.

On the drive back to town, I call Fry to let him know we'll be renting the cottage. "Glad to hear it. I'm at the cottage now, working on a couple of small projects. Come whenever you can, and I'll give you the key."

"I have a few errands to run in town, but I can be there in a couple of hours. Do you mind texting me the address? We came up from the beach the other day, and I'm not sure I can find it by road." I know exactly where the cottage is located, but I need the address to open my bank account.

"Sure thing. I'll send it as soon as we hang up."

My phone pings with the incoming text as I'm pulling into the parking lot at Blue Heron Savings and Loan. Everything goes miraculously smoothly at the bank. Gertrude, an adept customer service representative, walks me through the process of filling out the application. I cross my fingers when she runs the credit check, but my fake credentials pass the test. Rick Harvey answers his phone when I call. He sends the wire, and I leave the bank with three pages of printed checks to hold me over until my new checks and debit card arrive in the mail next week.

We stop by the preschool to drop off the paperwork and check for Conrad's tuition before continuing over the Merri-weather Bridge. My spirits soar as we park in front of the yellow cottage. After a rough few days, everything appears to be falling into place.

Fry greets us at the front door. "Welcome to your new home," he says stepping out of the way for us to enter.

I wave one of my temporary checks at him. "I'm ready to sign the lease."

"Very good. But first, we have a few things to discuss."

My heart sinks. I knew it was too good to be true. "Is something wrong?"

"Not at all. Just a couple of things I need to clarify. While the cottage comes fully furnished, towels and bed linens are not included. Nor are pots and pans and small appliances."

I mentally add up the costs of these items. I won't have to purchase everything at once. And these are things we'll take with us when we find our permanent home. "In that case, I need to go shopping. Where's the best place in town to find these things?"

"Coastal Hardware will have everything you need."

I raise an eyebrow. "Even sheets and towels?"

"Yes, ma'am. They carry everything under the sun except groceries. Now, let me show you a few of the mechanics of the cottage."

For the next ten minutes, Conrad and I follow Fry around the house as he shows us the fuse box, water main valve, and light switches that control both indoor and outdoor fixtures. "You're welcome to use the gas grill as long as you keep it clean."

"Yes, sir. I will." I write the check to cover the deposit and first month's rent, and he hands me a set of keys.

I muss my son's cropped hair. "Come on, Buddy. We need to go back to town to the hardware store."

"Aww. Do we have to? Can't I stay here with Fry?"

"Fry owns the cottage, but he doesn't live here," I explain to my son. "I'm sure he has other things he needs to be doing."

Conrad pouts. "Can't we go shopping tomorrow?"

"I'm sorry, son. But we have to go today. We don't have any towels or sheets for the beds. I promise it won't take long."

"But I want to swing in the hammock," Conrad protests.

Fry chuckles. "He's welcome to stay with me, as long as you're not gone too long. I have a few more chores to do here anyway."

Conrad presses his hands together under his chin. "Please, Mommy."

The idea of leaving my son with a total stranger terrifies me. We haven't been apart in months except for the brief period when I was testifying against Grady in court. What if Conrad accidentally tells him something about our old life? What if Fry gets busy and forgets to watch him? The ocean is just over the dunes. My son is an okay swimmer, but a wave could knock him down and the current could carry him out to sea. Fry seems like a nice man, but he could be a child molester for all I know.

As though reading my mind, Fry says, "Don't worry, Julia. I'll take good care of your boy. I have seven grandchildren of my own."

I look from Conrad's eager face to Fry's kind eyes. Against my better judgment, I give in. "All right. I won't be gone long, and you have my cell number if you need me."

As I leave the cottage, I convince myself this is a good warm-up for Monday, when Conrad goes for his first day at school. But after what we've experienced this year, I'm not sure I'll ever feel comfortable leaving him again.

TWELVE
WILL

The girls are a whirlwind of chaos, darting through the house with piercing squeals that make my head pound.

"Girls! Please! Quiet down! You're driving me crazy."

Caroline slides in socked feet to a halt in front of me. "But we're bored, Daddy. Come play with us."

"I can't right now, sweetheart. I have to finish packing. I'm moving our stuff to Marsh Point while you're at school tomorrow."

"Yippee." Caroline dances around, shaking her fanny with her arms in the air.

I fold my arms over my chest as I watch her. "Where did you learn those dance moves?"

"Alicia taught me," Caroline says about our next-door neighbor. "Do we get to spend tomorrow night with Aunt Ashton?"

"Indeed we do. Tomorrow night and every night after that for the foreseeable future. After I pick you up from school, we'll load up on groceries and drive out to Marsh Point. If you help me unpack and get settled, I'll cook steaks on the grill to celebrate."

"Yay!" Caroline screams and takes off again chasing her sister in circles around the center hallway.

Needing a break from the pandemonium, I text Sherry next door and ask if Alicia is free to watch the girls while I go to the hardware store. Five minutes later, the eleven-year-old appears at the front door.

"And no dancing," I tell Alicia in a warning tone. When she gives me a confused look, I say, "Never mind."

At Coastal Hardware, I spend a few minutes looking at fishing rods before filling my cart with packing supplies. I'm approaching the checkout counter when a young man jumps in line ahead of me. "Hey! What do you think you're doing?"

The man peers at me from around the mountain of towels and home goods in his cart. "Sorry. I was here first."

The *he* is really a *she* with super short hair and a trim figure with few curves. I roll my cart out of her way. "By all means, ladies first. Not that you look much like a lady," I say under my breath.

Her eyes mist over, and she lowers her head, staring down at the floor.

"Gosh. I'm sorry. I didn't mean to upset you. I'm in a hurry to get back to my children."

"Same," she says, sniffling as she dabs at her eyes with a tissue.

Guilt tugs at my heartstrings. Did I touch on a sore nerve? Or is she just having a bad day?

When the woman reaches the checkout counter, the clerk looks at her with pity. "Oh, honey. Are you okay? Do you need me to call for help?"

The woman shoots a death glare in my direction. "I'm fine. Just overly sensitive." She pays for her items with a check and wrestles her cart out of the store.

By the time I reach the small parking lot behind the store, the woman is finishing loading her items into her trunk. I approach slowly so as not to startle her. "I'm sorry about what I said in the store. I have a bad habit of putting my foot in my mouth."

"No worries. I'm used to jerks making fun of my appearance." She slams her trunk and turns to face me. Her big eyes are golden brown, the color of brandy, and she has a smattering of freckles across her nose. Her face is quite feminine despite her other boyish features.

"You have to admit, your short hair makes you look like a boy."

A smile tugs at the corners of her lips. "You should probably quit while you're ahead."

I laugh. "Probably."

As I hold her gaze, a connection passes between us. I sense a deep sadness in this woman that makes me want to know more about her, and I'm disappointed when she gets in her car and drives away.

I think about her on the way home, and she's still on my mind as I cook steaks on the grill the following evening at Marsh Point. I'm so lost in thought, I don't hear Ashton approach until she's standing beside me.

"You're a million miles away. What're you thinking about?" she asks, handing me a bottle of beer.

I set down my fork and take the beer from her. "A lot of things. Including your generosity in letting us stay here."

"The house belongs to our family, Will. You're welcome to live here as long as you like. Are you all settled?"

"Pretty much," I say, popping the cap off the beer bottle. "The girls pitched in. They've unpacked their suitcases, but I doubt their rooms are very organized."

Ashton glances past me at Caroline and Sophie, swinging hula hoops around their hips nearby in the yard. "Does my heart good to see them so excited about Marsh Point." She inhales a deep breath. "If you're like me, you'll find living on the water therapeutic."

"I never found peace here while Mama was alive. But I admit my nerves are already less frazzled."

"I wish I could help out more with the girls, but I'm crazy busy at work right now."

"I understand. We'll figure something out. Since it doesn't

appear any spots will open in the after-school program, they may have to hang out with me at work in the afternoons."

"They would probably like that. You could get them mini hard hats." Ashton lowers herself to a lounge chair. "Maybe I can take them a couple of afternoons a week. I could pick the girls up from school, feed them lunch, and send them to their rooms for quiet time while I work."

"That would be great if you're willing to give it a shot. They're usually pretty beat after school."

"We'll sit down with our calendars this weekend and come up with a schedule," Ashton says brightly.

I plop down in the chair beside her. "When're they starting on your pool?" I asked, wondering about the small pool and terrace she'd designed for the area off the kitchen where the girls are playing.

"They can't get to me until after the holidays. Depending on the weather, they hope to be finished by summer." She angles her body towards me. "So how did your meeting with the custody attorney go?"

"Not great." I take a swig of beer. "I've decided to look for someone else."

Ashton sits up straight in her chair. "Someone else? Are you crazy? Vanessa is the best in the state. Did she refuse to represent you?"

I shake my head. "She'll represent me as long as I agree to her conditions."

"Let me guess. She wants you to seek counseling for your anger management problem."

"Right. And you know how I feel about shrinks."

"You may not have any choice, Will. If the Beaumonts are using your anger issues as the basis for their custody suit, any attorney you hire will insist you get help."

I feel my sister's eyes on me, but I can't bring myself to look at her.

"Do you *want* Tracy's parents to have custody of the girls?"

"Of course not." I remember Vanessa's warning about not waiting too long. *Your in-laws mean business.*

"Then you're going to have to fight for them. Even if that means stepping outside your comfort zone and seeking counseling."

"Whatever." I get up from my chair to check on the steaks.

"I'm serious," Ashton says in a low hiss so as not to alarm the girls.

"Chill, Ashton. Vanessa gave me a few days to decide. I've been busy with the move. I'll call her first thing Monday morning."

"Ugh. You're being so hardheaded right now. This is important, Will. Call her now. I don't care what time it is. If she doesn't answer, leave a voice message."

Our sister's minivan appears in the driveway, saving me from having to respond. "Here comes trouble. Did you invite her over?"

Standing, Ashton says, "No. But be nice."

Carrie gets out of the minivan and strides angrily towards us. She gestures at the grill. "Thanks for inviting me to your family cookout. Or am I no longer considered a member of the family?"

"Don't be silly," Ashton says. "I would've invited you if I'd thought you'd come. Will and the girls moved in today. They're going to be living here for a while."

Carrie's mouth drops open. "How long is a while?"

"Don't worry about it," I say. "It's not permanent. Ashton has offered to help me with the girls until I get back on my feet."

"Saint Ashton to the rescue." Carrie glares at Ashton and then turns her attention to me. "Did you help yourself to Mom and Dad's old room?"

"As a matter of fact, I did. And why wouldn't I? No one else is using it."

Ashton's fingers graze Carrie's arm. "You know you're welcome here anytime. We still have two available bedrooms upstairs."

I turn my back on them as I transfer the steaks from the grill to a platter. Ashton has more patience than me for our sister's poor-me attitude.

"You promised to update the guesthouse for me," Carrie says about the two-story tabby structure across the lawn where Ashton lived during renovations.

"And I'll eventually get to it," Ashton says in a clipped tone. "I'm taking a breather after finishing the main house."

I turn off the grill and face my sisters. "Are you here for a reason, Carrie? Because our dinner is ready." I glance down at the platter of meat in my hands. "I'd invite you to stay, but I only bought four steaks."

Carrie lets out a humph. "No, Will. I'm not here for a *reason*. I happened to be driving by. When I saw you, I decided to stop in and say hi. Now I wish I hadn't." She spins on her heels and storms off.

"Yeah, right?" I say under my breath. "She was just driving by the last house on the street."

Sadness crosses Ashton's face. "She's probably just lonely. I wish she didn't feel such animosity towards us."

We eat at the table on the veranda, and after dinner, we play card games with Sophie and Caroline.

Exhausted from moving, I turn in with the girls, but I can't sleep from worrying about the pending custody case. Am I willing to risk losing my children because I refuse to seek therapy? Maurice's words come back to me. *Keeping all your worries bottled up inside ain't good for your soul. Miss Tracy left a big hole in your life. If you don't fill that hole with good stuff, the bad stuff will get inside you and eat you alive.*

Maurice is only partially right. Tracy's death left a void in my life. But I've had a hole in my soul for as long as I can remember. Since I was fifteen years old. I don't need a shrink to tell me my anger issues stem from Bert's accident. I've spent my lifetime trying to forget about the past. What good will come from dredging it all up?

I'm still awake when Sophie cries out in her sleep sometime around midnight. I hurry down the hall to her room at the back of the house.

"Daddy!" She extends her little arms to me. "I had a bad dream."

"I'm sorry, sweetheart. But I'm here now." I stretch out beside her on the bed. We snuggle until I'm certain she's fallen back asleep. But when I try to slip out of the bed, she stirs again.

"Please don't go, Daddy. I need you."

I wrap my arms around her small frame. "I'm right here. I'll stay as long as you need me."

I feel Sophie's heart beating against my chest. She's only two years old, an innocent child who needs nurturing and protection from the evil forces in the world. No one has ever needed me before. Tracy's independent nature was one of the things I admired the most about her. Her strength and determination attracted me to her from the beginning. I can only imagine what she'd think about her parents having custody of our children. She wasn't close to her parents, nor did she trust them. I'll never know why she'd turned to them for support during the days prior to her death. Perhaps because they were her only family. Or maybe she was planning to divorce me, and she needed her powerful daddy to help her get custody of the girls.

I am a flawed man with skeletons in the closet, but I am this child's biological father, and I will not give my children up without a fight. First thing in the morning, I'll call Vanessa and hire her as my attorney. Even if it means I have to see a shrink.

THIRTEEN
JULIA

Living at the beach has advantages. During the day, a clear view of my surroundings allows me to be on the constant lookout for predators. But at night, I can't see beyond the area around the cottage illuminated by outside sconce lights. Any person or thing could be lurking in that inky darkness.

I'm too on edge to sleep. I'm growing accustomed to the cottage's noises—the ice maker clinking, the toilet running, and the palmetto fronds rustling in the wind outside. But the other sounds, footsteps on the porch and the rattling of the doorknob, are figments of my imagination. Built for summer habitation, the cottage's exterior walls are paper thin. A strong man, a member of a cartel, could easily break them down.

All things considered, our first weekend in the cottage is pleasant. We cook hot dogs on the grill for every meal, not only because we're on a budget but because Conrad loves them. And we spend our days on the beach. Pure joy fills my heart watching my son splash in the surf. He's beginning to lose the weight he'd gained these past few months, and his skin has a healthy glow from the sun. The physical exertion wears him out, and he sleeps like a baby at night.

He's excited to start school on Monday morning, and I'm eager to have three hours to myself for the first time in as long as I can remember. On the drive to town, I remind him how he should respond if anyone asks about his father.

"Daddy lives somewhere else now," he says.

Conrad will eventually forget his father and everything that has happened these past few months. When he's old enough to understand, I'll tell him the truth.

"And where did we move here from?" I grill him.

"Colorado. I've got this, Mom," he says, sounding like a teenager instead of a preschooler.

On my way home, I stop in at Coastal Hardware for some preliminary shopping, for when Rick Harvey grants me access to my trust in a few days. I scrutinize the many items on the home security aisle—door jammer bars, motion detectors, window and door alarms. Fry wasn't joking when he said Coastal Hardware sells everything. Their assortment of guns is impressive.

I'm studying a glass case of handguns when a voice says, "Let me know if you would like to see any of our handguns."

I look up to see an attractive young woman with long mahogany hair behind the counter. She is not the type I would expect from a gun salesperson. "Thanks. But I'm not ready to buy."

She opens the case from her side. "Why not have a closer look for when you are ready?"

For the next few minutes, she shows me several small automatic pistols that would suit my needs.

"Have you ever shot a handgun?" she asks.

"Yes. Many times with—" I stop myself from telling her about my experiences shooting pistols with Grady on our farm. "But I'm rusty, and I would like to apply for my concealed carry permit."

"We can help you with that. Coastal Hardware operates a shooting range just outside of town. Coincidentally, I teach there two mornings a week." She hands me her business card. "You can reserve your space in the class online, but I wouldn't wait. On average, we book out a couple of weeks."

I read her contact information and drop her card in my purse. "Thank you, Courtney."

When I sit down with my computer thirty minutes later, I sign up for the next available class, two weeks from tomorrow. I create a new document in my writing software and begin typing the opening chapter of the novel I've been mentally plotting these past few months. I stop when I reach eight hundred words. Everything about this story feels wrong. The thriller novel in my head is based on my life of late. And it's entirely too close to home. I'm not a thriller writer at heart. I love my cozy mysteries. I need to find a genre more lighthearted and geared towards women.

Closing my computer, I go for a long walk on the beach, killing time until I have to pick Conrad up from school. I finally have some me time, and I'm counting the minutes until I see my son again. I hope his day is going well, and I'm relieved to see him wearing a big smile when he climbs into the car a few minutes past twelve.

When he climbs into the back seat, he thrusts a crumpled yellow flyer at me. "Here, Mommy. This is for you."

"What is it?" I ask, smoothing out the crumpled paper.

"The teacher is having an important meeting for parents tonight, and you have to go."

I fold the flyer and slip it into my purse. "Sorry, Buddy. But I can't leave you at home alone."

"You could get me a babysitter," Conrad suggests as we drive away from the school.

"I don't know any babysitters," I say, and think to myself, *I can't afford to pay for one if I did.*

When I stop at a red light, I shift in my seat to look at him. "So? How was your first day?"

He bobs his head. "Really good. I made a new friend."

The light turns green, and I return my attention to the road as we cross over the Merriweather Bridge. "That's exciting. What's his name?"

"It's a girl. Her name is Caroline. She's really pretty. And she's nice."

I chuckle. If my son is already interested in girls at age four, I'm in big trouble when he becomes a teenager.

"Can I invite Caroline over for a playdate soon?" Conrad asks.

"Give me a few more days to get settled first." I can't invite another child into our fold until I'm certain we're out of danger.

I've no sooner parked in front of the cottage than Fry pulls into the driveway. "What're you up to? I didn't expect to see you today."

"I finally got the part to fix the running toilet," he says, waving the packaged part at me.

Conrad runs over to Fry and hugs him around the waist. "Fry, can you babysit for me tonight? Mommy has to go to a parents' meeting at my new school."

I pry my son off our landlord. "Conrad! You're being rude. We can't impose on Fry like that."

"I don't mind. My wife has her book group tonight. I could use the company. What time is your meeting?"

I fish the flyer out of my purse. "At seven o'clock. I won't be gone long. I can have him ready for bed. You won't have to do a thing."

Fry smiles down at Conrad. "I'll bring a bag of popcorn, and we can watch some television."

———

I ARRIVE at school a few minutes late, and the meeting is already in progress. The door opens from the hall into the back of the classroom. Noticing all the seats are taken, I slip into the room and inch my way along the back wall towards the window.

"Hello again," says a voice near my ear.

I look up, startled to see the jerk who made fun of my hair at the hardware store leaning against the wall next to me. I say under my breath, "*You* again."

Directing my attention to the front of the classroom, I try to absorb what Mrs. Rogers is telling us about field trips, birthday treats, and what to do when your child is sick. But the jerk's presence distracts me, and I observe him out of the corner of my eye. He's tall and handsome with broad shoulders and blue eyes the color of an ice glacier. He wears a silicone ring on his left hand. Is that in place of a wedding band? If he's married, where is his wife? If one of them had to stay at home with their child, wouldn't the father be the obvious choice?

Another couple arrives late to the meeting, jostling me closer to the jerk. The heat of his body sends a jolt of electricity through me, landing in the pit of my stomach and sending a flood of warmth further south. What is this about? I can't possibly be attracted to him. He's a jerk. And he's married. And I don't even know his name.

When the teacher adjourns the meeting, I make my way through the mob. I'm almost to the door when a hand on my shoulder stops me. "Are you still mad at me about the hair comment?"

I turn to face the jerk's chest, my eyes traveling up his thick throat and across his scruffy chin to his face. He wears an aura of sadness that makes me want to know more about him. Alarm bells ring in my head, warning me to stay away from this man. "How can I be mad at you when I don't even know you?"

He cocks his head, those glacier eyes seeing right through me. "We can remedy that. I'm Will Darby." When I don't respond, he prompts me, "And you are?"

"Leaving. Goodbye, Will Darby," I say and slip through the crowd as I make my escape to the safety of my car.

I push the speed limit on the way home, putting as much

distance as possible between Will Darby and me. His pained face haunts me. He's suffering as much as I am, but whatever his story, I don't need any more trouble.

FOURTEEN
WILL

From the list of psychiatrists Vanessa provides, I choose the one she recommends most highly. Since she lives twenty minutes away in Beaufort, she may be unfamiliar with my illustrious family. If I'm going to paint my life's story to a virtual stranger, I prefer to start with a blank canvas and be the one holding the brush.

A member of Vanessa's staff schedules the appointment for me for the following morning. I arrive at a stunning historic waterfront estate on the Beaufort River. I assume I've been given the wrong address, but I ring the doorbell anyway, and I'm surprised when the doctor answers the door.

"Welcome. I'm Clementine Montgomery, but everyone calls me Clemmy."

Her physical appearance is befitting a woman with an old-fashioned name like Clementine. She's plump with rosy cheeks, and silver hair fastened loosely atop her head. She reminds me of Mrs. Claus or the Pillsbury dough girl. Her soft smile and twinkling blue eyes immediately set me at ease, an effect I've rarely experienced from a stranger.

I extend my hand to her. "Very nice to meet you, Clemmy. I'm Will Darby."

"Let's go to my office and get better acquainted."

As I follow her through the house to the veranda, I take in the priceless antiques and artwork adorning the center hallway. If she makes this kind of money counseling patients, I'm in the wrong profession.

A sitting area occupies the end of the porch nearest the water and includes a daybed swing, the proverbial shrink's couch. I choose to sit in a comfortable wicker lounger and the therapist sits down on the sofa next to me.

"I hope you don't mind my unconventional office. The water has a tranquilizing effect on the mind," Clemmy says as she pours sweet tea from a pitcher into two glasses of ice.

I stare out at the river. "Not at all. It is very peaceful here. And your home is lovely."

She hands me a glass of tea. "Tell me about yourself, Will Darby."

"I . . .um . . . I'm not sure where to start. Did Vanessa explain my situation?"

"She did not. I prefer to get to know you myself," Clemmy says, and settles back on the sofa.

I take a sip of tea and set the glass down on the coffee table. "Well, let's see. I'm a custom home builder and I have two daughters, ages two and four, Sophie and Caroline respectively."

Clemmy smiles. "Little girls are so sweet. How does their mother fit in the picture?"

"She died in a boating accident last summer."

Her breath hitches. "Oh goodness. I'm so sorry. Since you're working with Vanessa, I assumed you were involved in a custody dispute with your wife."

"My case is a little more complicated. The custody dispute is with Tracy's parents, my in-laws."

Her expression turns serious. "A judge would never take children away from their biological father without probable cause. And an attorney would be hesitant to represent the grandparents unless they have reason to believe they can win custody. What do they have against you, Will?"

My eyes fall to my lap. "They claim I have anger management issues."

She leans in closer to me. "Do you?"

I'm taken aback by her abruptness. "I admit I have a short fuse at times. That's the way I'm wired. But it's not as bad as everyone is making it out to be."

"Who is everyone, Will?" When I hesitate, she says, "I can't help you unless you tell me the truth."

"My in-laws are pressuring the police to bring charges against me for murdering my wife." Sinking back in my chair, I tell her about the accident and the police hounding me and the Beaumonts' influential connections. I lose track of time, and when I glance at my watch, I realize I've gone over my allotted hour. "I'm sorry. You should've stopped me when my time was up. You probably have another patient scheduled."

"Not today. At the height of my career, I had a booming practice with a month-long waiting list. But now I only counsel a few patients at a time. I can better serve you this way. We have a lot of work ahead of us, Will. And it won't be easy. Psychotherapy is the hardest thing you'll ever do. In the essence of time, because of your pending custody case, I recommend we meet twice a week. Are you free at the same time on Friday morning?"

I sigh, wondering how I'm going to fit one more thing into my hectic schedule.

Clemmy raises an eyebrow. "Is this schedule a problem for you?"

"No, ma'am. As a single parent, I'm still trying to figure out how to juggle everything. But I can make it work."

The doctor pats my knee. "I understand. And I'm flexible.

We'll take it as it comes. I prefer to meet in person, but, if necessary, we can video conference."

I smile at the doctor. "Thank you for being so accommodating."

I rush back to Water's Edge. By the time I arrive at the preschool, I'm fifteen minutes late in picking up the girls.

Betty scolds me. "I understand you're dealing with a lot right now, Will. But it's not fair to the teachers or your children for you to be late."

"Yes, ma'am. I promise it won't happen again. Have any spaces opened up in your after-school program?"

Betty gives me a sad smile. "Unfortunately, not. And it doesn't look like anything will. But you're at the top of the list for the spring term."

That won't do me any good if I don't have custody of my children come January.

As I drive off, Caroline says, "I invited my new friend over for a playdate after school on Friday."

I jerk my head around to look at her. "You can't do that without talking to me first."

"Why?" Caroline's chin begins to quiver. "Mommy never cared when I invited people over."

Of course she didn't. Tracy had been so easygoing she readily adapted to new situations and changes in plans. "Just give me a little more time, sweetheart. I'm still trying to adjust to being both Mommy and Daddy."

When we get home, I feed the girls lunch and send them off to their rooms for quiet time. I spend an hour cleaning up the house and folding laundry. I've just sat down at the desk in my room to return emails and make business calls when the girls enter the room.

"Daddy! We're bored. Can we go outside and play?"

Getting anything accomplished with these two around is proving to be impossible.

"Sure thing," I say, pushing back from my desk.

Truth be told, the fresh air will help clear my head and give me a chance to reflect on my first therapy session.

———

THE GIRLS and I are seated at the kitchen table—they are coloring and I'm returning emails on my laptop—when Ashton arrives home from work around six o'clock.

"Honey, I'm home!" Her voice echoes throughout the house and seconds later she appears in the doorway. "What's for dinner? I'm starving."

"What do you mean? It's your turn to cook." My eyes travel across the room to the whiteboard calendar Ashton bought to help keep us organized. "Ugh. It *is* my turn. I'm sorry." I get up from the table and open the refrigerator. "Looks like we're having scrambled eggs again."

Sophie moans. "I don't like eggs."

Caroline asks, "Can't we have pizza?"

Ashton and I exchange a look. We're both tired of pizza. "What would you eat if we weren't here?" I ask her.

"Hmm. I'd probably heat a can of soup or fix a salad."

"Then we'll have a salad, and I'll order a pizza for the girls." I return to the table and place the pizza order on my computer.

Ashton crosses the room to the calendar. "Speaking of schedules, I'm supposed to drive carpool tomorrow, but I have an important meeting with new clients. Can you switch with me for Friday?"

"That's fine. Friday is better for me anyway." I don't tell her I'm going for my second session with my new shrink.

Caroline perks up. "Does that mean my new friend can come home with me on Friday?"

Ashton turns away from the whiteboard. "I don't see why not.

Once I get through this meeting tomorrow, I'll have plenty of time to spend with you on Friday."

I remove two chicken breasts from the refrigerator and place them on the grill pan on the stove. "She can have her playdate another time if it doesn't suit you."

Ashton kisses the top of Caroline's head. "Friday is fine. We'll have a good time. What's your new friend's name?"

"Buddy," Caroline says.

Ashton's lips form an O. "I see. So, your new friend is a boy."

"The girls in my class are stupid," Caroline says.

"Caroline," I scold. "Stupid is not a nice word."

She folds her arms over her chest. "Well, they are. The boys are way more fun."

Caroline chatters on about the kids in her class while I cook the chicken breasts and slice them into strips for our salads.

When the doorbell rings, I say, "That's probably the pizza," and leave the kitchen to answer it.

Ashton's voice echoes throughout the house behind me. "Will! Your phone is ringing. Want me to answer it?"

"Sure," I call back to her.

By the time I return to the kitchen with the pizza, Ashton has ended the call. Joining me at the island, she transfers slices of pizza to two plates while I finish making the salads.

"That was Buddy's mom confirming the playdate," my sister says. "She seemed overly concerned about his safety, but I reassured her the kids would be fine."

"Thank you for arranging the playdate." I lower my voice so the girls can't hear me. "The list is endless—carpool and laundry, playdates and meals."

"I think we're doing great. This is only our first week," Ashton says in her usual upbeat tone.

"We're barely treading water. And I'm not getting any work done."

A pensive expression crosses Ashton's face. "Maybe we should hire a housekeeper."

I drop the paper plates on the table in front of the girls. "That's a great idea. If we can find someone, I will gladly pay her. I now understand what Tracy meant when she claimed she needed a clone."

FIFTEEN
JULIA

Late on Wednesday afternoon, Rick Harvey calls to inform me he's wired a large sum of money to my bank account. Relief floods me when I hear the amount. If I'm careful, the money will get us through until next spring, at which time I hope to be publishing a new novel.

In my previous life, I used royalties from my writing as extra spending money—not that I needed much. Life on the farm was simple, and I accumulated a substantial savings. Now, for the first time, I'm living on my own earnings, and that independence fills me with pride.

I'm doing it, Eleanor, I think. *I'm making it on my own.*

While Conrad is in school on Thursday morning, I confirm the deposit has arrived in my bank account and go on a shopping spree at Coastal Hardware. I purchase a basic security system but splurge on accessories for my handgun. I stop by the shooting range for a session on my way home. My aim needs work, but I could stop an intruder if necessary.

Conrad and I spend the afternoon installing our security system, and I feel slightly more at peace when I retire that night.

Since Conrad is going home from school with Caroline on

Friday, I plan to spend the entire day writing. I have a new idea for a thriller plot that has nothing to do with human trafficking and witness protection programs. But when I sit down at my computer with a cup of chai tea, my thoughts soon drift to Will Darby. He's been at the forefront of my mind since I saw him at the parents' meeting on Monday night. By the time I finish my tea without having written a word, I close my computer and decide to go for a walk on the beach.

Will Darby is married, and I'm not ready for a relationship. I can't be with him, but nothing's stopping me from writing about him. As I stroll along the surf with the sun warming my back, I daydream about a young woman returning home after a long absence to claim the inheritance her estranged mother left her—a waterfront inn in the South Carolina Lowcountry. The character's name is Anna. Simple and sweet. On her first day back in town, she encounters an old high school boyfriend, Jason Rainy. Anna and Jason has a nice ring to It. Sparks fly between my two characters. They still have chemistry after all these years. Her inn needs work and, ironically, he's a builder. Problem is, she's still furious at him for cheating on her with her best friend back in high school.

Hope blossoms inside of me as I hurry back to the cottage. I've finally come up with a plot I'm inspired to write. For the next hour, I research trending romance subgenres and tropes. Because the thought of writing sex scenes makes me blush, I'll stick to clean and wholesome romance with the second chance love trope.

After eating a ham sandwich for lunch, I take my computer out to the hammock where I spend the afternoon creating a rough outline for my novel.

I wasn't thrilled about the idea of my son having a playdate, but Caroline's mother promised to keep a close eye on them, and I ignored my fears and permitted him to go. I escaped WITSEC to give him a normal life. I can't hold him back. But when I arrive at Marsh Point, I'm disheartened to find the kids playing alone in the side yard with no grown-ups in sight. I walk around to the side of the house facing the marsh where an attractive woman is sitting in a rocker on the porch.

"Hello there!" I say as I climb the steps to the porch. "I'm Conrad's mom, Julia."

"Hi, Julia. I'm Ashton. Have a seat," she says, patting the arm of the chair next to her. "The kids have gotten along marvelously, but they've worn me out, and I'm taking a breather."

I laugh as I lower myself to the rocker. "Kids will do that. I see you have two daughters. Are they close in age?"

"That's Sophie. They are two years apart. But they aren't my daughters. They're my nieces, my brother's children. His wife died in a boating accident this summer."

I gasp as my hand flies to my mouth. "That's awful. I'm so sorry."

Ashton presses her lips thin. "It's been a tough time. They recently moved in with me so I can help him with the girls. I don't have children of my own, and we're like the blind leading the blind."

From inside the house, footfalls on hardwood floors echo through the open door. When I crane my neck to see behind me, my heart rate quickens at the sight of Will Darby standing in the doorway.

OMG, I think as I connect the dots. Will is Caroline's father. He's not married or divorced. He's widowed.

Will exits the house onto the porch. "What're you doing here?"

"I came to pick up my son from his playdate with your daughter. Your sister was just telling me about your wife's accident. I'm so sorry."

"I don't want your pity," he says with an icy glare.

Ashton stares horrified at her brother. "Don't be rude, Will."

Will's shoulders slump. "Forgive me. I've had a tough day. Let me change into shorts, and we'll go for a boat ride."

My eyes travel to the end of the dock where a small boat sits high on a lift. I wonder if this is the boat from the accident that killed his wife.

As though reading my mind, Will says, "Don't worry. I'll make sure you don't die." His smile fades. "I shouldn't joke about the accident. Tracy and I got caught out in a storm. She was driving. She handled the boat wrong, and it cost her her life."

"That must have been awful for you. I'm not worried about your driving. I'm from Colorado. I've never ridden on a boat."

"Then we need to fix that. Round up the kids, and I'll meet you on the dock."

The kids are thrilled at the prospect of a boat ride. We herd them over to a pile of life jackets in the carport. I locate the right size jackets for both Conrad and me. We slip them on over our clothes and zip them up tight.

Ashton laughs when she sees me. "You don't have to wear that unless you don't know how to swim."

"I know how to swim. I just feel better with this on," I say, hugging my life-jacketed self.

"Suit yourself."

Will gawks at the sight of me in the life jacket. "I have my captain's license, Julia. I never take chances with passengers onboard."

"I trust you. But I told you, I've never been out in a boat before."

He shrugs. "Whatever. As long as you feel safe."

Will is lowering the boat lift when Ashton receives a work-related call. "Y'all go ahead. I need to take care of something before five o'clock," she says and dashes up the dock towards the house.

Will helps everyone aboard the boat. The kids crowd onto the bench seat up front, and I stand awkwardly at the rear. "Where should I sit?" I ask Will as he pushes off from the dock.

He takes his place behind the steering wheel. "Wherever you want. You can ride with the kids up front or on the leaning post with me." He pats the seat beside him. "But you need to be holding on to something when I put the boat in gear."

I join him on the leaning post and grab onto the console railing.

"Can we go fast?" Conrad calls out to Will.

Will shakes his head. "Sorry. I don't want to scare your mom," he says, glancing over at me with mischief in his eyes.

"Puh-lease," Caroline and Conrad say in unison.

"We'll go fast for a minute. But then I want to show your mom the town from the water."

I hold on tight as he speeds up, and the boat rises out of the water. The hum of the motor and the whistle of the wind make it difficult to hear, and we don't speak until he slows again as we approach the bridge.

When he slows the boat, I say, "Tell me about this Merriweather person the bridge was named after."

"He was one of the town's founding fathers. Believe it or not, I come from a long line of Merriweathers. My mother was the last to bear the name."

I find this fascinating. I've never known anyone so rooted in a place before. "So, you're a true South Carolinian."

"Born and raised," Will says and recites the town's history as we putt-putt along.

When we reach the city marina, we turn around and head back in the direction we came. Will picks up enough speed to appease the children but not prevent us from talking.

"So, you're new to town. Water's Edge is off the beaten path. Did your husband come here for work?"

"No husband. I just went through an unpleasant divorce."

He casts a sideways glance at me. "That sounds serious."

"It was. Fortunately, he's out of our lives forever."

The heat radiating from Will's body makes me swoon. I can't help but think of him differently now that I know he's a widower. But his wife has only been dead a couple of months. I assume he's in no shape emotionally to start a new romance. I'll continue pretending he's Jason and I'm Anna. I commit what I'm feeling about him to memory to write about these feelings later.

When we cruise past the house, I ask, "Where are we going?"

"I thought we'd ride to the mouth of the ocean." He eyes my life jacket. "You'll be more comfortable if you take that off."

I fold my arms over my chest. "No way! Not until we get back to the dock."

He chuckles. "Suit yourself," he says and presses the throttle to increase speed.

I never knew being on the water could be so liberating. I feel free with the wind blowing through my hair and the salt air tingling my nose. When we reach the mouth of the ocean, I point at a sprawling modern house on a large spread of land. "Who lives there?"

"Cliff and Corey Matheson. They're from New England. That's their retirement home. Ashton designed it, and I built it. It's our largest project to date. Pretty amazing, isn't it?"

"Stunning. Tell me about it. Do you build many contemporary homes?"

He shakes his head. "This is the first. My sister is a traditionalist like me, but we both learned a lot from the project. The house is U-shaped with an interior garden courtyard and an infinity pool overlooking the mouth of the inlet. Ashton calls it her crowning achievement."

"I can see why. Maybe it'll be featured in a magazine one day."

"Maybe," he says, and I can tell he likes that idea.

We arrive back at the house to find Ashton starting the grill. "I figured we'd eat early. I'm sure the kids are starving. Julia, can you and Conrad stay for dinner?"

Before I can answer, Will chimes in, "Yes! Please stay! You belong in our house of misfits."

I look up at him from under furrowed brow. "You'll need to explain that comment."

Will blushes. "I didn't mean to offend you. But when you think about it, we're an interesting threesome. You've banished your husband to Siberia, Ashton sent hers to prison, and I'm a single dad struggling to make it through the day."

"That sorta makes sense. I guess," I say in a skeptical tone. "Thank you for the invitation. We'd love to stay for dinner. As long as the subject of husbands is off duty." I'm dying to know why Ashton's husband is in prison, but I won't ask for fear she'll question me about mine."

Ashton flashes her pearly white teeth. "Deal."

Preparing for dinner is a group effort. We chat like three old friends as we work. Ashton tells me about her career as an architect, and Will talks briefly about being a builder. I enjoy hearing about their joint projects and appreciation for historic preservation.

When Ashton asks what I do for a living, I tell her I'm a stay-at-home mom and wannabe author. This leads to a lengthy discussion about the novels we've recently read.

Our threesome feels like a group of people bonded by a common denominator. Although instead of misfits, I would label us the Wounded Hearts Club.

SIXTEEN
WILL

I'm at the sink rinsing dinner plates when I feel my sister's eyes boring a hole into the side of my head. I glance over at her. "What's wrong?"

"You're humming." She removes the meat platter from the sink and begins drying it with a dish towel. "Not that there's anything wrong with humming. Just out of character for you."

"I agree. I'm not one to sing. I'm distracted. I have a lot on my mind." I place the plate in the dishwasher and reach for another.

Ashton nudges me with her elbow. "Is Julia the object of these thoughts? You seem quite taken with her."

"Julia? No way. She's not my type. Her hair's too short."

Ashton stops drying. "Are you joking? She's stunningly beautiful. She can totally pull off the boy-short cut. What does a woman's hair have to do with her character anyway?"

"Nothing, I guess. Besides, it's too soon after Tracy's death for me to be thinking about another woman," I say more to myself than my sister.

Ashton opens a deep drawer and slides the platter in with the other serving plates. "I admit, I'm a little suspicious of Julia."

I glance over at her. "How so?"

"She says she's from Colorado, but earlier in the day, Buddy told me he moved here from Texas."

I wave off her concern. "He's four years old. I'm sure he's just confused."

"You're probably right. But if not Julia, what's with the good mood?"

I place the last plate in the dishwasher and close the door. "Is a guy not allowed to be in a good mood?"

"Yes. But you're not most guys." She drapes the damp dish-towel over the oven's door handle.

I lean back against the counter. "Truth be told, I have no reason to be humming. My therapy session this morning was tough. This was only my second session. I'm terrified of what's to come."

"I'm sorry, Will. Do you wanna talk about it?"

"Maybe. After I give the girls their bath," I say, pushing off the counter.

I drag my exhausted daughters up the stairs to the Jack and Jill bathroom that connects their two bedrooms. They whine during bath time and turn down my offer to read to them. We say prayers, and I tuck them into their respective beds, kissing each on the fore-head before turning out the lights.

When I go back downstairs, Ashton has opened a bottle of red wine and moved outside to the veranda. I grab a glass and join her. "I thought you quit drinking."

She looks up at me. "I have for the most part. But I see nothing wrong in having just one glass at the end of a hectic week."

"I agree." I hold my glass up to hers. "Cheers." I take a sip of wine and settle back in the rocker. "The days are getting shorter."

"Mm-hmm. And the nights cooler." Ashton rests her head against the back of the chair. "I love this time of year. It'll be Halloween soon. Being the last house on a dead-end street, I doubt we get many trick-or-treaters."

"Sophie and Caroline are already discussing their costumes," I say. "Barbie, due to the popularity of the movie, is the hot costume for girls this year. They already own so many dress-up clothes. Why can't they just wear one of those costumes?"

"Ha. Where's the fun in that?" Ashton rolls her head on the back of the chair to look at me. "Tell me about therapy."

I stare down at my wine. "Dr. Clemmy should be paying me. I'm the one doing all the hard work. She asks so many questions and expects me to have the answers."

Ashton barks out a laugh. "That's the nature of the process. You identify your life's defining moments. Scrutinize them ad nauseam. And then file them away in the back of your memory closet for good."

"You know the process well. I didn't realize you'd spent so much time in therapy."

"Oh yeah. I've spent a small fortune trying to get this brain straight." She taps her temple. "And after everything Owen put me through, I'm considering going back for more."

I run a thumb around the rim of my wine glass. "I don't see the point in dredging up all these memories. Our parents did a number on us. Dad neglected us while Mom was mentally and physically abusing us. We were raised in a nuthouse."

"You and Savannah had it the worst," Ashton says.

"Do you think she's still alive?"

"She's alive. I feel it in my gut. She's probably strumming her guitar and captivating audiences with her amazing voice in some remote part of the world where we'd never think to look for her."

I consider the possibility. "If that's the case, why hasn't your investigator found her? You've had him on retainer for years."

"I fired that guy. He bled me dry and did nothing to find Savannah. As soon as Carter gets some free time, he's going to look into her case," Ashton says in reference to the private investigator she'd paid to unearth her husband's nefarious activities.

"What if he finds her? How weird would it be if Savannah came home after all this time?"

Ashton leaves her rocker and moves over to the railing, staring out at the amber sky of the setting sun. "Weird in a good way. If the world hasn't hardened her up. She was always the sweet one. Mama's happy-go-lucky little angel."

"Until Mama took her baby away," I mutter.

A pained expression crosses my sister's face. "I wonder if Savannah had more children. We could have nieces and nephews we don't even know about."

"I never thought about that. Caroline and Sophie could have more cousins out in the world somewhere."

Ashton watches the sun make its final descent before turning to face me. "Having therapy sessions twice a week is intense, Will. You should count on things getting tougher before they get better."

I drain the last of my wine. "I'm aware of what's coming, and I'm dreading having to tell Clemmy about Bert. I've worked so hard to put the accident behind me. Nothing good will come from reliving it again after all this time."

"I disagree." Ashton comes to stand in front of me, pulling me to my feet. "In my opinion, your bottled-up emotions are more about the accident than our dysfunctional past. You blame yourself for what happened to Bert. And that is the source of your anger."

I hang my head. "You might be right."

She lifts my chin so that I have to look at her. "Trust me on this, Will. Once you work through these emotions, you'll be free of the ties binding you to the past. And you can finally lead a happy life."

"That life won't be so happy if my in-laws take my children away from me. If I'm in prison for murdering my wife."

"Keep the faith. You and I will face whatever happens together."

I pull her in for a hug. "Thank you, Ashton. For everything

you're doing for me. I don't think I could make it through this without you."

She hugs me tight. "I should be thanking you, little brother. For finally letting me be a part of your life."

———

THE WEEKEND IS a whirlwind of activity. When I'm not entertaining the girls, I'm cleaning, doing laundry, and helping Ashton with odd jobs around the house. Come Sunday afternoon, instead of feeling refreshed after a two-day break from work, I'm exhausted.

The girls are swimming in the sound with Ashton, and I'm cooking chicken breasts on the grill when Maurice's truck pulls into the driveway.

"Hey, boss. I hope you don't mind me stopping by on a Sunday. I had some extra time and thought I'd haul off the last of the building supplies." He looks down at the chicken. "Isn't it a little early for dinner?"

"I'm meal prepping for the week. Not only am I a mother and father to my children, but I'm chef and housekeeper, chauffeur, and handyman. Do you know where I can find another one of me?"

Maurice lets out a roar. "Not off the top of my head. But I know where you can find a housekeeper, babysitter, and part-time cook."

My ears perk up. "Do tell."

"My sister just moved back to town from Columbia. She divorced her husband and is looking for full-time work. She's never had a career. Keeping house and taking care of kids is all she's ever known."

"She sounds too good to be true. Does she drive?"

"Of course, she drives, boss. Who doesn't drive these days?" He pulls out his phone. "I'll forward you her contact information.”

“No! Get her on the phone now! If she’s still free, I’ll hire her on the spot.”

Maurice looks up from his phone. “But you’ve never even met her.”

“She’s your sister, Maurice. That’s the only recommendation I need.”

He hunches a beefy shoulder. “If you say so.” He places the call and steps away for a minute to talk to his sister. When he comes back, he hands me the phone. “Her name is Mia. I told her about your wife’s accident.”

I take the phone from him. “Hello, Mia. This is Will Darby. I understand you’re looking for work.”

“Yes, sir. My boys are both in high school. They’re involved in after-school sports, so I’m free all day. I can do whatever you need. Drive carpool. Clean. Cook. Laundry. I’m used to managing a busy household. Maurice thinks so highly of you, I’d be honored to work for you, Mr. Darby.”

“And I’d be honored to have you. And please, call me Will. Can you start tomorrow morning?”

“Yes, sir. I can come around eight-thirty after I drop my sons at school.”

“Wonderful. Thank you, Mia. See you in the morning.”

I end the call and hand the phone back to Maurice. “I owe you one, Maurice. I might finally get some work done, maybe even have some semblance of my life back.”

Maurice pockets his phone. “You won’t regret it. Mia’s a real hard worker.”

“I don’t doubt it if she’s anything like you.”

“That’s mighty kind of you to say.” Removing his cap, Maurice wipes the sweat off his forehead with the back of his hand. “Well, I’d better get to work,” he says and heads off to the carport.

I remove the chicken from the grill and take the platter inside to the kitchen. Grabbing a beer out of the refrigerator, I head for the beach where the girls are splashing in the water and Ashton is stretched out in a beach chair, reading a novel.

I drop down to the sand beside her. "I have amazing news," I say and tell her about Mia.

Ashton raises her chair to a sitting position. "That's amazing, Will! But don't you think you should've interviewed her in person first?"

I take a swig of beer. "If she were anyone else, I would have. But she's Maurice's sister, and I trust him with my life." As the words leave my mouth, a sense of foreboding overcomes me. These are my children. Why would I hire the first housekeeper who comes along without even checking references, let alone conducting a background check?

I hardly sleep that night for worrying about what I've gotten myself into. If Mia doesn't work out, I'll have to fire her, which will upset Maurice. And I can't afford to have my best foreman angry at me.

But all the worry was for nothing. I'm immediately captivated by Mia's friendly personality and quirky sense of humor. She's a lot like Maurice in both regards. When I arrive home from work on Monday afternoon, the house is clean, dinner is warming in the oven, and my girls are quietly working puzzles at the kitchen table.

"You're a godsend, Mia! Where have you been all my life?"

She beams. "Where have you been all mine? This is a dream job. I love being in your lovely home and looking out at the water while I'm doing my housework." She sweeps an arm at the high-end appliances. "I feel like a chef in a five-star restaurant cooking in this kitchen. Compared to my rambunctious boys, your daughters are angels sent from heaven." She moves over to the whiteboard. "And speaking of the girls, I hope you don't mind, but I added a couple of things to your calendar."

"I don't mind at all. That's what it's here for," I say, joining her at the whiteboard.

"Caroline's friend Buddy has invited her over for a playdate on

Wednesday after school. I spoke with Buddy's mother in the carpool line. If you want, Julia can bring Caroline home. Or I can pick her up, whichever works best for you."

"I'll text Julia and work out the details. What else?"

"Caroline has a field trip to a local herb farm on Monday of next week, and Sophie's teacher sent a reminder about bringing in a treat for her birthday next Friday." Mia points to the days on the calendar where she's neatly written in the events.

"Is it already her birthday? Time has gotten away from me. I guess I'll need to plan a party. The mere thought of entertaining a crowd of three-year-olds gives me a headache."

Mia chuckles. "I feel your pain." She looks over at my daughters. "Sophie's so young. Why not have a small party for family only?"

I comb my hands through my hair as I consider her idea. "I like that idea. And much less of a headache."

"I'm happy to help you plan it. And I'll make cupcakes for her to take into school for her birthday treat." Mia glances at her watch. "Look at the time. Unless you need something else, I should head out. I'm supposed to pick up my sons from football practice in a few minutes."

"Not at all. Go! I don't want you to be late."

Mia disappears into the laundry room. When she returns with her purse, I walk her out the kitchen door to the side porch. As her car disappears down the driveway, I thumb off a text to Julia, thanking her in advance for the playdate on Wednesday and offering to pick up Caroline on my way home from work."

As I hit the send button, I smile to myself. The idea of seeing Julia again excites me more than it should.

SEVENTEEN
JULIA

I'm thrilled with my progress on my new novel. The words flow effortlessly from my brain to the computer, forming sentences and scenes and chapters. Only a few times has the writing gone this smoothly this early in the process. But all those books became best-sellers, which leads me to believe I'm onto something big. A hit in this new genre would boost my confidence and establish my pen name, Bebe Bloom.

In addition to actually writing the book, I have a long list of other tasks to accomplish before I can launch it. I'll have to create a new website and social media profiles and accounts at all the major online bookstores. And since I can't show my face to the public, I'll have to use an avatar instead of an author photo.

On Wednesday afternoon, I'm so engrossed in creating the website header that I don't hear Will when he comes to pick up Caroline from her playdate with my son.

"Hello!" he calls out as he rounds the corner of the house.

I jump to my feet. "Hey, Will! I didn't know you were here. Did you ring the bell?"

He joins me on the porch. "I knocked. When you didn't answer, I figured you were on the beach."

I nod. "We've been back and forth to the beach all afternoon."

"They certainly seem happy enough," he says, his eyes on the kids who are kicking a soccer ball around in the yard.

"They've been great. And I've gotten a ton of work done."

He glances down at my open laptop, at the document full of words. "I can see you've been busy. Is your writing just a hobby or are you hoping to publish something soon?"

"My goal is to release my first novel early next year," I say, lifting my hands to show fingers crossed.

"That's exciting. Good luck with that. I admit, I'm not much of a reader."

I'm relieved to hear this. I'd be embarrassed for him to read my work in progress since he's the inspiration for one of my protagonists. "I doubt you'd like my books anyway. They're geared towards women." I close the laptop and cross the porch to the back door. "I'll grab Caroline's backpack for you."

Will follows me inside the house. "Charming cottage," he says as he circles the small living room. "I hope you're not planning to stay here through the winter."

I spin around to face him. "Is there a reason why I shouldn't?"

"The exterior walls aren't insulated. You can see the cracks in the siding." He points to a sliver of light creeping in through the shiplap joints. And the windows are paper thin." He taps on a window. "I'm a historic preservationist. I'm guessing this cottage was built during World War II when building materials were in short supply."

Dread overcomes me. "I don't have much choice. I've signed a nine-month lease. I guess we'll be wearing our sweaters and coats inside."

Will kneels in front of the fireplace and looks up the chimney. "I assume you know how to build a fire."

"Of course," I say, although I've never built a fire in my life.

He fiddles with the flue for a minute before straightening. "I would call a chimney sweep to make certain everything is in working order." He removes a red bandana from the back pocket of his jeans and wipes his grimy hands. "Be sure to order a cord of wood before the first cold snap. Coastal Hardware carries an oil-filled space heater. It has wheels so you can roll it from room to room. I'll text you the link."

I shiver, thinking about the long winter months ahead. "You're scaring me, Will. Are we gonna freeze to death?"

"Worst case scenario, I'll have one of my crews tack up some heavy plastic that will help keep out the cold. Did you discuss this with your landlord? I can't believe he'd rent this cottage to a woman and a child without pointing out its deficiencies."

I rack my brain trying to remember if Fry mentioned anything about the lack of insulation. "I don't think he did. But I will definitely be having that conversation with him."

"Lucky for you, we live in the South where our winters are usually pretty mild."

"Yeah, lucky me." I hand him Caroline's backpack and head back outside to the porch. "Caroline! Your daddy's here."

"Hi, Dad!" Caroline rushes over to the porch with Conrad on her heels. "Can Buddy and Miss Julia come for dinner again on Friday?"

Before Will can respond, I interject, "I'm sorry she put you on the spot. Please, don't feel obligated."

"I don't feel obligated. I would love for y'all to come. Ashton will be in Charleston, helping her boyfriend move, and we have no other plans."

"Can we go out in the boat again?" Conrad asks.

"Conrad! Don't be rude," I scold.

"It's fine." Will tousles my son's hair. "We will totally go out in the boat. Weather permitting, of course."

"Do you ever take the boat out in the ocean," I ask? "I'd love to see the cottage from the water."

"All the time. Will do it on Friday, as long as the ocean is calm."

"Yay," the kids cheer and run ahead of us around the side of the cottage.

As we follow them to the driveway, I say, "Please don't go to any trouble. I'm happy to bring some food."

"Why not make it a group effort? We'll decide on the menu together. Can you come around five? That'll give us plenty of time for a boat ride."

"Sounds perfect. I'm already looking forward to it."

When we reach his pickup truck, Will lifts his daughter into the back seat and goes around to the driver's side. He starts his engine, and Caroline rolls down her window. "Bye, Miss Julia. Thanks for having me over."

I wave to her. "Thanks for coming, sweetheart. See you Friday."

Will has no sooner left when Fry barrels down the driveway in his rusty truck. He gets out, slamming his creaky door, and lumbers over to us. "I see you got yourself a boyfriend. You sure didn't waste any time."

I glare at him. "He's not my boyfriend. Not that it's any of your business, but Will is Conrad's friend's father. He was picking her up from a playdate." I nudge Conrad towards the cottage. "Run along inside. I need to talk to Fry about something."

I wait until Conrad is out of sight before facing my landlord. "Coincidentally, Will is a builder. He noticed the lack of insulation in the cottage's exterior walls and is concerned about us staying warm this winter. You should've pointed that out to me."

"I set your rent low for a reason. The affordable rate doesn't include insulation," Fry says, his flippant tone sending a jolt of anger through me.

"I'm not joking, Fry. This is serious."

"Aw, come on, Julia. You're making a mountain out of a molehill. Besides, the Farmers' Almanac is predicting a mild winter."

"If you believe the Farmers' Almanac. What have your previous tenants done to keep warm?"

A flush creeps up Fry's neck. "I've never rented it for the entire winter. Although I had one couple stay through Christmas. They never complained about being cold. Then again, they were newlyweds. I'm sure they found plenty of ways to stay warm," he says with a chuckle.

I glance up at the roof. "Does the chimney even work?"

Fry kicks at some gravel in the driveway. "I can't remember the last time anyone built a fire in the fireplace. But I feel certain it does."

I plant my hands on my hips. "As my landlord, you need to *make* certain. I expect you to hire a chimney sweeper and buy a couple of space heaters. The good kind they sell at Coastal Hardware."

"And if I don't?"

"I'll contact the Better Business Bureau."

His expression grows serious. "We'll wait until the weather turns cold before deciding what you need."

"I was a Girl Scout, Fry. I like being prepared. I'll pay for a cord of wood, but I expect you to take care of the chimney sweep and space heaters." I don't give him a chance to argue. "Now, are you here for a reason?"

Fry appears confused, as though he can't remember why he came. Then he snaps his fingers. "I almost forgot. My wife made you a chocolate chip pound cake." He retrieves the cake from the front seat of his truck and hands it to me. "It freezes well if you want to cut it into chunks for later."

I lift the cake to my nose and sniff. "Smells delicious. Thank you. And please, thank your wife."

I should feel guilty, but I don't. He tried to pull a fast one over on me. Besides, his wife is the one who made the cake. I carry the cake inside with my head held high. I'm proud of myself for standing up to him.

EIGHTEEN
WILL

I'm distracted during my therapy session on Friday morning. I can't stop thinking about my plans with Julia for later in the day. I'm imagining our sunset boat ride with Julia perched beside me on the leaning post when Clemmy brings up the subject of Bert, jerking me out of my reverie.

I sit up straight in my chair. "Who told you about Bert?"

"You did. You've mentioned him several times."

I sink back down in my chair. "Oh. I didn't realize it."

She cocks her head to the side, her blue eyes like daggers on me. "Because he's at the forefront of your mind."

I look away from her piercing stare at the Beaufort River. There is not a cloud in the periwinkle sky, and the sun's rays are shimmering off ripples in the water. The conditions will be ideal for a ride in the ocean this evening.

I let out a heavy sigh. "I guess subconsciously, Bert is always at the forefront of my mind. I will eventually tell you about the accident, but does it have to be today?

She holds her hands out, palms up. "No time like the present."

I slowly rise out of the chair. "Do you mind if we walk? The movement will make my confession less painful."

Clemmy gets to her feet. "Whatever works for you, Will."

Leaving the porch, we head across the expanse of grass towards the water. "Bert was my best childhood friend. My *only* childhood friend. His were the only parents who allowed him to hang out at our House of Horrors."

"Because of your mother's drinking problem?"

I nod. "Word gets around. Especially in a small town. Everyone knew about her drunken tirades. Even Bert was afraid to spend the night."

"That must've been difficult for you?"

"Truth be told, I was ashamed of my mother. I couldn't bear for anyone to see what went on in our house. But Bert was different. He never judged us."

"He sounds like a genuine friend."

"Bert was the best." I stop walking when we near the river's edge. "One night, when Bert and I were fifteen, we attended a party we had no business going to. Some kids in the grade above us had broken into an abandoned house. I've never been much of a drinker. Even as a teenager, I shied away from booze. I was always afraid I'd turn out like my mother. I didn't drink a drop of alcohol that night. But Bert got sloppy drunk." My throat thickens, and I pause to collect myself. "He was making a fool of himself, and I tried to get him to leave. We were standing on the second-floor deck. I attempted to drag him over to the steps, but he refused to go. We wrestled, and Bert crashed into the railing. The wood was rotten, and he fell to the ground. He broke his neck on impact." My voice breaks, and I can't continue.

Clemmy places a comforting hand on my shoulder. "Take your time. We're in no hurry."

I swipe at the tears in my eyes. "I was inconsolable. The paramedics, who were unable to calm me down, strapped me to a gurney and drove me to the hospital where I was admitted to the psych ward. Because they assumed I'd been drinking, they refused to sedate me. They neglected to check my blood alcohol content."

The therapist's mouth fell open. "What?"

"Yep. They assumed the police had breathalyzed me. I was in the hospital for ten days. The worst part was missing Bert's funeral." I inhale an unsteady breath. I'm on the cusp of breaking down, but now that I've started telling the story, I can't stop until I get it off my chest. "The police charged me with manslaughter, and everyone at the party that night volunteered to testify against me. All kinds of rumors circulated. Some of them even claimed I'd been drunk and picked the fight with Bert."

"You poor kid. That's so unfair."

I lift my hand and let it drop. "I was the town drunk's son, guilty by association. Because I was underage, the case never went to trial." Feeling as though I might collapse, I make my way over to a nearby teak bench and plop down. Tears blur my vision as I look down at the colorful flowers planted around me.

Clemmy waits a few minutes before joining me. "Are Bert's parents still alive?"

"As far as I know. He has an older sister, Kristy. She was also at the party that night. She was furious with us for showing up uninvited. I told her I was worried about Bert. That he'd been drinking, and I was going to drive him home. But she was hanging out with her friends, and when I asked her to help me get him to the car, she told me to buzz off."

Clemmy's brow shoots up. "Wow. Talk about a heavy load of guilt. Where is Kristy now?"

"I have no clue."

"Did you ever have a chance to speak to his family about the accident?"

"I tried. I wanted to apologize. Even though it wasn't my fault, I felt responsible. I went to visit his family when I got out of the hospital, but they refused to see me. After the district attorney dropped the manslaughter charge, Bert's parents brought a civil lawsuit against me. My parents, who were worn out with the whole situation, paid them a very large sum of money."

"Did your parents send you to therapy?"

I give my head a solemn shake. "Nope."

"So, you never processed your guilt or grief, and it's been festering inside of you all these years."

I bury my face in my hands. "Pretty much."

———

I'M MENTALLY DRAINED by the time I leave Clemmy's. I'm even considering canceling my evening with Julia. But my spirits immediately brighten when she arrives at five with her arms laden with food dishes. My sister is right. Julia is stunningly beautiful. Her short hair highlights her delicate features, while her yellow sundress reveals her sun-kissed bare shoulders and dances around her shapely legs. Spotting her hard-sole sandals, I shake my head.

In response to my bewilderment, she asks, "What's wrong?"

"Nothing's wrong. But you have a lot to learn about the boating life."

I help her carry the bowl of salad and dish of warm cornbread to the kitchen. "We have chicken breasts marinating, and Mia made us a key lime pie for dessert."

"That sounds delicious," she says. "I met Mia in the carpool line. She seems wonderful."

"She's a lifesaver. Thanks to her, I was able to put in a full week at work for the first time in months."

The three children burst through the kitchen door chanting, "Boat ride! Boat ride! Boat Ride!"

I chuckle. "I'm ready. Go get your life jackets out of the carport," I say, ushering them back out of the door.

Julia calls after them. "Bring one for me."

My eyes travel the length of her dress. "You're not seriously going to cover up your pretty dress with a life preserver?"

Her cheeks turn a dainty shade of pink. "I probably won't wear it. I just feel better having one with me."

"What you really mean is you don't yet trust my boating skills." My teasing tone sounds foreign to my ears. This woman brings out a lightheartedness in me I haven't felt in a long time. I'm sure telling Clemmy about Bert had something to do with my improved mood. After holding it all inside for decades, getting it off my chest is liberating.

She flashes a brilliant smile at me. "Give a girl a break. This is only my second boating adventure."

"You'll learn. Are you ready for today's lesson?"

"Hmm. Depends on what it is."

I point at her sandals. "Never wear hard-sole shoes on a boat. Not only do they make it easier for you to slip, they scuff up the deck."

"Oops. I didn't know." Julia's eyes fall to her feet. "What should I do? I didn't bring any other shoes."

I give her a grim shake of my head. "I'm sorry. You'll have to stay behind at the house."

She appears wounded. "Seriously?"

I chuckle. "I'm just kidding. You can leave your sandals on the dock and go barefoot."

The kids return with their life jackets, and we migrate out to the dock. After lowering the boat, I help everyone onboard, and they resume their positions from our previous outing with the kids up front and a barefoot Julia beside me.

"Where to?" I call out to my four passengers as I ease away from the dock.

"The ocean," they respond in unison.

"All right. Hang on while I speed up," I say and slowly press the throttles forward.

My eyes are on Julia when the wind lifts the hem of her short dress. I catch a glimpse of her black lacy panties and have to cross my legs to hide my excitement. Casting an uncertain glance in my direction, she clambers onto the leaning post and tucks her dress between her legs.

What is wrong with me? How could I possibly be attracted to another woman so soon after my wife's death? Am I that shallow? Or were there worse problems in my marriage than I realized? I loved my wife, but I'm willing to admit I may not have been *in* love with her. Until now, I thought true love was a myth. I'm not suggesting I'm in love with Julia. We hardly know each other. But something about her moves me the way no other woman has.

Exhilarating is the word I'll use when writing about my boat ride experience in the ocean. Puffy white clouds hang low in the late afternoon sky, and the water is smooth as glass stretching beyond the horizon.

"Where would we end up if we kept heading east?" I ask Will.

"Somewhere in Africa depending on the ocean's currents. But we don't have the proper provisions for such a trip," he says with mischief in his blue eyes.

I give him a gentle shove. "Duh."

The boat glides over the swells as we cruise along the shoreline. The children are ecstatic when a school of porpoises appears, jumping and diving alongside us. They rush to the side of the boat, hanging over the bow, to watch them.

"They're not in danger of falling over, are they?" I ask Will.

"They're fine. We're barely moving," he says, but calls out to them to be careful.

After the porpoises have swum on, Will puts the boat back in gear and we ride slowly along the coast. I spot our small yellow cottage, nestled among the mammoth beach houses, and point it out to the others. "Look. There's our cottage."

"I'll try to get in for a better view," Will says and noses the boat up as close to the beach as he dare.

I'm snapping pictures with my phone when I notice a flicker of movement inside the cottage. *Is someone in my house?* I shield my eyes and squint, but I don't see anything out of the ordinary. Must have been the late-day sun playing tricks on my eyes.

I'm unaware Will is watching me until he asks, "Is something wrong?"

"Nope. Just looking to see if I remembered to leave lights on."

We continue south to the Sandy Island Club, a sprawling complex with a terrace-wrapped clubhouse, swimming pools, and tennis courts. On the way home, I'm once again in awe of the Mathesons' contemporary home and grounds on the northern tip of the island.

"What's the view like from inside the house?" I ask Will.

"Impossible to describe. With so many windows, it's like being inside a glass bubble and looking out in every direction around you. Maybe one day I'll sneak you in for a quick tour."

I smile at him. "I would love that."

By the time we arrive back at Marsh Point, the children are complaining of starvation. Will and I prepare dinner together as though we've done it hundreds of times before. We dine at the table on the veranda, and while we eat, the kids discuss what movie they'd like to watch afterward.

"Can Buddy and Miss Julia spend the night?" Caroline asks.

Will doesn't hesitate. "Sure! If they want. We have two spare rooms."

Conrad bounces on his bottom. "Can we, Mama? Puh-lease."

I pat his head. "Not tonight, sweetheart. But we can stay for the movie." When he starts to argue, I shoot him a warning look that silences him.

The children help me clear the table while Will rinses the dishes. Once the kitchen is clean, we set the threesome up in the family room with blankets, a mountain of pillows, and a huge bowl of popcorn. Will makes White Russians for us grownups—a mixture of vodka, coffee liqueur, and a dash of heavy cream—which we take outside to the veranda.

I touch my glass to his. "Thanks for having us. I had a nice time."

"Thanks for coming. I had a nice time as well," he says with a kindness in his smile I've never seen before. I can't put my finger on it, but he somehow seems different from the man I met at the hardware store a couple of weeks ago.

We stand at the corner of the porch, sipping our drinks in comfortable silence. He's easy to be with, as though I've known him for years. When a streak of lightning illuminates the darkening sky, I say, "Looks like a storm's coming."

"Mm-hmm. Ahead of a predicted cold front that's forecasted to bring us our first taste of autumn weather." Turning towards me, Will takes my glass, sets it on the railing, and tilts my face to his. He presses his soft lips to mine. "I've been wanting to do that all night," he says, his breath a whisper against my lips.

Drawing me close, he kisses me again with more urgency. Electric currents ripple throughout my body, sending tingles down to my toes. This man lights me up like a firecracker. Maybe it's because I haven't had sex in months. Or because I've endured such emotional turmoil, I'm desperate for human touch. Or maybe it's just the man himself. After the way Grady betrayed me, I never thought it possible to find love again.

I'm so lost in the kiss, in the warmth of his body against mine, that I don't hear Caroline approach until she's standing right next to us.

"Daddy?"

Startled, Will pushes me away. "Sweetheart! What is it? Why aren't you watching your movie?"

"I got up to go potty and saw you kissing Miss Julia." Caroline stares at me with her father's electric blue eyes, studying me as though in a new light. "Is she gonna be my new mama?"

Will cast an apologetic glance in my direction. "No, Caroline. Miss Julia and I are just friends. Sometimes grownups kiss their friends. Now run along back inside."

He marches her over to the double-paned doors. When he returns to my side, he says, "I'm sorry she saw that. I'm sure she's confused. And she's not the only one." He runs a finger down my cheek. "That kiss was . . . I don't know how to describe it except to say *wow*."

I'm the most confused of us three. I agree with Will. The kiss had the wow factor. But I don't want to be a friend with benefits to anyone. Most especially Will.

I grab his hand, pulling it away from my face. "I should go before the storm sets in," I say and hurry inside to collect my child and our belongings.

Will helps me carry my things to the car. After buckling Conrad into his car seat, he walks me to the driver's side. "I hope you're not upset about . . . you know . . . the kiss?"

"Not at all," I say with feigned nonchalance.

When he leans in close, I worry he's going to kiss my lips again, but he plants one on my cheek instead.

"Thanks again for having us. It was a perfect evening." I get in my car and close the door.

I assume Caroline told my son what she witnessed between her father and me on the porch. I fully expect Conrad to interrogate me, but his eyes are closed before we depart the driveway, and he's snoring softly by the time I reach the Merriweather Bridge.

With no moon or streetlights to offer illumination, Beach Drive is bathed in pitch darkness. As I drive slowly towards the cottage, I fantasize about a future with Will. Our children play together so well. How would they get along as siblings? He would move out of Marsh Point, and we would get our own home. Maybe an old house on the water with double-decker porches where I could spend my days writing. Maybe we would have a child together. At least one, maybe even two. We would be a happy couple, raising our four children in this peaceful town with no threat of outside danger. A pie-in-the-sky dream that is not likely to ever come true.

We arrive home to find the lights out in the cottage. My heart pounds in my chest as I help Conrad from the car.

"Why is it so dark, Mommy?" Conrad asks, as though sensing my tension.

"I'm not sure, son. I thought I left the lights on." I turn on my phone's flashlight, and as I'm taking hold of my son's hand, lightning cracks the night sky. "Stay close to me. We need to get inside before it pours."

The first raindrops splatter our faces as we run for the door. Using the flashlight for guidance, we make our way to the electrical panel in the kitchen. Several circuit breakers have been tripped. I flip the switches to restore the power in the cottage, and the lights blink on.

"What made the power go out?" Conrad asks.

"Who knows? Maybe the approaching storm had something to do with it."

I remember being out in the boat and thinking I saw someone moving around in the cottage. I check under the bed and in the closets for an intruder. Once I'm certain we're alone, I turn on the security system and help Conrad get ready for bed. After reading him a story, I go to the kitchen for a cup of tea. But my teacup isn't in the drying rack where I'm certain I left it with my salad plate from lunch. Goosebumps dot my arms as I search the kitchen. I find the two items in an otherwise empty dishwasher. I haven't run the dishwasher since we moved in. Because our ancient dishwasher on the farm rarely worked, I got in the habit of hand-washing my dishes. Someone was definitely in this cottage while we were gone. Did they intentionally trip the breakers so we would come home to a dark house? Are they lurking outside in the rain, waiting for an opportunity to break in?

The cup of tea forgotten, I remove my handgun from the

lockbox in my closet and insert a loaded magazine. I turn every light in the house on except the ones in Conrad's room and settle into the most comfortable chair in the living room. I'm using myself as bait. I want whoever is out there to see me. I want them to break in so I can shoot them. I'll tell the police it was a random intruder, but the killing will send a message to the cartel that I'm not to be messed with. I can and I will defend myself and my child. This is a reminder that we will never be safe from the threat of The Six. I can't drag Will into my drama, and I certainly can't put his innocent children's lives at risk.

TWENTY
WILL

With Ashton gone and Mia off for the weekend, I'm back to being a single parent and maid. There's more to do at Marsh Point than in our old home, which means the girls don't need as much entertainment. Unfortunately, this leaves me with too much time to think. And the subject of those thoughts is Bert. During the day, visions from our good times flash in my mind. But at night, I have vivid dreams about the accident. I was better off suppressing the memories. Instead of being less angry, I sense myself on the verge of a volcanic eruption.

The girls and I spend the afternoon on Saturday washing the boat, and on Sunday morning, we go to church. Afterward, feeling the need to be productive, I search the Internet for easy recipes. I stumble across a food blog for single dads—Sylvester's Solo Dad's Suppers. I appreciate the sense of humor in which Sylvester approaches single parenting. When I discover a recipe for sausage and ground beef chili, I load the girls into my truck, and we head out to the grocery store for the ingredients. The girls are playing a game on the porch outside the kitchen, and I'm attempting to dice an onion when Ashton returns home late afternoon.

She stops short inside the doorway. "I don't believe it. You're actually cooking?"

I look up from the cutting board. "I'm trying. I'm surprised onions actually make you cry." I put down the knife and dab my wet eyes with a paper towel. "What's that?" I ask, noticing the plastic jug in her hand.

"Homemade Apple Cider, fresh from Charleston's City Market." She places the jug in the refrigerator and comes to stand beside me at the counter. "What're you making?"

"Chili. How did the move go? Did Sully get settled?"

"Yes! His bungalow is charming."

I pick up the knife and return to dicing the onion. "Good thing you approve. You might be living there with him when you two get married," I tease.

"Stop!" She smacks my arm with the back of her hand. "It's way too soon to talk about marriage. Besides, I'm never leaving Marsh Point."

The children burst through the back door. "Aunt Ashton! You're back!" they say, throwing their arms around her.

Ashton strokes their hair. "Hello, girls. What'd I miss while I was gone?"

"Daddy kissed Miss Julia," Caroline says, and begins singing, "Daddy and Miss Julia sitting in a tree —

My temper flares. "Caroline!" I spin around with knife in hand. "I warned you not to bring that up again."

Tears fill Caroline's eyes as she looks from the knife to me. "I'm sorry!" she cries and flees the room with Sophie on her heels.

I exchange a look with my sister. "I shouldn't have yelled at her. But she's been going on like that ever since she saw me kissing Julia on Friday night. It was an impulse kiss. It didn't mean anything."

Ashton's hand shoots out. "You don't owe me an explanation. I'll go talk to her." She grabs her overnight bag from the counter where she left it and leaves the kitchen.

I stab the wooden cutting board with the knife. What was I thinking, pointing a knife at my daughter? I need to be more careful around my children. Caroline is just a kid. She doesn't understand why grownups might not find her childish teasing funny.

Ashton is gone for over an hour. By the time she comes back downstairs with the girls, the chili is simmering on the stove. I whisper to my sister, "Is everything okay? What took you so long?"

"Everything's fine. The girls helped me unpack, and then we spent some time organizing their closets." She lifts the lid and inspects the chili. "Shouldn't this be cooking in a Crock-Pot?"

"Sylvester suggested a Crock-Pot. But I couldn't find one."

Ashton narrows her eyes. "Who's Sylvester?"

I take the lid from her and return it to the pot. "Never mind. I'm giving you a Crock-Pot for Christmas."

Ashton goes to the refrigerator. "Does anyone want apple cider?"

The girls raise their hands. "Me! Me!"

"Count me in too," I say.

While Ashton is heating the cider, I pull my oldest daughter aside. "I'm sorry if I scared you," I say, kissing the top of her head.

"It's okay, Daddy. I'm used to you being angry all the time."

Guilt engulfs me. "I promise to work on that if you promise not to tell your friends at school about the kiss. I don't think Conrad would appreciate your classmates talking about his mom like that."

Caroline looks at me as though I've lost my mind. "Duh, Dad. I would never tell my friends. They would think that's gross."

Laughing, I give her ponytail a yank. "Okay then. Glad we got that straight."

Ashton heats the cider just enough to take the chill off. She fills four mugs and places them on a tray, which I carry out to the veranda. The girls quickly lose interest in the cider and take their Frisbee out to the yard.

"So, tell me about this kiss," Ashton says as she sips her cider.

I cut my eyes at her. "What happened to me not owing you an explanation?"

"Well, now I'm curious. I'm a woman. I'm allowed to be fickle."

"It was nothing. A heat-of-the-moment thing. But I haven't heard from Julia all weekend. I think I scared her off. I guess that's for the best. I shouldn't be starting anything with someone new so soon after Tracy's death. This town's gossipmongers would have a field day."

"Since when do you care what anyone thinks?" She takes another sip of cider and sets down her mug. "Love often has rotten timing, Will. If you stumble across an opportunity for happiness, don't let it slip away."

"I admit, I enjoy Julia's company. She's sweet and considerate and easy to be around. But she just ended a difficult marriage. I doubt she's ready yet either."

"You never know." Ashton plants her elbows on the table. "Let's talk about what set you off with Caroline. You overreacted to her teasing."

"I know. And I apologized. But she's been going on about the kiss all weekend, and I've asked her repeatedly to stop."

"She's a child. She doesn't understand. I was hoping counseling would help you manage your anger."

"My therapist is not a miracle worker, Ashton. I've been seeing her only two weeks," I say in my defense, but deep down, I'm worried I'm getting worse instead of better.

Caroline calls out from the yard. "Can we have a birthday party for Sophie next weekend?"

"Sure!" I yell back. "We'll have a family cookout, and invite Sully over."

"Aww. That's boring," Caroline says, crossing her arms over her chest.

Ashton gives me a look. "Yeah, Daddy. Grownups are boring. You should at least invite a few of her friends."

The girls come up to the porch. "Please, Daddy," Caroline says. "If Mommy were here, she would have a party for Sophie."

Here we go with the guilt treatment, I think. "That's not fair. Mommy was an expert at throwing parties. I wouldn't even know where to buy a cake."

"Let me do it," Ashton volunteers. "Throwing birthday parties is one of the things I missed out on in not having children."

"Fine. Have at it. But whatever you do, don't hire a clown. Kids are terrified of clowns."

"And rightly so. *I'm* terrified of clowns." Ashton turns her attention to Caroline and Sophie. "What do you think about arts and crafts with pumpkin painting and jewelry making?"

"Yes! That sounds like fun," Caroline says, and Sophie bobs her head.

I imagine myself surrounded by crying children. "The parents will stay with the kids, right? I don't want to babysit a bunch of two-year-olds."

Caroline crosses her eyes at me. "Sophie's turning three, Daddy. Duh."

"Yes, the parents will stay," Ashton assures me.

"Can we invite Buddy?" Caroline asks. "He's Sophie's friend too."

Inviting Buddy means Julia will come. And I would very much like to see her again. "Of course."

The girls dance around in front of us, shouting out ideas for the party.

Above the racket, Ashton yells, "I've been meaning to have Dad and May May over. This is the perfect opportunity."

I curl my lip. "Must we?"

"Yes, we must. He's Sophie's grandfather. Families are supposed to celebrate birthdays together. Besides, he and May May were good to you after Tracy's accident."

"All right," I say in a reluctant tone. "This will give me a chance to have a long overdue conversation with him about the past."

"Good luck with that," she teases. "I'll make certain I'm out of the room."

Caroline's eyes grow wide as though struck with a thought. She stops dancing and whispers something in Sophie's ear.

"Can I have a Barbie birthday cake?" Sophie asks.

Ashton laughs. "We'll see. Now run along. Go play Frisbee," she says, shooing them off the porch.

I wait for them to leave. "Don't you dare get her a Barbie cake. She's too young."

"Don't worry. I'll come up with something age appropriate."

Even though I won't be doing the planning, I have a feeling I'm in over my head with this birthday party.

———

THOUGHTS OF BERT'S accident continue to weigh heavily on me throughout the evening. On Monday afternoon, when my anxiety brings on a panic attack, I drive to Beaufort for an emergency session with Clemmy.

I plopped down in my usual chair on her porch. "Thanks for seeing me on such short notice. I haven't had a panic attack in years, and it scared me."

"I'm glad you called me. That's what I'm here for."

"I felt this enormous sense of relief on Friday after unburdening myself to you about Bert's accident. But it was short-lived. Now I can't stop thinking about Bert. All these emotions have built up inside of me. I feel as though I might burst."

Clemmy slips on her reading glasses and sits back in her chair with her notebook. "Tell me about your weekend. Did you do anything out of the ordinary on Friday afternoon? Anything that might've distracted you from thinking about Bert."

My mind drifts to my evening spent with Julia. "My daughter's friend and his mother came over for a boat ride. After dinner, Julia and I set the kids up with a movie and went outside to the porch. I surprised both of us by kissing her. I sense a strong chemistry between us. But it's way too soon after Tracy's death. This brings up the issue of how I could possibly be attracted to another woman only two months after losing my wife in a tragic accident." I bury my face in my hands. "I'm such a mess, Clemmy. When will things get better?"

"This range of emotions is normal, Will. You will have ups and downs as you work your way through the process. What would your wife think about you finding a new love interest?"

"We talked about that many times. She would want me to move on with my life."

"And that's what I think too. You're going through a lot right now, Will. I suggest you embrace anything and anyone who offers you happiness. Although I advise you to proceed with caution and to be honest with Julia about your therapy."

I sit up straighter in the chair as some of the guilt slips away. "I will. For her sake and mine. She just got out of an unhappy marriage. We need each other right now. And she makes me feel alive again."

"Good." Clemmy crosses her legs. "Now, tell me what you're thinking and how you're feeling about Bert."

"I've been remembering the good times we had as kids. But I've had these horrible nightmares about the accident. I'm just so angry." I tell her about the knife incident with Caroline. "I've denied it for so long, but now it's as clear as the light of day. The anger is a part of me, lying just beneath the surface and waiting for something to trigger it."

"And who are you angry with, Will?"

I dig my thumb into my chest. "Myself. I should've tried harder to save him."

"What else could you have done? You hadn't been drinking.

You tried to get him to leave. You told his sister you were worried about him, but she didn't do anything to help."

A moment of silence passes as I consider what else I could've done to save Bert. "I guess nothing, short of calling the police or his parents. The fight is a blur. He came after me, and we wrestled. The railing was rotten. It could've easily been me who fell off the balcony."

"It was an accident, no different than a car crash." Clemmy pauses a minute, letting this sink in. "Who else are you angry with?"

I rake my hands through my hair as I remember the months following the accident when no one would speak to me. "Everyone who was at the party that night who turned against me."

Clemmy chews on the end of her pen while she thinks. "Put yourself in their shoes." She jabs the pen at me. "If the situation were reversed, and you were the one who died, do you think those people would've turned on Bert?"

I hesitate before answering. I've never thought about the situation like that. "Probably. We were teenagers, and someone we knew had died. For many of us, that was our first experience with death."

She jots something in her notebook. "Are you still in touch with any of them?"

"Of course. Some of them are my friends."

"And these friends are no longer angry with you about Bert's death?"

I shrug. "I guess not. We never talk about it."

"So they've forgiven you?"

My eyes go wide. "I see where you're going with this. If they've forgiven me, why can't I forgive myself?"

"You have to give yourself permission. And you will in time." Clemmy leans in closer to me. "Who are you the angriest at, Will?"

"My mother." The realization strikes me so hard my head jerks back. "She didn't believe me. She insisted we settle the civil suit."

"Which was the same as an admission of your guilt," Clemmy says in a somber tone.

A kilowatt lightbulb blinks on inside my head. "Exactly. No wonder I hated her so much." I get to my feet and walk over to railing. "So many things in my life suddenly make sense. All these years, my anger has prevented me from seeing the forest for the trees."

"You were treated unfairly by many people. And you were just a kid. Even though Bert's parents were hurting, they should've given you a chance to apologize." Clemmy comes to stand beside me. "You did good work here today. You've identified the source of your anger, and you can now begin the process of healing."

I lower my head as I turn towards her. "How do I do that?"

"One step at a time."

TWENTY-ONE
JULIA

We make it through the weekend with no attempted break-ins. While I'm confident we're out of immediate danger, since I can't explain how the dishes got in the dishwasher, I continue about my life with a heightened sense of awareness.

On Tuesday morning, after completing Courtney's training, I receive my certification, and I'm ready to apply for a concealed weapon permit. I drive straight from the shooting range to city hall and fill out the paperwork. If approved, my permit will arrive via mail in ninety days. Three months seems like an eternity to wait when the boogeymen are after you.

I haven't heard from Will, and I wonder whether he regrets kissing me. I sent the wrong impression by freaking out. He took me by surprise, and I wasn't prepared. But that doesn't mean I didn't enjoy the kiss. Way more than I should have.

I'm disappointed when Ashton, instead of Will, calls to invite us to Sophie's birthday party on Saturday. So he's not interested in me after all. While the kiss meant nothing to him, I'm unable to forget the feel of Will's lips on mine. I continue to use my attraction to him as inspiration for my novel. I'm completing the first draft in record time, and I hope to be done by the end of the week.

Using my pen name, I place an order for the cover with my old designer. If all goes as planned, I'll launch *Sweet Temptation* by Bebe Bloom in mid-January.

Conrad is thrilled about attending Sophie's birthday party, and when we go shopping at the toy store on Main Street on Saturday morning, he spends an inordinate amount of time choosing her gift. He finally settles on a stuffed bassett hound he names Baxter.

"Shouldn't you let Sophie choose the name?" I say as we wait in line at checkout.

He holds the dog up close to my face. "But he looks like a Baxter."

"How do you know it's a he? I think *she* looks like a Daisy."

He studies the dog. "I can see that. I guess you're right. We should let Sophie decide."

I smile at him. "I think that's wise."

We arrive home to find Fry waiting in the driveway. He comes around to my side of the car, opening the door for me. "There you are. I was getting worried."

"We were at the toy store picking out a birthday gift. What's up?"

"I was in the neighborhood and thought I'd stop by for the rent."

Unaccustomed to paying my own bills, I'd forgotten the rent is due tomorrow. I'll need to set a calendar reminder for next month. "I was going to bring it to you tomorrow, but since you're here, come on in."

While I write the check, Fry looks around the cottage, making certain everything is in order. "I assume you noticed I fixed the leaky pipe under the sink."

I look up from my checkbook. "Why would I notice when I never knew the pipe was leaking? When did you fix it?"

"Last Friday evening. You weren't here when I stopped by. I was in and out in ten minutes. I figured you wouldn't mind."

My jaw goes slack. Wouldn't mind? Is he crazy? He put me through hell, thinking the boogeymen had located us.

"Did you put my cup and plate in the dishwasher?"

"Yep. You shouldn't leave dirty dishes in the sink. They attract ants and roaches."

"They weren't dirty, Fry. I washed them with soap and water and was letting them dry on the rack. Conrad and I don't dirty enough dishes to bother with the dishwasher. It saves on energy and water." I tear out the check and hand it to him. "We talked about you not coming in when I'm not here. I'll ask you again to respect my privacy."

"Yes, ma'am. I'm sorry. I'm just used to coming and going whenever I wish."

"You're violating my rights as your tenant. Do it again, and I'll have to find somewhere else to live."

"Understood." He folds the check in half and slips it into his pocket. "I'll be on my way."

Locking the door behind him, I go to my room to change clothes for the party. It's warm out today with afternoon temperatures expected to reach near eighty degrees. My two sundresses are too summery, and shorts are inappropriate. I finally settle on a pair of blue jeans and a black halter top.

I can hardly believe my eyes when we arrive at Marsh Point. The entire side yard off the kitchen is set up with seasonal games like bobbing for apples and corn hole tosses.

"Whoa! It's like a circus." Conrad says, his face pressed to the car window.

"Or a fall festival." I park my car haphazardly in the crowded driveway and help Conrad out. "Looks like they invited the entire town."

"I know! I see a lot of the kids from my class." After adding his gift to the overflowing table, Conrad runs off to find Caroline, leaving me standing alone. Noticing a harried-looking Ashton organizing the sack race, I make my way through the crowd of children and parents towards her.

"This is amazing," I say, sweeping a hand at the festivities. "You should charge admission."

Ashton bursts out laughing. "I may have gotten a little carried away." Her blue eyes search through the crowd for Mia, who is helping a group of children balance apples on their heads. "I blame Mia. She kept coming up with fabulous ideas for the games. I couldn't choose, so I decided to do them all."

I snicker. "I'll remember not to ask for her input when planning Conrad's birthday. Do you need some help?"

Ashton appears grateful. "Do I ever. Jump in wherever."

I pitch in to help with games like pinning the stem on the pumpkin and guessing the weight of the pumpkin. An hour passes before I see Will standing at the edge of the crowd near the porch. Our eyes meet, and he waves me over.

"Your sister has set the bar high. Thank goodness Conrad's birthday is in January."

Will gives me a peck on the cheek. "This is a spectacle. She literally invited every kid in town *and* their parents. No telling how much it's costing me."

"But the kids are having a blast."

"True. Come with me. I need to talk to you about something." Will takes me by the hand and leads me across the lawn to the water. "I've been thinking a lot about you this week. I hope you're not still upset with me about the kiss."

"Not at all. I hope you're not upset with me for running out on you."

"I don't blame you. I caught both of us off guard."

I wring my hands together. "I should've texted you to thank you for the boat ride and dinner. But I was worried you didn't want to hear from me."

"So that explains it." He wipes fake sweat off his forehead with the back of his hand. "I figured you were done with me." He sets his piercing blue eyes on my lips. "I very much enjoyed the kiss. I'd do it again if we weren't in the direct line of sight of a hundred children."

My face warms, and I have no idea what to say in response.

"Did Conrad ever say anything to you about the kiss?"

I shake my head. "I don't think Caroline told him."

"I'm glad for your sake. My daughter teased me mercilessly all weekend." His face brightens, as though a thought has just occurred to him. "Hey! Would you consider going on a proper date with me next Saturday? We'll leave the kids at home, and I'll take you out for a nice dinner."

"I'd like that very much. But I have no idea where to find a babysitter."

"Hmm." He strokes his chin. "I haven't thought of that. I can see if Mia's available, and she can keep all three kids here."

I smile at him. "That sounds wonderful if we can work it out."

"So, how's the writing coming?"

"Great! I finished my first draft yesterday."

He offers me a high five. "Excellent. Congratulations."

"Thank you. I'm excited. My editor is lined up, and the cover design is in the works. If all goes as planned, my novel will be on bookshelves in January."

His face scrunches up as though confused. "I thought this was your first novel, but you sound like a professional author."

Careful, Julia, I warn myself. *You almost gave yourself away.*

I chuckle with feigned indifference. "I could be a professional considering all the webinars I've attended. I've been planning for this moment for a long time."

Someone in the party crowd catches Will's attention, and he seems to tune me out as I ramble on about online courses and Facebook groups.

"Excuse me a minute," Will says, his fingers grazing my arm. "I need to speak with someone. I'll call you later in the week to work out our dinner plans."

An emptiness fills me when he leaves me standing alone. How can this man I hardly know have such an impact on my emotions? He asked me out on a date. He must sense the connection between us. Dinner will allow us to get better acquainted.

I watch Will approach an older couple, whom I assume are his parents. He shakes the man's hand and hugs the woman with the gray braid. Even from afar, I sense tension between Will and his father.

Rejoining the crowd, I accept a glass of sweet tea from Mia and mingle with the other preschool moms. But Will is never far from my line of sight, and I'm more than a little jealous at the way Ellie flirts with him. Conrad says Ellie's daughter, Zoe, is a show-off. Based on the few times I've met her mother, I'd say the apple doesn't fall far from the tree.

Ellie is overdressed in a peasant frock with her hair and makeup styled like a beauty queen. I glance down at my attire, my flat chest, and slim hips. Compared to her, I *do* look like a man. Ellie flashes Will a bright smile that makes me want to pull all the brilliant white teeth out of her mouth.

I'm so busy watching Ellie and Will, I miss the commotion at the scarecrow-making contest.

Ashton taps me on the shoulder. "We've got trouble. You'd better come," she says and I follow her through the crowd to where a group of children are gathered around Conrad and Zoe.

"You pushed me," Zoe screams.

"Because you deserved it," Conrad yells back.

I shove my way through to them. "Conrad! You know you're not supposed to hit girls."

"I didn't hit her," he says, his face red with anger. "I pushed her, because she called you a slut. She said you were making a fool of yourself by going after Caroline's dad."

Ellie appears on the scene. "My daughter would never say such a thing."

"She did! I heard her!" Caroline shouts angrily.

Tears fill Zoe's eyes. "I'm sorry, Mommy. But that's what you said about Miss Julia."

An audible gasp spreads throughout the crowd.

I place a hand on my son's head. "Consider the source, son."

Conrad looks up at me. "What does that mean?"

I glare at Ellie. "It means, she doesn't know any better." I take hold of my son's hand. "Come on, sweetheart. I think it's time for us to leave."

I expect Will to come after me as I march across the lawn, but Ashton is the one who follows me to my car. "Don't let Ellie upset you. She's just jealous. She's been shamelessly chasing after my brother since Tracy died."

"I'm not worried about Ellie. But I feel awful for causing a scene," I say opening the back door for Conrad to climb in.

I spot Will in the crowd as we drive off. He's distanced himself from Ellie and is now conversing with a group of dads. My throat swells as I drive away from Marsh Point. I'm a newcomer to town. Everyone here has known each other all their lives. Something tells me I will never fit in.

TWENTY-TWO
WILL

Against my better judgment, I take Ashton's suggestion and invite Dad and May May to stay for hamburgers after the party. I keep a close eye on my father and May May as we eat. They are like an old married couple. When she fusses at him about his table manners, he grumbles but complies to appease her.

Not only was May May my mother's closest friend, she was our surrogate mother during our formative years. While Dad and May May were devoted to my mother, I was not surprised when I recently learned they had a brief affair a long time ago. It happened during the height of my parents' troubled marriage, shortly after May May's husband passed away from a sudden heart attack. They were two close friends comforting each other through difficult times.

Now that my mother is gone, they are free to be together. May May appears to be a positive influence on Dad. He seems more lively, more outgoing, and much happier.

After the dishes are put away, Ashton volunteers to bathe the girls, my cue to have the dreaded conversation with our father.

He's gathering up his things to leave when I say, "Dad, if you can spare another minute, I have something I need to talk to you about."

"Sure thing, son." Setting down his belongings, he removes his felt fedora and takes his accustomed seat at the head of the table.

When May May tries to slip unnoticed out of the kitchen, I say, "Please stay, May May. This involves you too."

She stops in her tracks and turns back around. "All right, then. Can I interest anyone in a cup of tea? Sounds like we may need one."

Dad and I both decline her offer.

I sit down next to Dad, and as soon as May May joins us with her steaming mug of tea, we begin.

"You sound serious, son. What's this about?" Dad asks with concern etched on his face.

I lace my fingers together on the table. "I've been in counseling."

Dad places his hand over mine. "That's good, son. You've suffered a tragic loss. You *should* seek counseling."

"This is about more than Tracy's death, Dad. I've been coping with some anger issues. Anger issues that stem from my youth. From Bert's accident."

Dad retracts his hand. "Oh. I see."

"Do you think I was drunk that night, Dad? That I was responsible for Bert's death?" I watch Dad's face, anticipating his response.

His pained expression appears genuine, but his words are not what I want to hear. "Plenty of witnesses claimed you were."

"I don't care what those witnesses claim. They wanted to blame someone, and I was their scapegoat. I told you I was sober. I'd never been in trouble for drinking before. Why did you believe them over me?"

Dad hangs his head. "Kids make mistakes. We loved you despite what you might have done."

I bang my fist on the table, startling both them and me. "I did nothing wrong. Bert was the one who was drunk. When I tried to make him go home, he came after me. We wrestled, and he fell into the rotten railing. It easily could've been me who died that night."

Dad and May May exchange a look I can't interpret. "Your parents did the best they could in a difficult situation," May May says.

"Including paying Bert's parents hundreds of thousands of dollars to go away?"

She gives her head a solemn nod. "It seemed a small price to pay for your freedom."

I gawk at her. "My *freedom*? I was never in danger of going to prison. I was too young to stand trial. But settling the lawsuit was an admission of guilt. And that guilt has held me hostage all these years. I lost a different kind of freedom, but a freedom nonetheless." I realize I'm being unnecessarily cruel to them, but I can't help myself.

My father appears taken aback. "Watch your tone, son. May May is right. Your mother and I did the best we could in a difficult situation. Your mother couldn't take the pressure."

I throw up my hands. "Right. Everything in our lives has always been about Mom's disease. You covered for her, and made excuses for her, because poor Eileen couldn't help herself. Did you ever play the tough love card with her? Show her the potential consequences of her actions?"

May May reaches for Dad's hand. "Many times. You were too young to remember. I admit, your father and I enabled her. But only after we tried everything else."

Dad snatches a napkin from the basket on the table and dabs at his wet eyes. "The decision to settle wasn't just about your mother, Will. Your reputation was already destroyed. We were avoiding having your name in the press for another six months. We wanted you to move on with your life. We did what we thought best. If we had known this would have such a devastating impact on your life, we would've chosen another course."

Seeing my father cry makes my chest tighten. Why am I putting him through this? Blaming him for ruining my life gives me no satisfaction. Confronting him about the past hasn't changed my perception of the events. But I admit, I feel much better having gotten it off my chest.

Getting up from my chair, I pull Dad to his feet and into my arms. "I'm sorry, Dad. I didn't mean to hurt you. These difficult discussions are part of my therapy."

He holds me at arm's length. "I understand, son. You can talk to me anytime about anything. I want to help you. Knowing we were the cause of your suffering breaks my heart. But it helps me understand the adult you've become."

"It's a parent's job to screw up their kids' lives," I say with a chuckle, trying to make light of the situation. "I'm doing a superb job of ruining Caroline's and Sophie's." I turn serious again. "Deep down, I know you did the best you could in a difficult situation. Mom didn't make anything easy for any of us."

Dad gives his head a grim shake. "No, she didn't. But we sure loved her."

I give him a quizzical look. Did I love her? Kids are *supposed* to love their parents, but resentment is all I've ever felt towards my mother.

———

When I discuss the matter with Clemmy at my next session on Monday, she says, "Love comes in all shapes and sizes, Will. Surely, there were some good things about your mother that you loved."

I rack my brain but come up empty. "Maybe. But I can't think of any."

"Then think a little harder."

Clemmy's questions have grown increasingly more thought-provoking. Reflecting on my life helps me to see how many people I've hurt over the years. But it also reminds me of the good I've done. I've built houses for paralyzed vets, and I routinely hire men down on their luck. I'm a law-abiding citizen, and I attend church regularly. My anger problem is my one Achilles' heel. But boy is it a big one.

By the end of our third session on Friday, I'm feeling better about myself, and I'm beginning to forgive myself for Bert's accident.

"You've made enormous progress this week," Clemmy says. "But I caution you about being overly optimistic. The path ahead will not be lined with rose petals. You will still have some bad days. But next week, we'll begin to arm you with coping mechanisms to help you deal with the anger when it arises."

"Therapy is harder than I expected, but I'm doing everything you ask of me. Do you think I'll pass the psychiatric evaluation?"

"Let's hope it doesn't come to that." A mischievous smile appears on her lips. "Have you kissed any more of your daughter's friends' moms?"

"Haha. No. But I have a date with Julia tomorrow night," I say, making a mental note to call her on the way home about the logistics.

Clemmy rises out of her chair, signaling the end of our session. "I'll tell you like I told my boys when they were coming along. Mind your manners. Always think with your noggin and not your noodle."

I burst out laughing. "Clemmy! Shame on you."

She snickers. "Well, it's the truth."

"For a teenager maybe. But I'm a forty-year-old man. I may have anger management issues, but I know how to treat a lady."

TWENTY-THREE
JULIA

I'd given up hope of hearing from Will about our date when he finally calls on Friday afternoon.

"It's been a crazy week, and I'm sorry it's taken me so long to get back to you. If you'd still like to have dinner tomorrow night, I've lined Mia up to keep all three kids at Marsh Point."

I'm too relieved to hear from him to give him a hard time about not calling sooner. Men are often slack when it comes to making plans. "That sounds perfect. What time should I bring him over?"

"Around six thirty. I wanted to take you to the Sandy Island Club. Unfortunately, they are having a large wedding reception, and the dinner room is closed. There are only two restaurants in town I would consider. One has excellent food but a lousy atmosphere. And the other has a decent atmosphere but the food is only so-so. What's your choice?"

"I pick food over atmosphere," I say without hesitation.

"I agree. I'll make a reservation for seven."

I'm like a teenage girl getting ready for her first date on Saturday afternoon. I spend an hour trying on every item in my limited wardrobe. Now that I have some extra money, I should take the time to go shopping. I hold two dresses up for Conrad to choose from. One is cobalt blue with a high thigh slit, and the other is black with a V-neckline, skinny straps, and a flaring mini-length skirt.

He turns up his nose. "They're both yucky. What's the big deal? Why don't you just wear blue jeans."

"Geez. Some help you are," I say turning back to the mirror. "I'll wear the black. The blue is too dressy for a restaurant, and the black is . . ." I stop myself from saying sexy.

Conrad tilts his head quizzically. "The black is what, Mommy?"

I toss the chosen dress on the bed. "It can be dressed up or down." I dig in my closet for a pair of black booties. "In this case, we're going for casual."

I'm not nervous about having dinner with Will. He's easy to talk to, and I'm looking forward to getting to know him better. It's the thought of what might happen after dinner that has my stomach in knots.

The Clam and Claw is crowded when we arrive, and even though Will made a reservation, we have to wait for our table. We order a drink from the bar, but it's nearly impossible to carry on a conversation over the cacophony of noise.

When we finish our drinks and our table is still not ready, Will says, "Let's get out of here. I have a better idea."

"Fine by me," I say and let him lead me out of the restaurant.

When we exit left out of the parking lot, I assume he's taking me to his second choice, the place with better atmosphere but not so great food. I'm confused when he parks in front of the Fancy Pantry. "What are we doing at the grocery store? Are you planning to cook?"

"You'll see. Wait right here. I'll be back in a flash," he says and gets out of the truck.

He returns a few minutes later with a large shopping bag. He gives me the bag to hold, and I peek inside at the chilled bottle of bubbly, a loaf of French bread, gourmet salami, artisan goat cheese, and a container of apricot ginger preserves. "A picnic is a splendid idea. But where are we going?" I ask as we cross over the Merriweather Bridge.

"Since we can't eat at the Sandy Island Club, I figured we'd park at one of the public accesses and go out on the beach. We don't have a blanket. I hope you don't mind eating standing up."

"We can swing by my cottage. Or better yet, why don't we just *go* to my cottage."

He glances over at me. "I thought about that. But I didn't want to be presumptuous."

"Not at all. I'd prefer to eat sitting down," I say flashing him a mischievous grin.

At the cottage, I search for suitable glasses while Will pops the champagne. He pours some bubbly for both of us, and we clink glasses. "To first dates," he says.

"To first dates," I repeat. "A picnic is way more memorable than a noisy restaurant."

He leans down and kisses me. "I've wanted to do that since I first saw you in that dress. You look spectacular."

I flutter my eyelashes at him. "Not too much like a boy?"

"There is nothing boyish about you tonight." Setting our glasses down, he pulls me close and presses his mouth to mine. Our lips part and tongues meet, and the earth falls out from beneath me. Will smells like fresh pine air, and his body is rock solid against mine. I feel myself getting lost in him, and I'm disappointed when he draws away.

"We should have our picnic before we get carried away," he says, breathless.

"Good idea. I'll find us a blanket."

I locate an old quilt at the top of Conrad's closet, and a cooler in the pantry for the champagne. We take our provisions out to the beach and set up our picnic near the dunes. Even though we still have an hour of daylight left, the sky is already golden from the setting sun.

"Did you ever live in Texas?" Will asks as he slices the salami on a small cutting board.

A shiver travels my spine. "Texas? Why do you ask?"

"I thought I remember you saying you moved here from Colorado, but Conrad told Ashton you are from Texas."

"Probably wishful thinking on Conrad's part. I'm originally from Texas, and my parents still live there. Conrad loves to visit them on their farm." I'm probably giving too much away about our prior lives, but I need to provide an explanation in case Conrad slips again about our farm.

"That explains it." Will stretches out on the blanket, propping himself up on one arm. "Tell me about yourself, Julia."

"Why don't you go first?" He seems to want to talk, and I'm more than willing to listen.

His face becomes serious. "My life is complicated right now. I've been seeing a therapist."

"Because of the accident?" I ask as I drizzle apricot preserves on top of a cheese-covered salami slice.

"That's only part of it. I come from a dysfunctional family. My mother was a raging alcoholic."

As I suspected, his aura of sadness is about more than his wife's death. "I can't imagine how difficult that was for you growing up. Were those your parents I saw you talking to at the birthday party?"

"That was my dad and his girlfriend. My mom passed away in May from complications of her alcoholism."

"I'm so sorry. You've had a difficult year."

"For sure." Will drains the last of his champagne and sets his glass aside. "Anyway, I've been trying to sort through some issues.

I've come a long way in a short time. Three weeks ago, I refused to even consider therapy. But I'm learning so much about myself. You should try it sometime." His eyes widen. "That didn't come out right. I'm not suggesting you need therapy."

"Everybody needs therapy at some point in their life." As much as I would benefit from counseling, there would be no point when I can't tell the truth about myself.

"Just so you know, I'm not the kind of person who goes around talking about their therapist. But I have feelings for you, Julia. And I thought you should know I'm not at the top of my game right now." Will sits up and pinches off a chunk of bread. "Your turn? I want to know everything about you."

"Well, let's see. Blue is my favorite color. I love seafood. I'm a grouch in the morning before I've had my first cup of coffee. I've never had a real job. When I was married, I was a stay-at-home mom. And I've always wanted to be a writer. That's pretty much it."

"Geez. I tell you my biggest secret, and you tell me your favorite color in response."

I pick at a loose thread on the quilt. "I have skeletons in the closet too, Will. I'm just not ready to talk about them." I wonder if I'll ever trust Will enough to tell him the truth about Grady.

"Fair enough." Will scrambles up and pulls me to my feet. "Let's just enjoy each other's company for now. No pressure." He offers an arm. "Can I interest you in a stroll?"

I take hold of his elbow. "A stroll sounds lovely."

We stroll for what seems like miles, talking about our children and the pros and cons of small-town living. He tells me about growing up at Marsh Point, and I tell him about the farm through the eyes of a child, as though I lived there in my youth.

We turn around when we reach the Mathesons' property line at the northern tip of the island. As we head back towards the cottage, I summon the courage to ask him about Ellie. "I'm curious. Is something going on between you and Ellie?"

"No way. That woman drives me insane." He drops his smile. "I feel awful about what happened at the party. I would've come to your rescue, but I wasn't sure you wanted the entire town to know you really are making a fool of yourself by going after Caroline's dad."

I laugh out loud. "Right! Slut that I am. I hope Ellie learned her lesson. She should be more careful what she says around her child."

He cast a sideways glance at me. "Do you?"

"Do I what?"

"Do you care if the whole town knows we're seeing each other?"

Looping my arm through his, I lean into him. "Not at all. I'm proud to be seen on Will Darby's arm."

When we reach the blanket, we clean up from our picnic and return to the cottage. Will drops his armload on the dining table and pulls me close. Desire spreads throughout my body as he lays a passionate kiss on me. When we come up for air, I notice him glancing towards my bedroom, and it takes every bit of willpower I can summon to push him away.

"I'm sorry, Will. I'm not ready for more than kissing. I've only ever been with one man in my life."

Will jumps away as though burned. "Whoa. I didn't know. You should've said something."

My face warms. "I'm not a virgin. I just have limited experience."

"I understand, and I respect your wishes. You're in control. You tell me when you're ready, and I'll make sure it's special, a night you won't forget."

I cover my mouth to hide my smile. "That sounds like a corny pick-up line."

"My experience with women is also limited. Although maybe not as limited as yours." He places his hands on my hips. "We'll take it slow together."

"I'd like that," I say, resting my head on his chest.

I'm falling hard for this man. I'm tempted to throw caution to the wind and see where our relationship leads us. But my primary responsibility is to my son. I can't afford to make a move that might put our lives in danger.

TWENTY-FOUR
WILL

I'm leaving Clemmy's house on Monday afternoon when I receive a call from my attorney. Vanessa doesn't bother with pleasantries. "We need to talk, Will. In person. This afternoon. Now. Where are you?"

A knot forms in my gut. Her terse tone tells me whatever she wants to see me about is serious. "I'm leaving Clemmy's. Where are you?"

"On highway seventeen, heading south. I'll be in Beaufort in twenty minutes."

"Where should we meet? I don't know Beaufort very well. I'm sure there's a coffee shop in the downtown area."

"I'm googling coffee shops. There's one on Carteret. City Java and News. It's in the City Loft Hotel."

Locating a pen in my console, I scribble the name on the back of a teller machine receipt. "I'll find it. Can you give me a hint of what this is about?"

"I'd rather wait and tell you in person."

Beads of sweat break out on my forehead as I drive the short distance to town. My nerves are on end. Caffeine is the last thing I need. But I order a Chai Tea Latte because I don't feel right occupying space at the counter in the small coffee shop without buying something.

What could be so important for Vanessa to drive ninety minutes to meet with me in person? My imagination runs wild with possible scenarios, and by the time she arrives ten minutes later, I'm on the verge of a panic attack.

Vanessa stands just inside the doorway. She's extremely attractive in person and professionally dressed in a khaki pantsuit with a white silk blouse. Lifting her sunglasses, her blue-green eyes dart around at the shop's other occupants before landing on me. She motions for me to follow her. "Come on. Let's walk."

"Don't you want a coffee?" I ask, hustling to catch up with her.

She pats the tote bag dangling from her shoulder. "I have water. We need privacy for this conversation."

We walk in silence several blocks. When we reach the waterfront, she turns to face me. "You need to prepare yourself, Will. Your in-laws are coming after you with guns loaded."

"What do you mean by *guns loaded*? And how do you know this?"

"I have my sources. And I mean the Beaumonts are pulling out all the stops."

I toss my half-empty teacup in a nearby trash can. "Are these sources reliable?"

"Extremely. I have moles planted in various strategic locations around the Southeast. I have the name of an attorney for you." She thrusts a business card at me.

I read the information on the card. "A criminal attorney?"

"Alex is the best. I should be the one to reach out to her when that time comes."

My jaw slackens. "When what time comes?" I say, even though I suspect what is coming.

Vanessa sighs as she leans against the chain railing. "According to my intel, the local authorities in Water's Edge are preparing to come down hard on you. They will soon arrest you for your wife's murder."

I fall against the railing beside her. "Based on what evidence?"

"That part is a mystery. They claim to have new evidence in the case. We'll find out soon enough." Vanessa inspects the landscape around us. "I'm pretty sure you're being followed, which is why I wanted to meet in person. They know everything about you. That you've moved in with your sister at Marsh Point. That you've hired a housekeeper to help with your children. That you're receiving counseling three times a week, and that you're dating a woman named Julia."

I shake my head in disbelief. "They don't have to spy on me. My life is an open book."

"The Beaumonts have a reputation for being ruthless."

"That doesn't surprise me." My gaze once again falls to the business card in my hand. "Alexandria Stone. With all due respect, Vanessa, if I'm being accused of murdering my wife, I'm not sure I trust a woman to handle the case."

"Alex has a reputation for being one of the toughest criminal attorneys in the country. They call her Stone Cold Alex. Trust me, you want her on your team."

"If you say so." I remove my wallet from my pocket and slip the card inside.

Vanessa gives me a tight smile. "In the meantime, keep up with your therapy, and be aware of your surroundings at all times. If you need to reach me, send me a text, and I'll make arrangements to meet in person."

As we walk back to our cars, I have an eerie feeling we're being followed. And I cast frequent glances in my rear-view mirror on the drive home. I'm terrified I'm going to lose my children, and when they greet me at the door at Marsh Point, I lift both of them into my arms, hugging them tight.

Ashton appears in the doorway. She can tell from the look on my face something is wrong. She takes the girls from me. "Your daddy had a bad day. Let's go watch a movie in the family room and give him a chance to unwind."

I go into the kitchen and sit down at the table, staring blindly out at the marsh. When Ashton enters the room, she clicks on the television to drown out our voices while we talk.

I tell her about my meeting with Vanessa. "I don't get it, Ashton. What new evidence could they possibly have?"

The color drains from Ashton's face as she looks past me at the local news program on television. "It might have something to do with that."

I crane my neck to see a video of Julia and me emerging from her cottage on Saturday night.

I jump up from the table and hurry over to the television, but the segment has already ended. "Quick! Rewind it."

Ashton clicks a button on the remote to start the segment over. I recognize the reporter's mop of curly brown hair. He's the guy who accosted me in front of the police station. The banner across the bottom of the screen tells me his name is Ethan Striker. According to Ethan, I was having an affair with the mystery woman in the video, and I murdered my wife to be with this woman and keep custody of my children.

A series of photographs shows Julia and me together—returning from a boat ride and leaving the Clam and Claw on Saturday night. The last one is a fuzzy shot of us kissing in the corner of the veranda.

My temper flares, and I jab my finger at the television. "This dirtbag has been following me. He's been trespassing on our property. I didn't even know Julia when Tracy died. She wasn't even living in Water's Edge at the time."

The video of us emerging from the cottage replays. Our hair is windblown from our walk on the beach, but the context of the report gives the impression we had just spent hours in bed together.

I take deep breaths as I count to ten, the first coping mechanism for dealing with anger Clemmy taught me at our session earlier today. "Poor Julia. When she agreed not to keep our relationship a secret, I'm sure she didn't have this kind of coming-out party in mind."

Ashton sets down the remote and massages my tense shoulders. "How much have you told her about the custody hearing and potential murder charges?"

"I haven't told her any of that. Only that I've been seeing a therapist to deal with some stuff. I didn't want to scare her off." I tug my phone out of my back pocket. "I need to break the news to her before someone else does. She may have already seen the news story."

"Good luck with that," Ashton says, giving my shoulders one last squeeze.

"I need some air. I'm going out in the boat. Keep an eye on the girls and don't wait on me for dinner." I head across the room towards the veranda, stopping when I reach the door. I turn back to face my sister. "I'm sorry, Ashton. I'm being presumptuous in assuming you'll take care of my children. I don't mean to dump my responsibilities on you."

"That's what I'm here for." Striding across the room, she opens the door and motions me out. "Go! Take as long as you need. We'll eat now and save you some food for when you get back."

"You're the best. I don't know what I'd do without you." I peck her cheek before leaving the house. The fresh air clears my head, and I ride out to the mouth of the inlet before placing the call to Julia.

She answers on the first ring. "Will! This is a surprise. I didn't expect to hear from you so soon."

"I wish I was calling on a more optimistic note."

"I don't like the sound of that," she says, her cheerful tone now gone. "What's wrong?"

"You and I were the stars of the six o'clock news." I tell Julia about the custody case and about my in-laws pressuring the local police to arrest me for my wife's murder. She doesn't mutter a sound while I talk. "I'm so sorry. I never intended to put you in the middle of my drama." More silence fills the line. "Julia, are you still there?"

"I'm here," she says in a small voice.

"I don't blame you for being upset."

"I'm upset for you, Will. You've already been through so much."

Her tone gives nothing away, and I don't know her well enough to tell what she's thinking. "Where do we stand, Julia?"

"I can't answer that right now. I need some time to think about it. We'll talk soon," she says and ends the call.

I toss the phone on the console. Of course, she needs time. I just unloaded some heavy stuff on her. No woman in her right mind would want to be involved with me. Everything I have is at stake—my reputation, my family, my freedom.

TWENTY-FIVE
JULIA

I hear Conrad calling for me, and when I look up, I'm surprised to find myself in a rocker on the porch. I was so absorbed in my conversation with Will, that I don't remember coming out to the porch. I don't believe this. What a fool I am. Why didn't I ask more questions when Will spoke of sorting through issues and seeing a therapist? I've jumped from the frying pan into the fire. I've exchanged one man's problems for another's. If I didn't have such strong feelings for Will, I'd dump him right now.

Conrad appears in the doorway. "I'm hungry, Mama. What's for dinner?"

I ease myself out of the chair. "Soup and salad." I no longer feel like grilling chicken as planned.

I do my best to appear normal during dinner and afterward while I help Conrad get ready for bed. But my insides are churning. I'm distraught about the prospect of losing Will, but I'm terrified about what might now become of my son and me.

After tucking Conrad into bed, I turn on all the outside lights and sit down at the table with my computer and my gun. I locate the segment on the local news website and replay it over and over again. The footage is crystal clear. There is no denying I am the one in the videos kissing Will on the veranda and emerging from my cottage on Saturday night with hair and clothes a mess. I click on pause and zoom in for a closer look. Over my left shoulder beside the front door is the cottage's name, Golden Sands Hideaway, and address on Beach Drive.

The Six has access to the most advanced technology, and a Google search of facial recognition software tells me what I already know. Conrad and I are sitting ducks.

I'm tempted to reach out to Eleanor, but doing so would be admitting defeat. We've gotten this far. No turning back now. We'll have to move. But where will we go? Staying in the Lowcountry is out of the question. When the boogeymen find out where we are, they'll scour the area. We'll have to go to a different state. A different region would be even better. The Midwest, maybe? But I've grown accustomed to the ocean. Conrad and I are happy in Water's Edge. He's making friends, and I'm finally able to write again. These past few weeks have offered a glimpse of the happy life we could lead here, and moving would be an enormous setback.

I fall asleep with my head on the dining room table and my hand on my gun. The first rays of dawn creeping through the windows wake me the following morning.

All eyes are on me in the carpool line. The moms cover their mouths to hide their whispers, as though I can hear them from the distance. I long to roll down my window and scream, "I've done nothing wrong. I didn't even know Will back then."

But that would be a mistake. They'll video me with their phones and post the footage on social media with captions like *Will Darby's Secret Mistress Gone Mad.*

Leaving the school, I drive over to the shooting range where I spend two hours blasting bullet holes into paper targets. By the time I stop at the store for groceries, it's almost noon.

I'm waiting in the carpool line, searching the Internet for the top-ranking romance authors, when Ellie appears beside my car.

She motions for me to roll down the window, and I wave my phone at her. "I'm busy," I say, loud enough for her to hear me through the glass.

Ellie grabs the door handle, and discovering it's locked, she pounds her fist on the window. She yells, "I was right about you, Julia. You are a slut and a home wrecker."

I swing open the door and step out of the car. "Shh! Keep your voice down. There are children nearby."

Ellie lowers her voice to a loud whisper. "Tracy was one of my best friends, and she confided in me. She suspected Will was cheating on her." She jabs her finger at me. "It was you. *You* broke up their marriage."

I laugh in her face. "That's ridiculous. I wasn't even living in Water's Edge at the time."

"What're you hiding, Julia?"

Fear creeps up my spine. I tell myself she's bluffing and to remain calm. She couldn't possibly know anything about my past. "What're you talking about? I'm not hiding anything."

She squints her eyes at me. "There's something fishy about you. Water's Edge is the most out-of-the-way town in the Southeast. People don't randomly move here. They come here because they have connections. I believe Will was your connection."

"Not that it's any of your business, but I moved here from Colorado," I say, the lie sliding easily off my lips.

"You're lying. You were living in Charleston or Beaufort, somewhere close enough for Will to sneak away from his family to be with you. Then as soon as Tracy was cold in the ground, you moved to town and took over her life."

"Ask Will. We met at the hardware store after Labor Day." I notice the other moms gathering around us with their phones out, videotaping our altercation.

Ellie gets close enough to my face for me to smell her stale coffee breath. "Fair warning, I will find out what you're hiding, Julia Becker."

"Go ahead. But you're wasting your time," I say in a shaky voice. If Ellie starts digging into my past, she's likely to find out I don't have one. At least not in Colorado.

The school door bangs open, and the children file out. Ellie lowers her voice to a whisper. "You don't belong here, Julia. And you are not wanted. Do us all a favor and leave." She spins on her heels and disappears into the crowd of moms scurrying back to their cars.

My mind is too rattled to think straight on the way home. I'm too angry to even ask Conrad about his day. We arrive home to find the front door unlocked and my laptop open on the dining table. I password-protected my laptop, but a computer expert could easily hack into it. Checking the Internet browser's history, the last page opened was from this morning, when I ordered my favorite brand of coffee local stores don't carry from Amazon. I may have forgotten to close the laptop, but I most certainly did not leave the front door unlocked. A shiver travels down my spine as I click on Fry's number.

"Were you by any chance at the cottage this morning?" I ask when he answers.

"No. You asked me not to enter the premises when you're away. Perhaps your new boyfriend let himself in. I saw the segment on the news last night. I have a reputation to uphold, Julia. I don't need any scandals."

"Neither do I, Fry. I pay you money to rent this place. What I do while I'm living here is none of your business," I say and hang up on him.

Over lunch, Conrad says, "All the kids are talking about you being on TV with Caroline's dad last night." Fortunately, he appears more interested in his ham sandwich than the rumors about Will and me.

I pick at the lettuce in my salad without taking a bite. "Does that bother you?"

"Nah. Why should it? Mister Will is super cool." He grins at me before sinking his teeth into his sandwich.

"The photographs of me on television present a problem. The boogeymen might figure out where we are. We may have to move again."

"No!" he shouts as tears fill his eyes. "I don't wanna move, Mommy. I love it here. I want to live at the beach forever."

Seeing his devastated face makes my heart crumble into pieces. This year has been grueling for him. Making him move again hardly seems fair. Maybe I'm getting ahead of myself. I left the house in a fog of sleep this morning, having only had a few sips of coffee. Maybe I forgot to lock the door. Realistically, the cartel could not have found me so quickly anyway.

While Conrad plays with his new Lego kit, I go outside to the porch with a cup of tea to sort out my thoughts. I want to believe Will. Is he telling the truth about his in-laws pressuring police to arrest him? Or do the police have evidence that he killed his wife? I can't imagine Will hurting anyone, let alone murdering his wife. Then again, I never imagined Grady trafficking women and children. Thanks to that reporter, I'm smack in the middle of the investigation. The moms in the carpool line videoed Ellie accusing me of sleeping with Will prior to his wife's death. What if those social media posts go viral? What if the police bring me in for questioning? They'll want to know my whereabouts over the summer. If I tell them I was in Witness Protection awaiting my husband's trial for human trafficking, my cover will be blown.

As much as it saddens me, I have no choice but to put as much distance as possible between Will Darby and me. I send him a text. *I'm sorry, Will. Considering the circumstances, I don't think we should see each other anymore.*

TWENTY-SIX
WILL

I wait until the cleaning crew leaves before making my final inspection of the Mathesons' house. The owners are arriving tomorrow with their first moving truck of furniture, and I want to make sure everything is in order for them. I'm sad to see this project come to an end. I will miss the incredible views.

Making certain the doors are locked, I leave the house for the final time. I'm headed to my truck when a silver Tahoe pulls into the driveway. The vehicle screeches to a halt and Detective Marlowe jumps out. "There you are! You're a difficult man to track down."

"Ha! Ethan Striker doesn't think so."

Marlowe moans. "What a jerk. I seriously question that guy's ethics."

"What's up, Detective? I assume you're not here on a social call."

"I'm *not* here in a professional capacity today." Marlowe takes in the house. "Wow. That's some house. Who lives here?"

"No one at the moment. A couple from New England built it as their retirement home. They're driving down with their first load of furniture this weekend."

"Is there somewhere we can talk?"

"Sure! Follow me," I say and lead him around to the pool.

Marlowe shields his eyes as he looks out over the expanse of water, the ocean on his right and the sound to the left. "This place is amazing. The view is spectacular."

"Isn't it? I was just thinking how much I'm going to miss working here."

We walk around the pool and sit down on the steps leading to the beach. "I'm curious, Marlowe. Why *are* you here, if not in a professional capacity?"

"I've been relieved of my duties at Water's Edge Police Department."

My eyes widen. "You mean they fired you?"

"Yep. I defended you until the bitter end, and now I'm here to warn you. Prepare yourself, Will. They are coming after you."

"Wait a minute. Are you saying they fired you because of me?"

"Pretty much. Because I refuse to arrest you. They are trying to frame you. And they're doing a good job of it."

"Who is *they*? Who is coming after me, Detective?"

"Your in-laws are calling the shots. But they have some mighty powerful people doing their dirty work."

I hang my head. "I was afraid of that. What should I do?"

"Lawyer up for starters. Hire yourself the best criminal attorney you can afford. And get your life in order. Make arrangements for someone to take care of your children in your absence."

Chill bumps break out on my arms despite the warm afternoon. "What do you mean by my absence?"

"If you're arrested. I assume you already have a will that stipulates who gets custody in the event of your death."

"I do. Although I haven't updated it since Tracy died."

"Talk to your attorney. Make sure the proper provisions are made."

Panic grips my chest, and I squeeze my eyes shut as I focus on counting my breaths. "I can't believe this is happening. What will you do now? Will you look for work at a police station in a neighboring town?"

"Eventually, I will leave this Podunk town and not look back. But I have unfinished business to take care of first." Marlowe shifts his tall frame towards me. "Your case has gotten under my skin, Will. What your in-laws are doing to you is wrong. I want you to hire me to investigate them. You don't even have to pay me."

"I appreciate your interest in my case, and your defense of my innocence, but my custody attorney already has a team investigating the Beaumonts."

"And I'm sure they're doing a fine job. But they don't have skin in the game like me. The Beaumonts cost me my job, and I want revenge. Your in-laws are as crooked as the day is long. If I can dig up some dirt on them, we can use it against them to make them back off."

Leaning forward, I plant my elbows on my knees, burying my face in hands. "I don't know, Detective. I need to think about it. Everything is happening so fast. I don't want to make a wrong move here."

"I get it. But don't wait too long. Coincidentally, who is this woman to you? The one I saw on the news last night. She's all over social media today." Marlowe shows me his phone's screen where Ellie and Julia appear to be having a heated argument. He clicks the play arrow and hands me his phone. I watch in horror as Ellie accuses Julia of breaking up my marriage.

"I didn't even know Julia back then." I hand him back his phone. "I would never have cheated on my wife."

Marlowe points at Ellie. "Was she really one of your wife's best friends?"

My head jerks back. "No! Tracy couldn't stand her. Ellie's been hitting on me for months. Do you think she's trying to run Julia off to get to me? "

Marlowe stands and stretches his long limbs. "Maybe. I'm seeing a lot of mental illness in this world today. You can't have too many people in your corner right now. You have my number. Give me a call when you're ready."

I wait until I hear Marlowe's car leave the driveway before getting to my feet. On my way to my truck, I access my social media feed and scroll until I find a post of Ellie and Julia. I'm reading through the comments when a text from Julia appears on the screen. *I'm sorry, Will. Considering the circumstances, I don't think we should see each other anymore.*

My heart pounds as I speed down Beach Drive towards the bridge. Everything I've learned from Clemmy about anger management flies out the window, and I punch the roof of my truck several times.

At the next red light, I thumb off a quick text to Vanessa. *I need to see you. I'm leaving Water's Edge. I should be in Charleston by 3:30.*

She responds right away. *Meet you at the splash fountain in Waterfront Park.*

Highway traffic is heavier than usual, and Vanessa is waiting for me when I arrive ten minutes late.

"Let's walk. I can't hear myself think over all this racket," she says, gesturing at the children squealing and frolicking in the splash fountain.

As we stroll along the waterfront path, I bring her to speed on recent developments. "Can you create a legal document for me, designating my sister as temporary custodian if anything happens to me? The attorney who drew up my original will is a friend of Tracy's. I don't trust anyone in Water's Edge right now."

"That's wise. I'll draft it this afternoon and send it over for your approval."

"I think you should reach out to your criminal attorney friend. It may be premature, but I want to be on her radar if they arrest me. I'd prefer to spend as little time in jail as possible."

"I understand. No harm in being prepared."

She stops walking and grabs hold of my arm. "Tell me the truth, Will. Were you seeing Julia at the time of your wife's death?"

"No!" I jerk my arm away. "I swear. I didn't even know her then. She moved here from Colorado after Labor Day."

Vanessa gives a curt nod. "If necessary, we'll get her to testify to that effect."

I stare over her shoulder at a sailboat cruising across the harbor, its sails billowing in the wind. "I'd rather not involve Julia. She broke off our relationship this morning," I say and start walking back in the direction we came.

Vanessa steps into line beside me. "I'm sorry for you, Will. I can tell you really care about her. But it's for the best. Seeing someone so soon after your wife's death is not a good look."

While I agree with her, losing Julia hurts like the devil. If I feel this way about a woman I barely know, I can't imagine the agony of losing custody of my children. Suddenly eager to get home to them, I say goodbye to Vanessa and head back to my car.

I send Ashton a text, asking if she and the kids would like to go on a boat ride when I get home around five. She responds with a thumbs-up emoji, and the threesome is waiting for me on the veranda when I arrive.

As I navigate away from the dock, Caroline calls out to me from the front of the boat. "Can we go to town for ice cream, Daddy? Please?"

"Sure! Why not?"

Ashton shoots me a disapproving look. "You'll spoil their dinner."

"So what?" I want them to have some fond memories of me when I'm in prison.

Ashton eases herself onto the leaning post. "Why do I get the feeling this isn't a joy ride?"

"Every boat ride is a joy ride." I speed up enough to appease the girls without making it difficult to talk. "But you're right. I have something important to talk to you about. Detective

Marlowe came to see me today. He got fired from his job because he refused to arrest me. I'm in big trouble here, Ashton."

"We'll fight—"

"Let me finish. I have a lot to say. Marlowe warned me to get my affairs in order. I've just come from meeting with Vanessa in Charleston. I've asked her to create a legal document giving you custody of the girls if something happens to me. This is not an easy ask, Ashton. And I want you to take some time to think about it. There is a very real chance you could end up raising my children."

"I don't need to think about it, Will. Caroline and Sophie are my nieces," Ashton says, her eyes on the girls and her hand over her heart. "I promise to do everything in my power to nurture them into healthy adults. I will give them unconditional love and support them in all their endeavors."

"Wow. I wish you'd been my mama." I laugh. "Wait, you kinda were." I drop my smile. "What about Sully? Is he up for fathering two young girls?"

"*If* Sully and I get married, and in the unlikely event you go to prison, Sully would be a wonderful father. I've met his son. He's an impressive young man."

I give her a gentle shove. "Who are you kidding? You're totally into Sully, and you know it."

A sheepish grin spreads across her face. "Maybe. He's a really good guy, Will. I can't stop thinking how different my life would've been if we'd dated in high school."

I let out a humph. "After what we went through as kids, we should make a pact to never discuss what-ifs."

"Deal." Ashton extends her hand, and we shake on it.

We tie up at the city marina and walk over to the Velvet Spoon on Main Street for gelato. Ashton and I order scoops of pistachio, and the girls choose chocolate chip. We take our treats to the picnic table at the small playground on the waterfront. Caroline and Sophie take a few bites of ice cream before rushing off to the sliding board. The gentle breeze blowing off the water has a hint of the cold months ahead. If things were different, I might be sitting here with Julia, watching our three children play. I don't even know where I'll be come winter. I could potentially be in jail awaiting trial for murdering my wife.

"If I get arrested, Ashton, do you have the money to post bail? I'll pay you back of course. If not, I can add you to my bank account. I should probably do that anyway."

Ashton's tormented expression tells me how painful this discussion is for her. "I have plenty of money, Will."

"Thank you, Ashton, for everything. Knowing you're taking care of my girls gives me peace of mind."

"I'm glad. You have enough to worry about with your legal problems."

"Speaking of which, Marlowe wants me to hire him to dig up dirt on the Beaumonts."

Ashton's face lights up. "Do it! I have the utmost respect for Detective Marlowe after the way he handled Owen."

As I finish the last of my gelato, I type out a text to Marlowe. *You're hired. And you're definitely not working for free.*

Three dots appear in the message bubble, followed by his response. *Great. Let's meet first thing in the morning. I'll be at Marsh Point at nine.*

I give his text a thumbs-up and drop the phone on the picnic table. I immediately feel better having him on my case.

I slide over on the bench closer to my sister. "I owe you an apology, Ashton. I've been hard on you for the last thirty years. Not only are you the best sister a guy could ask for, you're also an amazing friend."

Tears well in her eyes as she smiles at me. "Thank you, Will. That's the kindest thing anyone has ever said to me. I'm grateful to be in a position to help. This is why Mama left me the house."

I toss my empty gelato cup into a nearby trash can. "Give me a break. She left you the house because you were her favorite. Why do you always give her so much credit?"

Ashton shoots back, "Why do you always give her *no* credit?"

"Because she ruined my life."

"She made your childhood difficult, but you've allowed her to ruin your life by harboring so much resentment towards her."

"You sound like Clemmy. If you decide to quit architecture, you have a career as a psychotherapist waiting for you."

"I'm serious, Will. Mama is dead and buried in Mossy Oak Cemetery. It's time you take back control of your emotions from her."

"And how do I do that, Dr. Ashton?"

"By forgiving her," Ashton says, pushing her empty cup away.

Her response hits me like a ton of bricks. I realize the path to emotional freedom is through forgiveness. And I'm making great strides towards forgiving myself for Bert's accident. But forgiving my mother for all the bad stuff she did to us is one avenue I'll detour.

TWENTY-SEVEN

JULIA

Late on Tuesday afternoon, I'm poring my heart out to my computer while Conrad plays with his trucks in the dunes at the edge of the yard. I hear a loud rapping on the door and freeze, my fingers poised on the keyboard. Who could that be? I know so few people in town. The boogeymen wouldn't bother knocking. It must be Fry, finally respecting my privacy.

I'm on my way to the door when more loud knocking is followed by a harsh voice saying, "Police! Open up!"

My immediate thought is that something has happened to Will. I swing open the door to find two young men standing on the small front porch, a baby-faced officer in uniform and an intense-looking guy with thick dark hair and menacing black eyes.

"Are you Julia Becker?" asks the man in plain clothes.

I grip the doorknob. "I am."

"I'm Detective Max Rourke." He flashes me his credentials and tosses a thumb at his sidekick. "And this is Officer Porter. We need to talk to you about your relationship with Will Darby."

Glancing over my shoulder, I see Conrad coming inside with his trucks, leaving a trail of sand across the porch floor. I close the door tighter, so my son won't see our visitors, and lower my voice.

"Now is not a good time. You'll have to come back in the morning when my son is at school."

Rourke's dark brow hits his hairline. "Excuse me, Miss Becker. But this is not a social visit. We can either talk here or we can go down to the station. Either way, we're having this conversation now."

I consider my choices. There's no one I trust to keep Conrad, and I can't take him to the police station with me. "Come in." I step out of the way for them to enter the cottage. "I need to start a movie for my son. You can wait for me on the porch."

Conrad's eyes grow wide when he sees the police officer. "Is that a real gun?" he asks, pointing at Porter's holstered weapon. My son appears more fascinated than intimidated by the officer. Has he already forgotten that cold night last spring when an army of police officers arrested his father?

Porter smiles down at Conrad. "Yes, son. It is. You're a cute kid. What's your name?"

My son tilts his face upward. "Conrad. But my friends call me Buddy."

Porter holds out his hand to Conrad, and they shake. "Nice to meet you, Buddy."

Clearing my throat, I motion them towards the porch. "I'll be out in a minute."

"Why are the police here, Mommy? Did you do something bad?" Conrad asks as I scroll through the PBS app for a suitable program.

I smile. "No, son. I'm not sure why they're here. Whatever it is, I don't want you to worry. I'll handle it." I tune into *Arthur*, one of Conrad's favorites, and tuck a blanket around him on the sofa. "I'll be right out on the porch, but you shouldn't interrupt us unless you really need me."

"Okay," Conrad says, already engrossed in the show, the excitement of the police officer now forgotten.

I made the mistake of leaving my computer open when I went

to answer the door. And I'm more than a little irritated to find Rourke seated in my abandoned chair, scrolling through my document.

"That's none of your business." I snap the laptop shut and snatch it away from him.

"That's some pretty steamy stuff. Are you a writer?" he asks, with a note of sarcasm in his tone.

"Something like that." I don't tell him my romance is clean compared to a lot of other authors. Hugging my computer to my chest, I sit down in the chair between the two men. "I'm in the middle of something. Can we just get this over with?"

"Fine. As I mentioned, we're here about Will Darby. What can you tell us about your relationship?"

I shrug. "There's not much to tell."

Rourke narrows his dark eyes. "We can sit here all night while I ask you a litany of questions. But you'll get rid of us a lot sooner by telling us what we want to know."

"How can I do that when I have no idea what you want to know?" I'm intentionally being difficult. But he's right. I do want to get rid of them.

Rourke falls back in his chair. "Why don't you start at the beginning? When did you meet Will Darby?"

I set the laptop on the table and fold my hands on top. "At Coastal Hardware a few days after Labor Day."

Rourke exchanges a look with Officer Porter. "According to our sources, you and Will were seeing each other at the time of his wife's death."

"Well, your sources are wrong," I say in a defiant tone. "I know when I met Will."

"Let's assume for a minute that our information *is* incorrect. What happened at this meet-cute in the hardware store?"

I stand abruptly. "I resent your innuendo, Detective. I've done nothing wrong. And neither has Will. Our children are in the same class at school. They became friends. When I went to pick up my son from a playdate with Will's daughter one Friday afternoon, Will and his sister asked me to go on a boat ride. I ended up staying for dinner. Will invited my son and me for a cookout the following weekend, and Will asked me on a date a couple of Saturdays after that. Because the restaurant was crowded, we picked up a few items at Fancy Pantry and had a picnic on the beach. We've kissed a few times, but we haven't had sex. And now we've broken up. End of story."

Rourke stands to face me, and following his lead, Porter scrambles to his feet. "When did you break up?"

"Yesterday." My throat thickens, and I wait for my tears to pass before continuing. "We were never really together, so *breakup* is not the right word. Will just lost his wife, and I just got divorced. We were friends, comforting each other through difficult times. I don't want to be a distraction for Will with all he has going on right now."

Rourke appears unmoved by my sentiment. "Where did you move here from, Miss Becker? And why Water's Edge? It's not exactly a hot spot."

"You're not the first person to say that to me, Detective. I moved here from Denver. After an unpleasant divorce, I needed a fresh start. I was looking for a quiet place on the coast. Water's Edge seemed to fit the bill. It appears I was wrong."

Rourke looks from me through the window at Conrad who has fallen asleep on the sofa. "I assume you don't share custody with the kid's father?"

I hold my chin high. "I don't see how my marriage relates to this situation."

"I'm interested in the timing of your divorce. If you and Will were having an affair when his wife died, and the two of you conspired to kill her, you're an accessory to murder."

The bottom falls out of my stomach as I realize I'm being framed. "That's ridiculous."

"Not according to our sources," Rourke says.

"And who are these sources, Detective?"

"I'm not at liberty to say."

"Whoever these people are, they are lying to you. When you figure that out, I'll expect an apology."

"Don't hold your breath." He extends his hand to me. "I need to see your driver's license."

"What for?" I ask in a defiant tone.

His beady eyes pin me against the side of the house. "So I can run a background check, to verify your story."

"Fine. I'll get it." I take my computer with me, leaving it on the kitchen counter when I retrieve my wallet from my purse.

As I give Rourke the license, I say a silent prayer that Eleanor did a thorough job creating my fake past.

With a glance at the license, Rourke hands it over to Porter, who photographs it with his phone before giving it back to me.

"That's all for now. If you think of anything else that might be helpful," he says and shoves a business card at me.

I shrink away from the card. "I won't. I've told you everything already."

"Don't leave town, Miss Becker," Rourke says and moves towards the house.

I hold the screen door open for them. "You can leave this way. My son's asleep, and I don't want you waking him up."

As they pass by me, Officer Porter smiles, but Rourke avoids meeting my gaze.

I listen for the sound of their car engine starting and the crunch of gravel from their tires before lowering myself to a rocker. I woke up from one nightmare to find myself in another. I'm being framed for the murder of a woman I never even met. To prove I wasn't having an affair with Will at the time of her death, I would have to blow my cover. Even if I wanted to leave town, doing so would make me appear guilty. I'm stuck with no choice but to wait for the cartel to come after me.

TWENTY-EIGHT
WILL

When Marlowe arrives promptly at nine, I offer him coffee and we walk onto the veranda.

"What is your first name?" I ask him. "Since we're going to be working together, I should call you something other than Detective."

He chuckles. "Technically, I'm no longer a detective. My name is Brice."

I give him a curt nod. "Brice it is. So where do we start?"

He looks around, surveying the property before zeroing in on the dock. "Why don't you show me your boat, the scene of the accident?"

The police impounded the boat for weeks after Tracy's death. His forensic team went over the boat with a fine-tooth comb and found nothing. I assume he has an ulterior motive for wanting to see my boat.

Marlowe waits until we're at the end of the dock before he says, "I don't need to see the boat. I personally went over every inch of it. But I wanted to talk out of earshot of the house. Before I leave, with your permission, I'd like to sweep the interior for listening devices."

My head rears back, as though I've been slapped. The thought of someone listening to my conversations with my sister and children makes my skin crawl. "You think my in-laws have bugged my house?"

"I wouldn't be surprised." He leans back against a piling, crossing his long legs. "Before we move forward, I have some questions for you." The hesitancy in his voice makes me wonder if he's having second thoughts about working for me.

"Sure. You can ask me anything."

"I wasn't aware until recently that your kids were with your in-laws at the time of your wife's death. Did they babysit for you often?"

I pause, considering how to respond. He'll find out the truth anyway. He might as well hear it from me. "Tracy took the girls to stay with her parents in Savannah without my permission. We were having some problems in our marriage, although it's not what you think. I was *not* having an affair."

"What was it, then?" His calm demeanor leads me to believe he already knows the answer, and he's testing me.

"Tracy found out about something that happened in my past. My best friend died in a freak accident when we were fifteen, and I was blamed for his death."

Marlowe nods. "I know about Bert."

"I'm not surprised. You don't miss much. Tracy got it in her head that I have anger management issues. She wanted me to check myself into a mental health facility that specializes in anger issues."

"You *do* have anger issues, Will. I've witnessed them myself."

"I'm aware. I took your advice, and I'm getting help. I assume you already know this, too."

"Yep." He chuckles. "I've spent some time on Clemmy's daybed swing myself."

I might think this funny if I weren't so irritated. Why is he grilling me when he already knows everything? Because he's testing me. To see if he can trust me.

Marlowe pushes off the piling. "Walk me through the events of the accident again. This time, don't leave out the part about the argument with your wife."

I turn away from him, staring out across the water as the memories from that dreadful day come rushing back. "Tracy shanghaied me. I came home from work that day to find my children gone and my suitcase packed and waiting beside the front door. She said if I didn't check myself into the mental institution, she would leave me. When I refused, she got livid and took off in her car. I followed her here." I repeat the rest of the story, which he's already heard a dozen times. About the storm and Tracy refusing to let me drive the boat. About the wave crashing into the boat and her falling overboard.

"How did you react when she asked you to commit yourself to the mental institution?"

Turning away from the water, I looked him straight in the eyes. "I was more upset about her taking my children to Savannah without asking me. When Tracy got something in her head, she refused to let it go. As was the case with my anger management issue." I pause to take the last sip of my coffee. "Tracy was the angry one that day, Brice. I can still see her whipping the steering wheel away from the oncoming wave."

We stand for a minute in silence, each of us lost in thought.

Finally, Marlowe slaps my shoulder. "Sorry to put you through all that again. I've always believed in your innocence. I lost my job because of it. But I had to make certain I hadn't missed anything before I go out on a limb for you."

"I understand. If you have any other doubts about me, let's clear them up now. I'm no angel, but I'm not the devil either."

Marlowe shakes his head. "I'm all in. Do you have any questions for me?"

I stare down at the ground, my mind a jumble of thoughts. "I'm sure I do. I just can't think of them right now."

"You can text me anytime," he says, and we stroll back towards the house. "Coincidentally, I need to warn you about my replacement. Max Rourke is a first-class jerk."

I stop walking. "You mean they've already hired someone?"

"Yep. They should've promoted Jimmy Riley. Jimmy's a hard worker with keen instincts, and he's earned the opportunity. Everything about Rourke's hire makes me suspicious. His timely arrival in Water's Edge, and his apparent lack of experience. I would be willing to bet Rourke is on Beaumont's payroll."

I frown. "Seriously? He's a law enforcement officer. How corrupt is this world?"

"More corrupt than you can ever imagine, my friend." He starts walking again. "Rourke paid your friend Julia a visit yesterday evening. My informant inside the department tells me he threatened to arrest her as an accessory to murdering your wife."

My heart skips a beat. "That's ludicrous. I didn't even know Julia at the time."

"I hope she has a strong alibi to clear her name."

"She does! Three months ago, she was living two thousand miles away in Colorado."

Deep lines appear between Marlowe's brows. "I wouldn't be too sure. How much do you know about Julia's past?"

I massage my jaw. "Very little, now that I think about it. She recently got divorced and has full custody of her son."

"Sounds suspicious to me. Why does she have full custody?"

"I'm not sure." I think back to the brief discussion Julia and I had about her husband. "She told me her divorce was unpleasant, and her husband is out of their lives for good."

"And why did she move here? To Water's Edge?"

"Because she wanted a fresh start." I lock eyes with the detective. "What are you suggesting, Brice?"

"That maybe she's a plant. I wouldn't put it past your in-laws to pay someone to lie about having an affair with you."

"But that makes no sense. Why would she risk being accused as an accessory to murder? If convicted, she could go to prison for life."

Marlowe raises a finger. "Unless she cuts a deal with the district attorney to testify against you in exchange for her freedom."

"I can't believe Julia would do something so awful. She seemed to genuinely care about me."

At the end of the boardwalk, Marlowe stops walking and turns to face me. "We could use more manpower on the case. How do you feel about me bringing Carter Leach on board?" he asks, referring to the private investigator Ashton hired to uncover her husband's underhanded dealings.

"Carter's a good guy. I'm fine with it if you think it's necessary."

"Since I'll be in Savannah tracking leads, I would feel better having someone on the scene in Water's Edge. He could start by looking into Julia's past."

"Fine. Hire him." My insides churn in anger. What if Julia really is a plant? What if she's been using me all this time? To bring our children into her dirty little scheme is twisted.

Marlowe tenses when Mia's minivan appears in the driveway. "Who's that?"

"Don't worry. It's only my housekeeper returning from taking my children to school."

"Is she aware of the situation? I don't want to alarm her when I scour the house for listening devices."

"She doesn't yet, but she needs to know. I'll talk to her while you conduct your sweep."

I walk around the side of the house and help Mia carry grocery bags into the house. While she's unloading them, I explain about Tracy's parents' unethical attempts to get custody of my children.

"I don't blame you if you want to look for employment elsewhere," I say. "Although we'd all be sad to see you go."

"No way, Mister Will. I love my job, and you need me right now."

"You're right about that." I give her a half hug. "I want you to be on heightened alert. If you see anything that concerns you, I want you to call me immediately. If I'm not available, get in touch with Ashton."

"Yes, sir. I understand."

I brew another cup of coffee and take it outside to the veranda. I make several business calls while I wait for Marlowe to finish inside.

Ninety minutes later, he emerges from the house. "As I suspected, I found several different state-of-the-art listening devices." He riffles through the backpack and pulls out a handful of tiny gadgets. "These are extremely costly. They were planted by professionals. My curiosity about your in-laws is growing by the minute. I can hardly wait to expose them."

TWENTY-NINE
JULIA

I live in constant fear of being ambushed. I'm always looking over my shoulder and in my rearview mirror. I'm fairly certain Ethan Striker is driving the old silver Honda Accord that is often tailing me from several cars back. But the driver of the ever-present black Tahoe never gets close enough for me to see either the person behind the wheel or the license plate. I pray it's the people working for Will's in-laws and not the boogeymen.

After dropping Conrad at school in the mornings, I head over to the shooting range where Courtney from Coastal Hardware instructs me on improving my aim. While she doesn't press me for details, she senses my concern for my safety and teaches me some basic self-defense moves.

Most days when I return home with Conrad at noon, I find something out of order. A carton of milk left out on the kitchen counter. The television on. The screen door unlatched. I attribute these to my frazzled state of mind. So far, I've seen no evidence the boogeymen are stalking me.

My work in progress takes an abrupt turn when I decide to make major changes to my first draft, brought on by current events in my life. I surprise my characters with a plot twist, and they are scrambling to save their relationship from the outside forces threatening them. My sweet romance has transitioned into a romantic suspense. But that's okay by me. I'm a mystery writer at heart.

I spend my afternoons on the porch writing while Conrad plays at my feet with his Legos or in the yard with his trucks. He's playing in the dunes, driving his dump truck in the sand, on Friday afternoon when Detective Rourke and Officer Porter appear from the side of the house. Conrad waves at them, but he doesn't get up to greet them.

I remain seated at the table as well. "And here you are again. Like déjà vu. You could've called first to let me know you were coming."

Rourke grunts. "Why would we do that, Miss Becker?"

"Out of respect, Detective," I say, and motion for them to join me at the table. "What's this about?"

"Your background check." Rourke opens his tablet on the table in front of him. "It's clean."

My mouth goes dry at the mention of my fake background. "Of course, it's clean. I'm a law-abiding citizen. Is that a problem?"

"It's too clean, Miss Becker. If you don't mind, I'd like to go over your history." Rourke taps his tablet, and the screen comes alive.

I mind, but I'm in no position to argue. "Fine. But can we make it quick?" I gesture at my computer. "As you can see, I'm working."

"Your romance characters can wait," Rourke says in a derogatory manner that tells me how little he thinks of my career.

For the next ten minutes, he grills me about the life Eleanor invented for me in Denver. Where I went to school from kindergarten through college. The address of my childhood home. The grocery store where I worked as a clerk. The hospital where Conrad was born.

"Very good, Miss Becker. Your memorization skills are excellent. Now tell me about your husband."

My *memorization* skills? The room begins to spin, and I worry I might faint. The detective knows I'm hiding something. If I don't appear calm, I'll give myself away. Inhaling a deep breath, I sit up straighter in my chair. "My husband is a sore subject for me. I was married to Ralph Becker. He became abusive and we divorced. The judge granted me full custody, and I moved to South Carolina to start a new life. End of story."

"The funny thing is, we couldn't find any evidence of a Ralph Becker in Denver. At least not a Ralph Becker married to a Julia Becker with a son Conrad. Now tell me the real truth. Who are you?"

I ignore his question. "What does my background have to do with Will Darby anyway?"

He closes the cover on his tablet. "Because I think you're lying. I believe you were living in Water's Edge this summer. And I believe you were having an affair with Will, and you two conspired to kill his wife."

Conrad looks up from his truck, concern etched on his young face.

"Shh! Lower your voice," I hiss at the detective, and call out to Conrad, "It's okay, sweetheart. Detective Rourke is helping Mommy with research for her book."

"I'm impressed, Miss Becker. You think fast on your feet."

Truth be told, I invented that excuse days ago in anticipation of another visit from him. "Are you going to arrest me, Detective?"

"Not today," he says in a tone that indicates an arrest is forthcoming.

"Then I'll have to ask you to please leave." Pushing back from the table, I stride across the porch and open the screen door.

Rourke stops in front of me on his way out, his face close to mine. "This isn't over, Miss Becker. I suggest you hire yourself a lawyer."

I'm tempted to tell him the truth, to clear my name and end

this nightmare. But I don't trust Rourke to keep my secret. I certainly don't expect him to help me.

I wait until Rourke and Porter disappear around the side of the house before stumbling back to my chair. But as my butt hits the seat, I notice movement in the row of shrubbery separating our yard from the neighbor's. I'm back on my feet, hurrying inside for my handgun. I sprint out the front door just as the now-familiar silver Honda Accord is speeding away.

How long had Ethan Striker been hiding in the bushes? Was he close enough to hear our conversation? Why is he stalking me? What does he want?

My questions are answered two hours later when I turn on the television to the evening news. Ethan leads the news with his story about me. He's standing at the end of my driveway, the cottage visible in the background. I peek out the kitchen window, but there's no sign of a news crew. He must've recorded the footage earlier this morning before we got home at noon.

"Julia Becker is the subject on everyone's minds and lips these days," Striker says to his audience. "Just who *is* Will Darby's mystery woman? Our investigation suggests she's hiding something. We have more questions than answers. We'll tell you what we've found out so far when we return from this commercial break."

Ethan's image fades to black, and a commercial for a nutritional supplement comes on.

Conrad is working on a puzzle at the dining table, seemingly oblivious to the news. But I can't take any chances of him hearing Ethan talking about me. Turning off the television, I leave the living room and go into my room to continue watching. I lower the volume and stand close to the small TV.

Footage of Rourke and Porter getting out of their patrol car and walking down the side of my house fills the screen. "Police interrogated Miss Becker for over an hour today," Ethan tells his viewers.

"Learn how to tell time, you jerk," I say to the television. "They were here less than fifteen minutes."

As Ethan talks, he shows photographs and footage of me driving Conrad to school and shopping for groceries at Fancy Pantry. "On the surface, Julia Becker seems like your ordinary stay-at-home mom, who spends her days making up fairytale romances. But her story doesn't check out. The police background check reveals gaping holes." An image of Conrad on the playground at school appears. "Is this boy her biological child? If so, who and where is his father?" The last clip is of me entering the shooting range. "And why, if Miss Becker has nothing to hide, does she spend her mornings target practicing at the local shooting range?" The camera pans to Ethan. "Stay tuned. We'll have these and more answers for you soon."

Anger consumes me, pumping through my veins and stealing my breath. As I grip the remote, powering off the television, I yearn to wrap my hands around Striker's throat and choke the life out of him. Then Rourke would have a legitimate reason to arrest me.

I sit down on the bed while I wait for my anger to subside. I'm tempted to pack up our belongings and leave Water's Edge under the cover of darkness. But sneaking out of town would make me look all the more guilty. Rourke would undoubtedly come after me. We wouldn't get far with the police and the boogeymen on our tails. I have no choice but to wait it out.

THIRTY
WILL

Caroline enters the kitchen before I can power off the television.

"Was that Buddy's mommy?" she asks as the screen goes black.

I feign ignorance. "What, sweetheart?"

Her little arm shoots out, finger pointed at the television. "Buddy's mom was on the television just now. Did you not see her?"

"Sorry. No. I wasn't paying attention. They were probably interviewing her about the book she's writing."

Caroline's eyes widen. "She's writing a book? That's so cool! She might be famous one day. Wait until I tell Sophie," she says, and dashes out of the kitchen.

I wait until I'm certain she's out of earshot before I turn the television back on. I'm rewinding Striker's segment when there's a knock at the back door.

"Hey, man," Carter Leach says. "I hope you don't mind me stopping by. Since Marlowe's out of town, I thought I'd check on you."

I step out of the way for him to enter. "Come on in. You've

gotta see this." I return to the television. "Did Marlowe ask you to look into Julia Becker's background?"

"He did. But I haven't had much time."

I click the play arrow on the remote, and Ethan Striker appears on the screen. "On the surface, Julia Becker seems like your ordinary stay-at-home mother, who spends her days making up fairy-tale romances," Striker says. "But her story doesn't check out. The police background check reveals gaping holes."

When the segment ends, I power off the television. "What do you make of that?"

"I'm not sure. Are you still seeing this woman?"

"Nope. She broke up with me. Not that we were ever really together." I remove two bottles of Miller Lite from the refrigerator and hand one to him. "We had a couple of cookouts with our kids, and we've been on one date. We weren't sleeping together, but I really liked her. She seemed normal. I just lost my wife. I wasn't looking to start anything with anyone new. But we hit it off. I figured why not?" I pause to take a sip of beer. "I need to know what's going on with her, Carter. Why does she spend her mornings at a shooting range? Is she colluding with my in-laws to destroy my life? I'm not even sure her name is Julia Becker."

"Don't worry. I'm on it. If she's hiding something, I will find out what it is."

"You're a good man, Carter. Thanks." Setting down my beer, I place a pot of water on the stove to boil. "Can you stay for dinner? My housekeeper makes the best marinara sauce. Although this time she's trusting me to boil the noodles. We'll see how that goes."

Carter laughs. "I appreciate the offer. But I'm meeting friends later."

We talk about my case while I'm waiting for the water to boil. Carter seems hopeful Marlowe will find something to use against my in-laws. "He's on a mission. I've never seen him this determined. This isn't just about you, Will. The case became personal for him when he lost his job."

"I'm sorry for him, but it definitely works in my favor," I say, dumping a box of thin spaghetti noodles into the boiling water.

Carter drains the last of his beer and hands me the empty bottle. "I'll be in touch as soon as I find out more about Julia," he says and lets himself out the back door.

As the noodles boil, I replay Striker's news segment in my mind. Who is Julia? And where is she really from? Buddy told Ashton they moved here from Texas, but Julia claims they are from Colorado. Was she ever married? Is Buddy really her son? And why is she spending so much time at the shooting range? Who or what is she afraid of?

Thoughts of Julia prevent me from sleeping a wink that night. Crazy scenarios assault my imagination as I toss and turn. But only one makes sense.

When the first rays of dawn creep through my blinds, I give up on trying to sleep and get dressed. I smile to myself when I see Ashton's bedroom door open and her bed still made. I'm glad one of us is enjoying ourselves.

I go down the hall to check on the girls. As I'm tucking the covers tight around Caroline, I happen to glance out the window and notice Ashton getting out of her convertible in the driveway. Her dreamy expression tells me everything I need to know about her night with Sully. Good for her. I wish those two all the best.

As Ashton approaches the front stoop, two figures in dark clothing dart out from around the side of the house. His brown curly mop identifies Ethan Striker. The other trespasser with him is built like a weightlifter and carries a professional video camera.

I fly down the stairs and sprint through the center hallway. By the time I get out the front door, Striker has a microphone shoved in Ashton's face, and he's spewing questions at her about me.

"How much do you know about your brother's mystery woman? And what is Julia Becker hiding? You must be hiding something as well, sneaking in here at the crack of dawn. Where did you spend the night last night, Miss Darby? Do you have a mystery man as well?"

I spin Ethan around and punch him square between the eyes. He collapses to the ground like dead weight.

Ashton lets out a scream. "Will! Stop!"

I drop down on top of him, pummeling him with my fists.

"Easy there, buddy." The cameraman pries me off of Ethan, lifting me to my feet. "We're leaving. Go inside and cool off."

When I try to go after Ethan again, Ashton drags me inside the house. "Come on. They're leaving."

"Get off my property before I call the police," I yell at them seconds before Ashton slams the front door.

I fall back against the door. "I'm so sorry, Ashton. I can't believe he treated you that way."

"I can. After what he did to Julia, I'm not surprised. So many journalists are scum these days."

"Come on. I'll make us some coffee." Taking me by the hand, she leads me through the dining room into the kitchen.

She fills the Keurig's water reservoir while I open a new box of Pumpkin Spice K-cups.

"You went off like a cannon on him, Will. I've never seen you so angry. You should call your therapist. Does she have weekend hours?"

My brow shoots up. "I have a right to be angry. They were trespassing on our property, and Striker was way out of line in what he said to you."

Her shoulders sag. "Still, I think you need to talk things over with Clemmy."

"What I need is to take a day off from all this drama."

Ashton pops in a K-cup and pushes the button to brew. "I can help you with that. Come sailing with Sully and me. We were going to ask you anyway."

"I can't. I have the girls."

"Duh. I meant for you to bring them with you," she says, handing me a cup of steaming black coffee.

I'm suddenly intrigued. The idea of spending the day on the water appeals to me. "Is Sully's boat big enough for all of us?"

"It's thirty-five feet," she says as she sets the second cup of coffee to brew.

"Then count us in. That sounds like fun."

"Maybe we can cook out here afterward," she suggests.

"That's a great idea. I can run to the market while the girls are still asleep."

Ashton glances at the wall clock. "I doubt anything's open this early."

"You're probably right. I'll wait a bit."

We take our coffees out to the porch and sit in silence as we watch the world come alive around us. Pelicans dive for fish. Heron search for food in the marsh. And schools of minnows skim the surface of the water.

Ashton breaks the silence. "I saw the segment about Julia on the news last night. Do you think she's hiding something?"

I massage my jaw, the beard stubble rough against my palm. "I was up all night trying to make sense of it. Marlowe thinks she may be a plant. That Tracy's parents are paying her to lie about having an affair with me."

"Come on, Will. That seems extreme, even for the Beaumonts."

The pitter-patter of tiny feet in the hallway through the open door saves me from having to answer. Caroline climbs into my lap and Sophie into Ashton's. In a sleepy voice, Caroline asks, "Aunt Ashton, will you make us waffles for breakfast?"

"You bet. And then we're all going sailing on Sully's boat."

Suddenly alert, the girls slide off our laps to their feet, dragging us out of our chairs and inside to the kitchen.

It's nine o'clock by the time we finish eating and cleaning up. I head out to the grocery store with my list, leaving the girls with Ashton to get ready for sailing.

I return home from the market an hour later to find a police car in my driveway. Two officers are speaking with my sister at the door, my daughters peeking out at them with wide eyes from behind Ashton's legs.

The officers turn to face me. Both are burly figures with angry scowls. One wears thick, black-framed glasses and the other has a shiny bald head shaped like an egg.

Officer Four Eyes snatches away my grocery bags, thrusting them at Ashton. "Mr. Darby, you're under arrest for the aggravated assault of Ethan Striker. You'll need to come with us."

I scoff. "Since when does punching someone equate to aggravated assault? Besides, he deserved it. He was trespassing on my property and verbally abusive to my sister."

Officer Chrome Dome places handcuffs on my wrists. "Save it for the judge, buddy."

Caroline lets out a high-pitched screen. "No! You can't take my daddy!"

"Is this really necessary, Officer? You're scaring my children."

"After what you did to Ethan Striker, we have to treat you like a dangerous fugitive. Now get moving," he says, manhandling me down the steps.

"What do you want me to do, Will?" Ashton calls after me in a tone of desperation.

I yell over my shoulder, "Call Vanessa and Carter. Tell Carter to get in touch with Marlowe."

The officer wrestles me into the back seat of the patrol car, and we speed off towards town. When we arrive at the police station, Four Eyes drops us at the back door and Chrome Dome leads me to the booking room.

"I've never been arrested before. How does the process work? When can I get out on bail?" I ask as he's logging my personal property.

"On Monday morning when the magistrate court goes into session."

"Wait. What? I have to stay here all weekend?"

"Afraid so, pal."

After fingerprinting me and taking my mug shot, Chrome Dome guides me into the cell block. He slides open a cell door and shoves me inside, clanging the door shut behind me.

"Hey! Wait. I have a right to make a phone call."

"You'll get your phone call. After I've eaten my lunch."

I glance around at the cinderblock walls, stainless steel toilet, and metal cot fitted with a thin mattress and flat pillow. I'm prone to claustrophobia, and I immediately feel the walls begin to close in on me. With no watch or wall clock, I have no way to mark the time. I stretch out on the bed and begin counting in sixty-second increments. Exhausted from lack of sleep and the events of the morning, I soon doze off. When I wake, I have no idea what time it is, how long I slept, if it's even night or day.

On an orange tray just inside the door is a bowl of chicken noodle soup that has gone cold. Presumably my lunch. Fortunately, I ate extra waffles for breakfast, and I'm not yet hungry.

Based on the eerie silence, I'm the only prisoner currently occupying the cell block. Then again, we don't have much crime in Water's Edge.

I resign myself to spending the weekend in here. With nothing to occupy my mind, I lie on my cot, staring up at the ceiling, and think about how I got myself into this situation. I am a victim. I've done nothing wrong. Yet a lot of people are determined to ruin me and send me to prison for life. Tracy's parents. Detective Rourke, whom I've never even met. Ethan Striker, an opportunist who is willing to destroy a man for a lead story. And Julia. Although I have yet to figure out how she fits into the picture.

My anger festers into rage. My head pounds and my vision blurs. None of Clemmy's coping mechanisms work. Punching the walls is the only thing that releases the fury consuming me.

I tell time by the delivery of meals. While I'm lying on my bed, fantasizing about the awful things I would like to do to Tracy's parents, an officer delivers my dinner on Sunday evening.

"I have your dinner, sir."

I sit bolt-upright in bed. Did he just call me *sir*? A young officer with a baby face and blond hair is standing on the other side of the bars with a tray.

"I pulled a few strings and got you a home-cooked meal," he says.

I move closer to the bars. The hunger pangs have been gnawing at my belly for hours. "Seriously?"

"Yes and no. Yes, your sister sent the lasagna. It smells amazing. But no, I'm too far down the totem pole to ask for favors. I could get fired for sneaking this in here."

I look from the silver-domed plate to him. "Then why did you?"

He glances around, making sure no one is in earshot. "Don't tell anyone, but I'm working undercover for Detective Marlowe. He sent a message. He said for you to keep the faith. Your attorney will arrange your bail first thing in the morning."

My shoulders sag as some of the tension leaves my body. I hope this attorney is the woman Vanessa recommended. I glance down at his nameplate. "Thank you for being one of the good guys, Cody Porter. I will not forget your kindness."

Sliding the door open, he hands me the tray. Noticing my bloody knuckles, he asks, "What happened to your hands?"

"I had a run-in with a cinderblock wall." My face warms. "I would say it's not what you think, but it is totally what you think. My anger got the best of me. The whole world is out to get me, and I can't seem to catch a break."

In a sympathetic tone, he says, "I get it, man. You may feel like the lone wolf, but you have a lot of people on your side. Do you think anything's broken?" he asks about my hands.

I rub my sore knuckles. "No. They're just cut and bruised."

"That's good." He clangs the bar door shut. "Hang tight. I'll be right back with something to clean them up."

I sit down on my bed and dig into the lasagna. For the first time since my arrest, I'm hopeful I may eventually get out of here.

THIRTY-ONE
JULIA

The weekend brings glorious weather with warm days and chilly nights. We spend our days on the beach. The sun's rays sparkle diamonds off the calm ocean as Conrad plays in the sand, and I lounge under our pop-up beach tent, a recent purchase from Coastal Hardware. To an outsider, we're mother and son enjoying our last warm days of autumn. Strollers passing by would never guess we're in imminent danger of a human trafficking cartel.

With miles of open beach in both directions, I'm able to be on constant lookout for suspicious people. My holstered gun is tucked inside the waistband of my shorts, and one of Fry's butcher knives is hidden in my beach bag.

Work on my novel has come to a screeching halt. My appetite has vanished, and I only manage a few hours of sleep at night. Every creak in the cottage's old floorboards sends a jolt through me. I get up several times a night to check the house, to make certain nothing is lurking in the shadows.

On Saturday evening, I sneak off to my room to watch the six o'clock news. My heart breaks into a million pieces when I see the footage of Will attacking Ethan Striker. He goes after the reporter with vengeance, the anger on his face and hate in his eyes chilling me to my core and staying with me long after the segment ends.

By Sunday afternoon, every nerve ending in my body is standing on end. I don't know how much more of this pressure I can take. When we come off the beach around four o'clock, we rinse the sand off our gear and toys and store everything neatly on the porch. I unlock the back door and enter the cottage, stopping dead in my tracks at the sight of a distinguished-looking gentleman seated on my sofa. I pull out my gun and aim it at his head. "Who are you? And what do you want?"

The man raises his hands as he slowly rises from the sofa. "Easy there, Miss Becker. Put the gun down. I mean you no harm."

Conrad inches closer to me. "Is that gun real, Mommy?" he whispers.

"Yes, son. It's real. Now go to your room and don't come out until I call you."

My serious tone sends Conrad scurrying off to his bedroom.

I wait until I hear my son's door close before repeating myself. "Who are you? And what do you want?"

"I'll tell you after you put down the gun."

I tighten my fingers on the gun's grip. "You first." I give him the once-over while I wait for him to make his next move. He's nice-looking, around sixty years old, with salt-and-pepper hair and chiseled facial features. His clothes are casual but expensive—gray flannel slacks and a slate-blue, quarter-zip sweater with a pink-checked dress shirt underneath—not the attire I would expect a member of the cartel to wear.

The man lets out a frustrated sigh. "My name is Landon Whitfield. I'm an attorney representing Clarence and Loretta Beaumont."

I crinkle my nose. "Who? I've never heard of them."

"The Beaumonts are the late Tracy Darby's parents. I'm here to offer you a deal."

I sit down in the chair opposite him with the gun resting in my lap. "Start talking."

The attorney lowers himself to the sofa. "I'm aware of your predicament. I know your real name is Casey Bishop, and you recently escaped Witness Protection after testifying against your husband for human trafficking."

I work hard to keep a straight face. "I don't know what you're talking about. Who is Casey Bishop?"

"You are. And your son's real name is Levi. I know everything about you, Mrs. Bishop. You're originally from Austin, Texas. Your parents and two sisters still live there. Your husband was involved in a cartel controlled by The Six. I can either protect you, or I can turn you over to them."

A wave of nausea overcomes me at the mention of The Six. There's no point in pretending. My cover is blown. "How can you protect me?"

"In much the same way as WITSEC. In exchange for your testimony, I will help you and your son start a new life."

Bile rises in my throat. "What testimony, Mr. Whitfield?" I ask, even though I have my suspicion.

"Your testimony stating you were romantically involved with Will Darby at the time of his wife's death."

I glare at him. "That's not a testimony, Mr. Landon. That's a bold-faced lie. You're asking me to perjure myself. I could go to prison for that."

Whitfield places his hands in his lap. "I'm prepared to offer you a very large sum of money."

When he tells me the amount, my eyes pop. With that kind of money, Conrad and I could disappear to a remote part of the world where the cartel would never find us.

After seeing him attack Ethan on the news last night, I've had some serious reservations about Will's innocence. It's possible a man harboring that kind of anger could've hit his wife over the head or pushed her overboard. But that's between Will, his wife, and God. I want no part of it.

"Tempting, isn't it, Mrs. Bishop?" Whitfield says, jerking me out of my reverie.

"My name is Julia Becker. And no, I'm not tempted. If I lie in court, I'll be accused of accessory to murder. When I'm sent to prison, the Beaumonts are off the hook for the bribery payout."

He gives his head a grave shake. "That's not the way it works. I can guarantee you will not be charged."

"How can you guarantee that?"

"You have to trust me on this."

"I don't trust you. I don't even know you." I jump to my feet. "Now, you need to leave."

"I understand you need time to think about it. I'll be back in touch in a couple of days." Whitfield stands and takes a business card out of his wallet. "In the meantime, if you have questions, you can reach me at any of these numbers." He hands me the card.

I take the card and tear it in half. "I won't have any questions and I won't lie in court. My integrity has a very high price, a price even your wealthy clients can't afford."

Whitfield places another business card on the coffee table. "You'll change your mind in due time. But don't take too long. The amount of our offer will decrease with every passing day."

I march across the room and open the front door. "Please leave. And don't come back."

I wait until his fancy sports car has disappeared from the driveway before closing the door and collapsing against it. Conrad comes flying out of his room and flings himself at me, wrapping his arms around my legs and crying, "Mommy, are we in trouble again?"

I stuff the handgun back in its holster and wrap my arms tight around him. "I don't know for sure yet, son. Maybe. I need to figure out a few things first. But I don't want you to worry." I hold him at arm's length. "Are you hungry? What say we order pizza?"

The offer of pizza usually works with my son. And this time is no different. His lips turn up in a sad smile, and I get the impression he's being brave for my benefit. "Pizza sounds good, Mommy."

I paste on a fake smile as we go about our evening. Conrad is unusually quiet, and I can tell his mind is occupied with troubled thoughts. When I'm tucking him into bed, he says, "It's okay if we have to move again, Mommy. Just don't let them take you away from me like they did Daddy."

My throat swells, and I force back tears. "No one is going to take me away from you, sweetheart." Kissing his forehead, I stretch out beside him and wait until I'm certain he's asleep.

Locating my phone, I go outside to the porch to call Eleanor. The minute I hear her voice, I burst into tears. "I'm in big trouble, Eleanor." In between sobs, I fill her in on everything that has happened. "I made a huge mistake in leaving WITSEC. Is there any chance Conrad and I can come back?"

"I'm sorry, Julia. Helping you escape nearly cost me my job."

Eleanor goes silent, and the sound of my uncontrollable sobs fills the line.

"Let me see what I can find out. Try to get yourself together. I'll call you back in a few minutes."

Despite my best efforts to calm myself, I'm hiccup sobbing when Eleanor calls me back thirty minutes later. Between breaths, I manage to choke out, "I'm sorry, Eleanor. The dam burst, and the emotion I've been holding in for so long is overflowing."

"I understand. You've been through a lot. After we hang up, lie down on your bed with a warm washcloth covering your eyes. You'll feel better in the morning."

I wouldn't dare cover my eyes with a washcloth. I need to be on the lookout for intruders. "Did you find out anything?"

"Based on our intelligence, the cartel has not yet discovered your location. Of course, that could change at any minute. I suggest you reach out to Delilah Hart. She's an independent journalist investigating The Six. Be honest with her. Tell her your story. She may be able to help."

I have no intention of contacting the journalist, but I don't want to be rude to Eleanor. It's not her fault she has nothing else to give me. "Do you have her contact information?"

"No. You can message her through social media. She's on nearly every platform."

"Okay. Thanks, Eleanor." I end the call feeling worse than before. I knew it was a long shot, but I was hoping WITSEC would accept me back into the program. I'm truly on my own now.

THIRTY-TWO
WILL

Officer Chrome Dome arrives early on Monday morning to escort me to magistrate court.

"What happened to your hands?" he asks, noticing my bandaged knuckles as he handcuffs me.

"I was locked in a cinderblock cage all weekend. What do you think happened?"

"You really need to learn to manage your anger." Chrome Dome leads me out of the cell block and through the back entrance to a patrol car parked just outside the door with Four Eyes behind the wheel.

"Where is the magistrate court?" I ask once we're on our way.

Four Eyes looks at me through the rearview mirror. "In the municipal building."

"Will I get to speak with my attorney before my hearing? I'm not even sure I have one, since you've denied me my one phone call."

"You have one. She's already at the municipal building," Four Eyes says and returns his attention to the road.

I say a silent prayer this *she* is Stone Cold Alex.

Several members of the press and their camera crews are

waiting in the front of the municipal building when Four Eyes parks alongside the curb. As the officers usher me through the crowd, the reporters shout questions at me.

"Will you plead guilty to aggravated assault, Mr. Darby?"

"Did you murder your wife?"

"Is an arrest in your wife's case forthcoming?"

"What happened to your hands, Mr. Darby? Did you suffer those injuries during your assault on Ethan Striker?"

A furious Alex Stone holds the door open for us as we enter the building. She's an imposing figure in a stark black suit with her black hair fastened at the nape of her neck. She glares at the officers. "Why didn't you bring him in through the back entrance instead of subjecting him to that media circus?"

"We're in a hurry," Chrome Dome says. "We don't have time for the parking deck. We just got word that Darby's case is up next."

"I need a moment alone with my client." Alex glances around the lobby. "Is there a private room nearby?"

Four Eyes shakes his head. "There's no time. The magistrate is waiting for him."

"I only need one minute." Alex holds up a finger with a red-lacquered nail pointed at the ceiling. "I'm not asking you. I'm telling you."

"Fine. You've got sixty seconds," Chrome Dome says, setting the timer on his Apple Watch.

Alex pulls me aside. "This is one ass-backwards town you live in. I've been trying to get in touch with the prosecutor all weekend." She eyes my bandages. "Did that happen during the assault?"

"Nope. In jail over the weekend."

"Well, it's not a good look." She tugs the gauze off my hands, wads it into a ball, and tosses it at Four Eyes. "Get rid of that."

"Yes, ma'am," Four Eyes says, and slinks off to locate a trash can.

Alex returns her attention to me. "Now listen carefully. When we get inside the courtroom, I want you to follow my lead. Hide your hands as best you can, and don't speak unless I tell you to. I hope it won't go that far, but if given the chance, I want you to plead not guilty."

"Time's up," Chrome Dome says, and motions for us to follow him down the hall.

Inside the courtroom, a white-headed man with a heavily wrinkled face looks down his nose at us. In front of him on his massive bench, a nameplate identifies him as The Honorable Luther Carr. "You're late," Judge Carr says.

"With all due respect, your honor, I've been given exactly one minute to converse with my client."

He gives her the once-over. "Who are you, anyway? I've never seen you before in my courtroom."

"Alexandra Stone. Google me."

The judge pulls out his cell phone and puts on his reading glasses. He hems and haws as he stares down at his screen. When he looks up again, he says, "Impressive."

"Thank you, your honor," she says, as though she could care less what he thinks of her.

Seated at one of two matching tables is Ethan Striker with a gentleman I assume is the prosecutor. From afar, I see no signs of the assault on Ethan's face, not even a black eye.

As soon as Alex and I have sat down at the other table, she's on her feet again. "Your honor, may I approach the bench along with opposing counsel? We need to address a recent development in this case. Despite my best efforts, I've been unable to reach the prosecutor over the weekend."

The judge looks over at the prosecutor. "Is this true, Mr. McGee?"

McGee, a heavyset man with a helmet of bushy brown hair, stands to address the judge. "I was out of town, your honor. I got back late last night."

The judge's brow raises above his reading glasses. "Did you not have cell service on your weekend getaway?"

"Yes, sir. I had cell service. I assumed the matter could wait."

The judge gestures at the empty courtroom. "You may speak freely, Miss Stone. As you can see, there's no one here but us."

"If you say so. My client, Will Darby, was simply defending himself when he struck Ethan Striker on Saturday morning." Alex leaves our table and walks over to the prosecutor, handing him a sheath of papers. "We're pressing charges against Ethan Striker for harassment and trespassing."

The prosecutor snatches the papers from her and thumbs through them. "Based on what evidence?"

"Surveillance video from Mr. Darby's home." She flashes him her cell phone. "I have a copy if you care to see. Striker ambushed Mr. Darby's sister upon her arrival home early Saturday morning. He was out of line in the things he said to her. In fact, I'd go as far as to say he was verbally abusive towards her."

McGee's hand shoots out. "Let me see."

Alex accesses the video and hands him the phone. The prosecutor's face goes pale as he watches the video. From where I'm sitting, I can hear Striker insinuating Ashton is hiding something by sneaking into the house at the crack of dawn. I wouldn't necessarily call it verbal abuse. But what Striker said to Ashton was definitely inappropriate.

The prosecutor gives Alex back her phone, and she returns to our table.

McGee has a brief hushed conversation with Striker before announcing, "Given the circumstances, I believe we can settle this matter out of court. We're willing to drop the charges if the defense is as well."

Alex gives a curt nod. "Agreed."

The prosecutor's face beams red as he flees the courtroom with Striker on his heels.

Alex turns to me. "One down. One to go. I realize the timing is inconvenient, but I have a couple of hours before I need to head back to Columbia. While I'm here, we should discuss the investigation into your wife's case. I'm afraid an indictment for her murder is imminent."

My stomach knots, and I'm afraid I might puke. I have a million questions for Alex, but this is not the time to ask them.

We leave the courtroom together and part ways in the hall. "The officers will transport you back to the police station and process your release," Alex says. "I'll wait for you in front of the station and drive you home. Your sister was instrumental in getting me this video. I look forward to meeting her."

I remain silent on the drive back to the police station and while they process my release. My anger simmers just beneath the surface. It won't take much for me to erupt. How could this be happening when I did not kill my wife?

More reporters are gathered outside the station, and I'm relieved when I spot Alex working her way through the crowd towards me.

"Stick close to me," she whispers. "If we get separated, I'm in the silver Volvo parked on the curb."

Taking me by the arm, she guides me towards her car. The reporters call out questions about both the assault and murder cases to which she responds repeatedly, "No comment."

We're emerging from the throng when a dark-headed man with an evil glint in his black eyes steps out in front of us. "Will Darby? I'm Detective Max Rourke, and you're under arrest for the murder of your wife, Tracy Darby."

Before I can react, I'm in handcuffs again and being led back inside the station. I keep my eyes glued to the ground as reporters flash their phones and cameras at me. My timely arrest provides the detective the perfect opportunity to gain exposure with the press.

For the second time in forty-eight hours, I'm fingerprinted and photographed. But instead of taking me back to my cell, I'm shown to a small, windowless interview room. I wait alone for what seems like hours, but according to the clock, only thirty minutes pass before Alex appears.

She paces angrily around the room. "Of all the dirty-handed stunts, this one takes the cake. And I've seen a lot in my day. How dare they arrest you in front of all those reporters! I encounter a lot of jerks in my line of work, and I don't usually let them get the best of me. They are messing with the wrong criminal attorney."

Despite the seriousness of the situation, I can't help but chuckle. I can see how she got the nickname Stone Cold Alex.

Alex rants on, "Their case is circumstantial. The evidence against you is weak. With friends like Julia Becker, you don't need enemies."

Dread overcomes me. "What does Julia have to do with anything?"

Alex sits down opposite me. "Their case is based on her testimony. She claims you two were romantically involved at the time of your wife's death, although there is zero evidence she was living in the Lowcountry over the summer."

"I hardly know Julia. We met after Labor Day through our children. I took her out once. We haven't even slept together. I can't imagine why she would lie. Have you actually seen her statement?"

"Beaumonts' attorneys haven't gotten her statement yet, but they've assured me it's forthcoming. For now, my primary concern is getting you before the magistrate so you don't have to go back to jail."

There's a tap on the door, and Cody Porter, the kind officer who provided bandages for my hands, sticks his head inside. "Miss Stone, I just got word from the magistrate. He will hear your case now."

The second trip to the magistrate court takes less time than the first. I plead not guilty, the judge pronounces an exorbitant amount for bail, and Ashton arranges to pay it.

On the way out to Marsh Point, Alex says, "The second arrest took up all our time. I need to get on the road to Columbia. But I'll be in touch soon. Just so you know, Will, I plan to throw every resource I have at your case."

"I hope your resources include a magician. Because it's gonna take a bag of tricks to get me out of this mess."

THIRTY-THREE
JULIA

While Conrad is at school on Monday morning, I pack up all our belongings and load them in the trunk of my car with the overflow in the back seat. I leave a check for next month's rent on the kitchen counter and hide my key to the cottage under a planter on the back porch. Once we're safely out of town, I'll text Fry and explain the situation.

With a few minutes to spare, I walk through the sand dunes to the beach to say a final goodbye to the ocean. I feel silly when tears stream down my face. I've grown accustomed to the ocean's presence in my life, and I will miss it.

I'm heading down Beach Drive on my way to pick up Conrad when a black sedan with a blue light flashing in the dashboard speeds up behind me. I slow down and pull over to the side of the road.

Detective Rourke appears beside my car, and I roll down the window. "What do you want? I'm certain I wasn't speeding. Do I have a taillight out?"

"I'm a detective, Miss Becker. I don't do traffic violations." He glances in the back seat. "Where are you headed?"

"Not that it's any of your business, but I'm on my way to pick my son up from school."

He opens the back door and pokes around in the bedding. "Looks to me like you're going on a camping trip."

"That's just stuff we're not using anymore. I've been meaning to take it to Goodwill."

He slams the back door shut. "You can't fool me, Miss Becker. I know what you're up to. You're leaving town."

"What choice do I have? I would rather die before perjuring myself."

"And die you might. And so might your son." The detective flashes his phone at me. "I have a member of The Six on speed dial. He would love to know your whereabouts."

I give his phone a skeptical look. "You're bluffing."

"Are you willing to take that risk?"

I look from the phone to his face. "You're asking me to lie under oath, Detective. What you're doing is unethical. Your duty is to uphold the law, but you're intentionally breaking it."

"My tactics may be *unconventional,* but my intentions are honorable. I'm using whatever means necessary to get a guilty man off the streets."

"Nothing about you is honorable. You're the scum of the earth."

Leaning over, he stares me in the eye. "If you try to leave town, we will hunt you down. Go home, Casey. Give this situation some more thought. Once you've carefully considered your options, you'll see that my way is your *only* way out."

"Don't hold your breath, Detective." I stomp my foot on the gas pedal, spewing gravel on him as I swerve the car back onto the road.

Dread turns my gut to stone. Detective Rourke means what he says. There is no escaping this situation for me.

I'm the first to arrive in the carpool line. I lean my head back against the seat and close my eyes while I wait for the bell to ring.

I'm at a complete loss. There is no way out of this situation. I could accept Mr. Whitfield's bribe. In addition to the large sum of money, he offered protection and a new life.

Who am I kidding? Beaumont would wash his hands of me once he gets my testimony. Besides, I meant what I said to Rourke. I'd rather die than perjure myself.

When Conrad gets in the car, he asks, "What's all this stuff doing here, Mommy? Are we going somewhere?"

I wait until we drive away from the church before answering. "I'm not sure, sweetheart. I'm considering our options. How was school?" I ask in the rearview mirror.

His chin quivers. "Caroline cried all day. Everyone is being mean to her and making fun of her daddy. Is Mister Will a bad guy? Did he kill Caroline's mommy?"

I grip the steering wheel. "No, sweetheart. He's not. But sometimes good people do bad things. This is all confusing grownup stuff, son. Nothing for you to worry about."

Conrad kicks the seat in front of him. "But I am worried. Caroline is so sad."

"I'm sure she is, sweetheart. She needs your friendship now, more than ever."

In my heart, I know Will is not a bad guy. He has some problems. Don't we all? But did he kill his wife in a fit of anger? I'm not sure.

Back at the cottage, I retrieve the key from under the flowerpot and remove our belongings from the car, including the cooler with our food from the refrigerator. I make Conrad a PB&J for lunch and go to my room to unpack. Turning on the television, I click on the app and replay the local noon news.

From in front of the municipal building, a journalist reports on the morning's breaking developments in the Will Darby case. A patrol car pulls up, and with the help of two police officers, Will emerges from the back seat. He looks awful, unshaven with dark circles under his eyes, wrinkled clothes, and the knuckles on both hands bandaged in gauze.

The camera pans back to the reporter. "Will Darby has just arrived for his arraignment in the aggravated assault case involving news correspondent Ethan Striker."

In the next segment, the same reporter is standing with a crowd in front of the police station. "We're awaiting a statement from Will Darby's attorney. According to our sources, charges against Will in the aggravated assault have been dropped."

Subsequent footage shows Will with his attorney. Instead of making a statement, the attorney replies *no comment* to the barrage of questions the reporters call out to her as they make their way down the steps. Will and the attorney are approaching a silver Volvo when Rourke appears. "Will Darby? I'm Detective Max Rourke, and you're under arrest for the murder of your wife, Tracy Darby."

I watch in horror as Detective Rourke handcuffs Will and takes him back inside the police station. Based on the time stamp at the bottom of the screen, the arrest happened prior to my encounter with Rourke on Beach Drive.

The camera pans to the reporter one last time. "At eleven o'clock this morning, Will Darby has pleaded not guilty to the murder charges and has been released on bail."

I turn off the television and lower myself to the edge of the bed. Rourke is framing Will for murder. Is he working for Beaumont? Probably. They are banking on my testimony to convict Will. Escaping is my only way out. It's only a matter of time before Rourke comes for me. I don't have the luxury of waiting another day.

I pull up the Greyhound Bus schedule on my phone. There's one leaving tonight at nine thirty. After transferring a half dozen times, we'll arrive in Minneapolis. I thought I wanted a warmer climate. But the option to either hide under fluffy scarves and stocking hats when outside, or to spend the long winter months inside, has its own appeal.

I return to the living room to find Conrad asleep on the sofa, and I try not to disturb him while I gather our belongings. He'll need to be well-rested for the long trip ahead. I stuff clothes, an extra pair of shoes, and a few toys into his backpack, making certain it's light enough for him to carry.

I organize my things on the bed before placing them in my backpack. I choose two changes of clothes and several pairs of underwear. My toothbrush makes the cut but not my makeup bag. I pack my handgun, two boxes of ammo, our identification documents, and the envelope of emergency cash I withdrew from the bank last week.

When Conrad finally wakes up late afternoon, he's alarmed to see our backpacks waiting beside the back door.

I sit down on the sofa and pull him onto my lap. "As much as I love our cottage, I don't think it's safe for us to continue living in Water's Edge. My friendship with Caroline's daddy has dragged me into his troubles. My picture has been all over the news, and I'm worried the boogeymen will find us."

"Where will we go?" Conrad asks, his brown eyes wide.

"I'm not sure yet. We'll head north and see where we land. Think of it as another adventure."

A single tear rolls down his cheek. "Can I say goodbye to Caroline?"

"I'm sorry, son. I don't think that's a good idea."

He buries his face in my chest and cries. I feel my son's pain. I'm leaving behind a piece of my heart with Will.

We eat a hearty dinner of vegetable soup, salad, and homemade buttermilk biscuits. I pack four extra biscuits to take with us on our journey.

I schedule an Uber to pick us up from the Sandy Island Club at eight thirty. At eight o'clock, leaving a few interior lamps on but turning off the outdoor spotlights, we sneak out the back of the cottage. Crouching down until we've cleared the dunes, we walk hand in hand in silence down the beach towards the southern tip of the island.

Our Uber is waiting at the club's entrance, and the ride to the bus station is uneventful. As I planned, we arrive with only moments to spare before our departure. We're waiting in line to board our bus when someone taps me on the shoulder. I turn slowly around, and my heart sinks at the sight of Detective Rourke.

"I thought I made myself clear earlier. Escaping is not an option, Julia. The sooner you accept your fate, the better for you and your son."

THIRTY-FOUR
WILL

Caroline cries out several times during the night. But instead of me, she seeks comfort from Ashton. She's grumpy at breakfast, and when she begs Ashton to let her stay home from school on Tuesday, I tell her a firm *no*. "You can't run from your problems, sweetheart."

"You're my problem, Daddy," she says, sticking her tongue out at me and fleeing the room, leaving her breakfast untouched.

I wait until Ashton has left to take the girls to school before calling Betty Bleaker and reading her the riot act.

"Watch your tone, Will. Your anger problem is what got you into this mess."

Betty is more than the head of my children's school. She's a long-time client and friend. Her warning is both warranted and appreciated. "I'm sorry, Betty. I'm just frustrated. Caroline is really struggling."

"Her teacher has made me aware of the situation, and we're on top of it. Parents should not let their children within earshot of the news. They are too young to process world events."

"Unfortunately, I've been in the news too much these last

couple of days. My children are my priority, Betty. Call me if you need anything. I will make myself available."

"You have my word. Hang in there, Will. Things will get better."

Ending the call, I say to myself, "I'm not so sure about that, Betty."

When I arrive at my office, my staff greets me with cold stares. Even my assistant speaks to me in a curt tone. As I make my rounds to the job sites, I receive the same chilly reception from both workmen and project managers. With the exception of Maurice who envelops me in a bear hug.

"Ignore them, Will. I'm sorry for the way they're acting. I don't know what's gotten into them."

Close to tears, I mumble, "I do. They think I killed my wife."

"Nobody thinks that, Will," he says in an unconvincing tone.

On the way back to the office, I stop by Custom Crust to pick up lunch. Judy, who takes my order for the same sandwich nearly every single day, looks at me with a blank stare, as though she doesn't know me. "What can I get you, sir?"

"Never mind. I lost my appetite."

Instead of returning to the office, I retreat to Marsh Point. It dawns on me that this is how my mom must have felt when ostracized by the locals for her alcoholism.

Mia is in the kitchen stirring a pot of beef stew when I arrive. I open the refrigerator door and close it again without removing any food items. I let out a heavy sigh as I plop down in a chair at the kitchen table.

"Can I fix you some lunch, Mister Will?" Mia asks, placing a lid on the soup pot. "I have some leftover rotisserie chicken. I can make you a pesto chicken panini."

My world may be falling down around me, but after spending the weekend eating jail slop, I would be a fool to turn down home cooking. "That sounds delicious, Mia. Thank you."

"I'm surprised to see you home from work so early," she says as she goes about making the sandwich.

"I needed a break. The whole town has turned against me, including my staff. Whatever happened to assuming a man is innocent until proven guilty? Heck . . ." I throw up my hand and let it drop. "Maybe you feel the same way. I don't blame you if you do."

"No, sir. I don't. In the short amount of time I've worked here, you've shown me nothing but kindness. That's good enough for me. I think it's a crying shame the way the police and reporters have been treating you." She slices my sandwich in half, places it on a plate, and sets it on the table in front of me. "Can I fix you some sweet tea to go with that?"

"That would be wonderful." I take a bite of sandwich and sit back in my chair. "Where is everyone? Shouldn't the girls be home from school by now?"

"Miss Ashton picked them up from school and took them to lunch at The Nest. She thought they needed some special attention."

Of course, they did. Because everyone in town, including their friends, thinks their father is a murderer.

After lunch, I go outside to the porch, and stretch out on the daybed swing. When I close my eyes, my thoughts turn to the days following Bert's accident when everyone turned against me. When even my family didn't believe in me.

At the sound of gravel crunching in the driveway, I sneak around the opposite side of the house to avoid seeing Ashton and the girls. My emotions are near the surface, and I can't risk falling apart in front of my children.

Tears sting my eyes as I drive off in my truck. I have no destination in mind, but I'm not surprised to find myself in front of Clemmy's house in Beaufort. Her car is in the driveway, and when I text her that I'm here, she instructs me to let myself in.

She meets me in the front hall and takes me in her arms. "I expected to hear from you sooner."

"I spent the weekend in jail," I say into her shoulder.

"I'm aware. I've been following you on the news." With one arm around my waist, she walks me outside to my favorite chair on the porch.

Sitting down in the chair next to me, she eyes the scabbed-over wounds on my knuckles. "What happened to your hands?"

"You know what happened. I thought I was better. But I'm so much worse. I'm on edge all the time. I feel like a ticking time bomb."

A grave expression crosses her face. "Do you want to try medication?"

I hang my head. "Not really. I just want to feel normal. To be normal. To live a normal life."

She chuckles. "There's no such thing, my friend. Everyone has problems. Some are better at hiding them than others."

"So I'm doomed to a lifetime of being angry."

"Not at all. You were making great strides. This is just a setback. While you've learned coping mechanisms for handling your anger, you never fully addressed the source."

"And how do I do that?"

She raises an eyebrow. "You tell me."

I'm silent for a long time before responding. "By apologizing to Bert's family."

"And . . ." She gestures for me to continue talking.

"How can I forgive a dead woman?"

"It's not about your mother, Will. This is about you. You know where to find her."

I jump to my feet, suddenly eager to get these things off my chest. "I need to go."

She rises from her chair and follows me to the door. "I'm hesitant to let you leave. Are you sure you're okay?"

"I'm fine. I'll text you later. Thank you, Clemmy." Pecking her cheek, I hurry out to my truck and speed off back towards Water's Edge.

————

I'M surprised when Bert's sister answers the door. Kristy hasn't aged well. She's put on weight, and her skin has an unhealthy pallor, as though she spends too much time indoors. While she's too old to be living with her parents, the ring finger on her left hand is bare.

"Will! What're you doing here?"

"I'd like to speak with your parents if they're around."

She casts a nervous glance towards the kitchen. "They're here. Mom's in the kitchen. We were making pumpkin bread. Dad's taking a nap though."

Mrs. Lewis sticks her head into the living room from the kitchen. "Kristy? Who's at the door?" Her face falls when she sees me, and she moves towards me, wiping her hands on her apron. "What're you doing here, Will?"

"I'd like to talk to you about Bert's accident."

"Now that you've been accused of another murder? Whatever it is you want from us, we can't possibly help you."

Kristy appears horrified. "Mom! That's uncalled for."

"Why *are* you here?" Mr. Lewis grunts as he rolls his walker into the room. He's hunched over with a drawn face and stringy gray hair. Like his daughter, the years have not been kind to him. Losing his only son took a lot out of him.

Mrs. Lewis glares at me. "He wants to talk about Bert's accident. Now, after all these years."

"I came once before. After I got out of the hospital. But you refused to see me. I want to apologize for my part in Bert's accident."

Mrs. Lewis lets out a humph. "What good will an apology do now? Except clear your conscience before you go to prison for life."

Kristy shoots her a warning look. "Mom! Stop! You're being rude."

"I'll only take a minute of your time. Bert was the best friend I've ever had. I miss him to this day."

Mrs. Lewis's face reddens, as though she's going to bless me out. But her husband doesn't give her the chance. "Let the boy have his say," Mr. Lewis says, pushing his walker towards his worn brown recliner in the corner.

Not much has changed since I was last inside the house. I sit down on the same damask-covered sofa and look up at the same old cuckoo clock hanging above the mantel. The time is wrong though. My watch says it's three fifteen. The shorthand on the cuckoo is pointed at nine and the long hand at four.

Kristy catches me looking at the clock. "It hasn't worked since the night Bert died. It's as though he stopped the clock as he left this earth. We can't bring ourselves to take it down."

Goosebumps break out on my skin as I think back to that night. Nine twenty is about the time of the accident.

I wait until everyone is seated before beginning. "Despite what you may have been told, I had not been drinking that night. I tried to get Will to go home, but he refused to leave. When I tried to force him, he came after me. We wrestled, and he crashed into the railing. The railing was rotten. It could just as easily have been me who went over." When I hear sniffling, I look over at Kristy to see tears streaming down her cheeks.

"There are some things about that night I never told you," she says to her parents. "Will's telling the truth. Bert was drunk that night. Embarrassing himself and me. When Will asked me to help him get Bert to the car, I told him to buzz off. The accident is more my fault than Will's. I was older. It was my responsibility to look after my younger brother."

Mrs. Lewis stiffens. "Why have you never told us this?"

Kristy lowers her gaze to her lap. "I saw how you treated Will. I was afraid you'd treat me the same way. My guilt has been my prison sentence. But I can't live like this anymore. I'm sorry if you hate me. I made a horrible mistake that night. Bert's accident wasn't Will's fault. It was mine."

The atmosphere in the room has gone from hostile to awkward. Mr. and Mrs. Lewis are devastated to learn of their daughter's part in their son's death. But this is a family matter. None of my concern. I doubt any of the three Lewises notice when I see myself out.

I leave the historic section and drive back through town to the cemetery. Clemmy meant for me to find my mother in my heart. But the cemetery seems like a fitting place to have this one-sided discussion.

Our family's plot takes up a large portion of the old section of the cemetery. As children, when we came here to visit our grandparents, my siblings and I played a game to see who could find the oldest tombstone. We could never find one older than Yancy Jedidiah Merriweather, born in 1818 and died in 1867.

I haven't been here since my mother's funeral. Her footstone is now in place and the mound of dirt on her grave is covered in lush grass. Everything I want to say is at the forefront of my mind, and the words flow effortlessly off my tongue. An onlooker might mistake me for a lunatic, pacing around the grave, talking to myself while gesturing wildly with my hands. Fortunately, there is no one else in sight.

As a Christian, I believe in life after death, and I sense my mother's presence. She may not have been the best mother in the world, but she didn't deserve to go to hell. I don't waste any time lamenting about the awful things she did to us. She knows. By now, she's repented for her sins.

I talk mostly about Bert's accident, and how much it hurt when she refused to believe in my innocence. When I run out of things to say, I drop to my knees and sob. I don't feel the enormous relief I'd hoped for. But I feel as though I've finally made a step in the right direction.

I've stopped crying, and I'm looking around at the nearby headstones when Carter calls. "Where are you?"

"The cemetery. Why?"

"I have news. Stay where you are. I'm three minutes away."

I lean against my family's headstone and wait for the investigator to arrive.

Carter parks his silver truck and wanders over to me. "Afternoon."

I stand to face him. "What's the big news? Has Marlowe experienced a breakthrough in the case?"

Carter slaps my shoulder. "Not yet. But he's working on it. I've just returned from Texas. As best we can tell, Julia and Conrad Beck did not exist prior to August thirty-first."

"What do you mean they didn't exist? And why Texas?"

"She's not who she says she is." He tugs a folded sheet of paper from his back pocket. "Do you recognize this woman?" On the paper is a computer-generated picture of Julia with lighter and longer hair. "That's Julia."

He jabs his finger at the paper. "This woman is Casey Bishop. She has a four-year-old son named Levi." Carter shows me another picture, this one on his phone. Despite his longer hair, the child is undeniably Conrad.

I scrunch up my face in confusion. "I don't understand. Why is Julia . . . Casey . . . pretending to be someone else?"

"She escaped from Witness Protection," Carter says and tells me a wild tale that makes sense of what little I know about Julia.

"We've confirmed that Rourke is working for your father-in-law. They know Julia's secret, and they are using it to coerce her into testifying against you."

I palm my forehead as the last puzzle piece fits into place. "By threatening to turn her into the cartel."

Carter nods. "Exactly. But we've been keeping an eye on her these past couple of days. I'm afraid to say, her life is in very grave danger."

THIRTY-FIVE
JULIA

I stalk my sisters on social media. Both have children near Conrad's age, and both would be excellent substitute mothers to my son. And he would be raised by family instead of strangers. I consider the logistics of flying him out to Texas. The nearest airport is in Charleston. But with Rourke on my tail, there's no way I can get him there without being spotted.

Then there's the matter of my family's safety. The Six is ruthless. Having Conrad living with them places my sisters, their husbands, my parents, and their children all in danger. Since my family is out of the question, I have only one choice left.

Conrad is four years old. He will eventually forget about me and his father and everything that happened to us this year. He has a fifty-fifty chance of landing in a good home. A better chance of making it to adulthood than he would living with me on the run.

"How was Caroline today?" I ask Conrad when I pick him up from school.

"She's still sad. I feel sorry for her. I was sad, too, too when the police took Daddy away."

"Her father is going through a rough patch, but he'll eventually be fine." I pray that he will. Without my testimony, there is no case against Will.

While he naps on the sofa after lunch, I pack Conrad's clothes in a small suitcase and store it in the trunk of my car. I sit in the chair beside him, committing the details of his face and tiny body to memory while he sleeps.

I'm a monster for even considering giving my child away. But I see no other way out of this mess I've made. I long for my mother. If only she could make this right. I pick up my cell phone to call her. I tap on her number. My finger hovers over the green call button. Rourke has probably bugged my phone. He would threaten to harm her if I don't testify against Will. I set the phone down again.

It's a dreary day, cold and rainy with a strong breeze blowing off the ocean. Around three thirty, I wake Conrad from his nap and ask if he wants to go to town for a hot chocolate.

He bounds off the sofa. "Yes! Please! Can we go now?"

"Sure thing! Let me get our coats."

We bundle up in our raincoats and head out in the car. I cast frequent glances at Conrad. He's smiling as he stares out the window. He's thinking about hot chocolate. He has no idea what's in store for him.

We linger over our tasty warm beverages at Corner Cup, the coffee shop located at the intersection of Main Street and Second Avenue. When I can no longer delay the inevitable, a few minutes before five, I take Conrad's hand and lead him across the street to the municipal building, the same building where Will appeared in magistrate court twice yesterday.

"Where are we going, Mommy?" Conrad asks as we ride in the elevator to the third floor.

I left his suitcase in the trunk so as not to alarm him. I'm grateful he can't read well enough to make out the writing on the door. *Child Protective Services.* The waiting room is crowded. I give my name to the receptionist, explaining I have a private matter to discuss with a caseworker, and take the only available seat, pulling Conrad onto my lap.

I look around the room at the other downtrodden women and their scraggly children. The women appear either angry or bored. The children have dirty faces, runny noses, and torn clothes. Some are crying while others doze in their mothers' arms.

Burying my face in my son's warm neck, I close my eyes and pray to God for strength and guidance. My heart crumbles into pieces. By giving my child away, I'm admitting failure as a parent. Everyone expects me to fail, but I will prove them wrong. I'm stronger than I give myself credit for. I turned my husband in to the police, testified against him in court, and escaped Witness Protection. We were doing fine until I fell into this trap. This situation is not of my making. I was simply in the wrong place at the wrong time. Luck is not on my side. I'm responsible for my own fate. Mine, and my child's.

Conrad wraps an arm around my neck, pulling my ear close to his lips. "I don't like this place, Mommy. Can we go soon?"

"I don't like this place either, son. Let's get out of here."

Conrad slides off my lap, and we quickly exit the waiting room. Hand in hand, we hurry past the elevator, down the stairs, and out the front of the building. As we're making our way to the car, I vow to stand strong against Rourke. I will refuse to testify against Will, and I will not leave town. If the boogeymen come after me, I will fight to my death to protect my child. I can't guarantee his safety. But I can promise to do my best.

I'm scared out of my mind but feeling courageous in my ability to take care of my son when we arrive home to find our house has been ransacked. Broken dishes litter the kitchen floor and down feathers from knife-slashed pillows float about the living room. The refrigerator door is open and puddles of ketchup, spilled cartons of yogurt, and last night's leftover turkey Tetrazzini cover the countertops.

Conrad tugs on my raincoat. "Mama? What happened?"

Before I can answer, a loud crashing sound echoes from my bedroom.

Clamping my hand over my son's mouth, I walk him into his room and whisper in his ear, "Hide under the bed. Don't come out until I tell you." I watch him scramble under the bed before pulling the door closed on my way out.

Removing my gun from my purse, I press my body against the wall and inch my way towards my bedroom. I grip the gun tightly with my finger on the trigger and and brace my arms in front of me. I'm prepared to kill to protect my son.

I inhale a deep breath, and as I turn the corner into my room, I shout, "Don't move!"

I'm squeezing the trigger, preparing to unload the magazine, when Will steps out of the closet with hands in the air. "Don't shoot, Julia! It's me."

My heart leaps in my chest as I raise my arms over my head with the gun aimed at the ceiling. "My god, Will. I almost shot you. Is anyone else here?"

He shakes his head. "I don't think so."

"I didn't see your truck in the driveway. Where'd you park?"

"In the bushes at the house across the street. I detected movement inside the cottage when I got here. I assume I scared them off. By the time I parked and came back, they had fled."

I uncock the gun and shove it into the waistband of my jeans. "I don't understand. Why are you here?"

"I came to see you. I think we need to clear the air."

The realization that I could've killed him hits home, and I begin to shake all over. Will takes me in his arms. "Shh! It's okay. I'm here now."

I cry into his chest, "I'm in so much trouble, Will."

"I know, sweetheart." He kisses my hair. "But I'm here now. And we're going to figure this thing out together."

I look up at him. "They are framing us. But despite what

Striker is saying on the news, I have no intention of testifying against you."

He kisses the tip of my nose. "We can talk about all this later. Where's Conrad?"

"Hiding under his bed," I say, and we hurry to my son's room.

Will helps me pull a trembling Conrad from beneath the bed. Holding him tight, I coo, "It's okay, Buddy. It was only Mister Will in the other room."

Swiping at his eyes, Conrad asks, "Why did Mister Will make our house a mess?"

I look at Will over the top of my son's head. "He didn't sweetheart. Someone else did. But I'm not sure who." The boogeymen are the obvious culprits. But it could just as easily have been Detective Rourke.

"We need to get you someplace safe," Will says.

I shake my head. "There *is* no place safe. Rourke is watching my every move. Twice, I tried running away. Both times, he found me."

Will presses his finger to his lips. Cupping his hand around his mouth, he whispers in my ear, "They're probably listening to us. Let's go outside to the porch."

I nod, and for the benefit of the eavesdroppers, I say out loud, "Give me a minute to get a movie started for Conrad, and I'll make us some hot tea."

"Hot tea sounds great," he says and points at the porch, letting me know he'll wait for me outside.

I locate a juice box in the refrigerator, open a bag of popcorn, and get Conrad situated on the sofa in front of a movie.

I'm far from out of danger, but I feel enormously relieved having Will back in my life.

THIRTY-SIX
WILL

Julia and I stand close together on the porch. I long to take her in my arms, but I need to stay focused. "We have to assume your cottage is wired. The rain pounding the roof will help drown out our voices, but we still need to whisper."

She leans in closer. "I understand."

"You can stay in the Mathesons' house for now. Until we come up with a better plan."

Julia scrunches up her nose. "You mean the compound at the tip of the island?"

"Exactly. It'll be dark soon. The rain plays in our favor. You'll need to go alone on foot. I doubt anyone will spot you but walk close to the dunes just in case. I'll take Conrad with me. We'll pretend he's spending the night with me at Marsh Point. Once I'm sure no one is following me, I'll bring him to you."

"Are you sure the Mathesons aren't there?"

"Positive. I spoke with Cliff last week. They aren't coming back until Thanksgiving."

"I don't feel right staying in their house."

"They won't mind. But if it makes you feel better, I'll call them tomorrow." I take Julia by the arms. "Listen carefully. We don't have much time. There's a lock box on the railing. The code is 7-6-5-4. The key fits the front door. Inside the door to your left is a hallway that will take you to the mudroom. The door in the mudroom leads to a three-bay garage. On the wall beside that door is a control panel for the garage doors. Press one of the buttons, doesn't matter which, so I can hide my car inside the garage when I arrive."

"What about their security system?"

"They haven't installed it yet. Do you have a flashlight?"

She pats her back pocket. "The one on my phone."

"You'll need to leave all your electronic devices here so they can't track you."

A pained expression crosses her face. "That makes sense. But I don't like not being able to get in touch with you."

"I don't either. But people survived hundreds of thousands of years without cell phones. We will too."

She sucks in a breath. "Right. I'll check in the kitchen. I think Fry keeps a flashlight in the junk drawer."

"The Mathesons' house is all windows. Whatever you do, don't turn on any lights once you're inside. Pack small bags for you and Conrad. I'll take those with me."

"But Conrad's suitcase is in the trunk of my car with all his clothes in it."

I furrow my brow. "What—"

"I'll explain later. But you'll have to get it out of my trunk. He needs his things."

"I understand." I know better than to argue with a Mama Bear.

"How long before you meet me?"

"I'm not sure, Julia. Don't be alarmed if it takes me a couple of hours."

When her chin starts to quiver, I pull her in for a hug. "I promise I won't let anything happen to you. Most of the houses on the beach have been vacated for the winter. If you get spooked, hide out in the dunes. I will eventually come for you."

"If anything happens to me, you have to promise to take care of my son."

I hold her at arm's length. "You have my word."

Julia swipes at her eyes. "Let's get this over with."

I kiss her lightly on the lips. "Follow my lead." When we get inside, I sit down on the edge of the sofa next to Conrad. "Hey, Buddy. How would you like to spend the night with us at Marsh Point? I haven't told Caroline yet, but she will be thrilled."

The boy looks uncertainly at his mother. "But what about Mama?"

"We'll leave her here to clean up this mess," I say, winking at Julia.

"Gee, thanks," Julia says and disappears into her bedroom.

I give Conrad's knee a squeeze beneath his blanket. "We'll take you to school in the morning, and your mom will pick you up afterward. How does that sound?"

"Okay, I guess," he says in a reluctant tone as he peels back the blanket.

I help him to his feet. "How about if we stop for pizza on the way home?"

He perks up. "That sounds great. But I need to pack." He gestures at his bedroom.

"Your mom is one step ahead of you. Your bag is already in the trunk of her car. We'll grab it on the way out. Let's get your raincoat."

I'm helping him into his rain gear when Julia emerges from her bedroom with a black backpack. She hands me the backpack and goes into the kitchen, rummaging through the drawers. A minute later, she waves a flashlight at me, and I give her a thumbs-up.

Conrad throws his arms around his mother's neck. "Bye, Mommy. Sleep tight. Don't let the bedbugs bite."

She musses his hair. "You too, sweet boy." She kisses the tips of her fingers and presses them to my lips. "Thank you," she mouths.

Nodding, I lean in close and whisper, "Good luck. I'll see you soon."

I scoop up Conrad and dash out of the cottage into the driving rain. By the time I stop by Julia's car to get the suitcase and sprint across the road to my truck, Conrad and I are both soaking wet. Fastening him into Caroline's car seat, I climb into the front and start the engine, cranking up the heat. I have a knot in the pit of my stomach as I drive away. There's no turning back now. My plan will either work or cost Julia her life.

I keep one eye on the rearview mirror as I cross over the Merri-weather Bridge, but it doesn't appear anyone is following us. I call in our order for three pizzas to Sal's Pizzeria and drive around downtown until the pies are ready. The streets are deserted. On a rainy night like tonight, anyone in their right mind is staying at home.

I text my sister, letting her know I'm bringing home pizza, and Conrad will be joining us for dinner. The girls are thrilled to see their friend, and when I open two of the pizza boxes on the table, they dive in, paying no attention to us when I lead Ashton out to the side porch for a word in private.

I quickly explain everything that's happened. "If Rourke is following me, he'll be on the lookout for my truck. Just to be safe, I'll drive Conrad to the Mathesons' in your car. If you don't mind."

"Of course. But be careful. Julia's is in a lot of danger. I don't want you in the line of fire."

I let out a heavy sigh. "I hate to say it, but we're all in danger from multiple forces. Including you and the girls. Keep the doors locked at all times and always be aware of your surroundings."

"You're scaring me, Will."

"Good. For the time being, you should be on heightened

alert." I pull her in for a half hug. "I'm sorry I brought all this on our family, Ashton."

"None of this is your fault, Will. We will find a way to get out of it."

"I hope you're right."

I wait until Ashton goes inside to check on the kids before I call Carter. "Are you by any chance near Marsh Point?"

He chuckles. "I'm at the end of your driveway, making my nightly rounds." His tone turns serious. "Why? Do you need me?"

"Come up to the house, and I'll explain."

The rain has slowed to a drizzle as I walk around to the front of the house. Carter parks his truck beside mine and gets out. "Can you check Ashton's car for tracking devices? I need to drive it, and it's important I'm not followed."

Carter narrows his eyes. "What's going on?"

I'm tempted to tell him everything, but my inner voice warns me to wait. "I'd rather not say just yet."

"If you're in danger, Will, I need to know about it."

"I need to figure out a few things. Then I'll tell you everything."

Carter gives me a skeptical look. "All right. But I'm not thrilled about you going off on your own secret mission."

"You need to trust me on this. I know what I'm doing."

He spends a few minutes going over every inch of Ashton's car with his phone's flashlight. "Her car appears clean. But you need to stay in touch." He flashes his phone at me. "I'll be waiting to hear from you."

I salute him. "Understood."

The kids have finished eating when I return to the kitchen. I remove the third pizza from the warming drawer. "Ready to go home, Buddy? I need to get this pizza to your mom. She must be starving by now."

He crinkles his nose. "But I thought I was spending the night."

"Change in plans. Your mom wants you to come to her. Is that okay with you?"

Relief replaces confusion on the kid's face. "Yes, sir. I wanna see my mom."

My armpits dampen with perspiration, and I white-knuckle the steering wheel on the drive back to Sandy Island in Ashton's car. If something has happened to Julia, I will never forgive myself for putting her in danger. I offer up a prayer of thanks when I pull into the Mathesons' driveway and see an open garage door. I park inside the garage and help Conrad out of his car seat.

Julia comes out of the house to greet us. Her hair is wet from the rain, and her damp clothes cling to her body. "I'm so glad to see you. I've been frantic with worry," she says, engulfing her son in her arms.

My heart swells seeing mother and son interract. They have a special bond, strengthened by the hardships they've experienced this year. "Did you encounter any problems?" I ask her.

She locks eyes with me over the top of her son's head. "No, aside from getting soaked to the bone. I've been hiding in the laundry room, so as not to get anything wet."

"I'm sorry it took us so long. I wanted to make sure we weren't followed. We need to get you into dry clothes."

Julia reluctantly lets go of her son and grabs her backpack out of the truck. I follow her inside the dark house with Conrad's suitcase and the pizza box.

The outside spotlights provide illumination as I lead Julia and Conrad through the living room and kitchen to the guest wing. "The primary suite is upstairs. The Mathesons designed the downstairs so each of their two daughters will have her own bedroom suite with sitting area. You can have your choice."

Julia enters the first one we come to and tosses her backpack on the bed.

I park Conrad's suitcase just inside the door. "These rooms all have blackout shades in the windows. As long as the shades are drawn, you're safe to turn on the lights. I'll leave you to get settled." I back out of the room, holding up the pizza box. "Take your time. I'll meet you in the sitting room across the hall when you're ready to eat."

Stumbling around the dark kitchen, I manage to reheat the pizza and locate some paper plates. When Julia joins me in the sitting room thirty minutes later, she's wearing dry jeans and a gray hooded sweatshirt.

"Sorry that took so long. I had to get Conrad settled. Once he closed his eyes, he was out like a light." Sitting down on the sofa beside me, she helps herself to a slice of pizza. "This looks delicious."

"It's hours old, definitely past its prime, but it's better than nothing." I settle back against the cushions. "I have a confession to make. I had one of my investigators look into your background."

She freezes with the tip of the pizza slice near her lips. "How much do you know?"

"Enough. Your real name is Casey Bishop, and you recently escaped Witness Protection after testifying against your husband for human trafficking. I'd like to hear the rest from you."

She takes a bite of pizza and sets the slice down on the plate. "Have you ever heard of The Six?"

"I only know what Carter told me earlier today."

"I think of them as the modern-day mafia. They are a corrupt group of six men who have somehow kept their identities a secret from the world. My husband got involved with one of their human trafficking cartels. I turned him in and testified against him in court. I was in Witness Protection during the trial. The plan was to remain in WITSEC after Grady's conviction, but I decided I didn't want to live in isolation. They provided us new identities, and we came here to start a new life."

"Then you got mixed up with me, and your face ended up on the news."

She shrugs, because what can she say? She's in even more

trouble because of me. "Why was Conrad's suitcase in your trunk?"

Julia's chin quivers, and it takes her a minute to pull herself together. "I almost turned my son over to Child Protective Services today. I considered sending Conrad to live with my sisters, but they both have children, and I couldn't put their lives in danger." She looks over at me. "I can't protect him, Will. As evidenced by what happened today."

"What made you change your mind?"

She sighs. "I've never been on my own. I moved from my father's house to my husband's. I wanted to prove I could make it. Giving up my child was the ultimate failure. But I didn't see any other way with Rourke blackmailing me. He claims to have a member of The Six on speed dial. If I don't do as he says, he'll turn me over to them. Your father-in-law's attorney threatened to do the same. I assume they're all working together."

My eyes widen. "You mean Landon Whitfield?"

"Yes, he paid me a little visit on Sunday."

I shake my head. "I'm so sorry. I can't believe what you've gone through because of me."

Unshed tears glisten in her eyes. "I considered perjuring myself to save my son, but I couldn't do it. I draw the line when it comes to sacrificing my principles."

Julia leaves the sofa and wanders around the room, stopping in front of the bookcases. Corey Matheson is an avid reader. Her husband jokingly claims she's kept every book she's ever purchased. Based on the books now lining the many custom-built shelves in the house, he may be telling the truth.

I go to stand beside Julia. "Regardless of how we got here, we're in this situation together. I suggest we combine our resources to find a way out."

"That sounds lovely, Will. Unfortunately, I'm fresh out of resources."

"Well, I'm not. I have two attorneys and a team of investigators. With your permission, I'll tell them what we're up against, and let them come up with a plan."

"Okay. I guess. I have nothing to lose. But if they fail, I have no choice but to go on the run again."

I draw her in for a hug. "They won't fail. I promise you, we're going to beat this. I won't stop until I'm certain you're safe."

She looks up at me. "Thank you. I can't tell you how much your support means to me. For the first time since discovering my husband's illegal activities, I feel like someone is finally on my side."

I kiss her lightly on the lips. "I'm sorry for all you've been through. I wish I could stay. I'd love nothing more than to hold you all night. But people are watching me. And for the sake of appearances, I need to adhere to a normal routine. Will you be okay here alone?"

She pats the bulge on her hip. "I have my gun. I'm not afraid to use it, and I'm a decent shot."

"Thatta girl!" I say, kissing her again before turning her loose.

Julia walks with me to the garage. "When will I see you again?"

"As soon as it's safe. I'll send Maurice over first thing in the morning with some provisions. He's a very large man. Don't let his appearance alarm you. He's worked for me for many years, and I trust him explicitly. I consider him my best friend." I punch the button, raising the garage door. "Don't forget to lower this when I leave." I give her one last, lingering kiss. "I wish I didn't have to go."

She smiles softly. "We'll have time for more kissing later. I hope."

"I'm certain of it."

Hurrying out to Ashton's car, I back out of the garage and pull slowly away from the house. As I navigate the long and winding driveway, I'm on close lookout for hidden cars. Fortunately, I see none. My heart is heavy as I continue onto Beach Drive. I've fallen head over heels in love with Julia, and I'm terrified for her safety.

THIRTY-SEVEN
JULIA

Despite being in a strange house, I sleep soundly on the luxurious mattress, made up with Egyptian cotton sheets. Conrad is still asleep when Maurice arrives in a Darby Custom Homes van a few minutes before eight on Wednesday morning. If anyone is watching, they'll assume he's here to work on the house.

Will warned me Maurice was a very large man. *Giant* would've been a better way to describe him. Despite his menacing presence, his warm hazel eyes and kind smile set me at ease. He dumps several grocery bags on the counter, removing a white box from the top of one.

"I brought you some warm scones from Fancy Pantry. I hope you like them. I chose my favorite flavors, chocolate chip and orange cranberry."

I peek inside the box. "These look divine. You're a good man, Maurice. Just like Will said."

Maurice beams. "Oh! I almost forgot. This is for you." He tugs a cell phone free of his back pocket. "It's prepaid. I stored both mine and Will's numbers in there in case you need to reach us."

I take the phone from him. "Thank you. Knowing I have contact with the outside world gives me peace of mind. Speaking of which, I noticed a desktop computer in the downstairs sitting room across from the bedroom where we're sleeping. Would it be okay if I used it?"

Maurice runs a hand across his cropped gray hair. "I don't see why not. Mr. Matheson had me set up all the computers in the house. There are three of them, brand new straight out of the box. One for each of his daughters and one for his study upstairs. I doubt anyone has even used them yet. If you like, I can make sure it's still connected to the Internet before I go."

I bob my head. "That would be great." If I can get online, I can access the Dropbox folder with my novel documents. I have much to write about, both good and bad. And since I'm sequestered here, I might as well work.

A few minutes later, Maurice pronounces the Internet online and computer in working order. After seeing him out, I set a pot of coffee on to brew while I put away the groceries. The kitchen is the hub of the house, adjacent to both living and dining rooms. While I can see out in every direction, from Catawba Sound to the ocean, the kitchen is set far enough back from the window for anyone to see me. Last night's rain has ended, leaving behind low-hanging gray clouds. A cozy day to stay inside.

I place a plate of scones, my mug of coffee, and a cup of juice for Conrad on a bamboo tray and deliver it to our sitting room. When I call for Conrad, he comes running.

"This house is so cool, Mommy! Can we live here forever?"

I chuckle. "I wish." As much as I love this house, I'm eager to put our problems behind us and return to our cottage.

"Are you hungry?" I gesture at the tray. "Mister Will's friend brought us some breakfast."

Conrad drops to his knees beside the coffee table and grabs a chocolate chip scone off the plate.

As I watch him eat, I think about how close I came to placing him in foster care yesterday. Pain rips across my chest. He's my child. I gave birth to him. I'm responsible for protecting him and providing for him. I remember Will's comment about combining our resources. There is one resource I haven't yet tapped.

I move over to the computer and jiggle the mouse. I don't have to search hard to find Delilah Hart on social media. She has profiles on several platforms, but Twitter, now known as X, seems to be her preferred method of communicating with her million followers.

After yesterday's drama, Conrad is content to play with his cars on the patterned rug while I work. I spend hours scrolling through Delilah's feed, reading her posts and watching her videos. An authority on The Six, she provides in-depth reporting on their involvement in countless crimes. I had no idea of the extent of the corruption. They have a hand in practically everything currently wrong with this country.

I finally muster the courage to direct message Delilah, introducing myself as Eleanor Hudson's friend and asking to speak with her as soon as possible. She responds within minutes, requesting a video call and providing a Zoom link. I click on the link and Delilah appears. She's as pretty as her profile picture with shoulder-length honey-colored hair and bright green eyes. I estimate her to be in her midthirties, although she wears the air of someone much older.

"Nice to meet you, Julia. Eleanor said I might be hearing from you. I was getting worried something might have happened to you."

I rake my fingers through my matted hair. I must look like a mess. I rolled out of bed and threw on some clothes. I haven't showered since yesterday morning. "Honestly, I've been hesitant to reach out. I'm not sure how you can help me."

"I have many influential contacts, Julia. I've used those connections to help lots of people in your position."

"I have nothing to offer in return. I can't identify any members of The Six."

Delilah barks out a laugh, a harsh sound coming from such an attractive woman. "I'm not sure anyone can identify The Six. I certainly can't, and I've been investigating them for over a decade. There are two men I'm fairly certain about, but so far, we haven't come up with the evidence to bring charges against them."

I wonder who she means by *we*, but I don't ask. "My house was ransacked last night, but The Six may not be responsible. I'm involved in this other situation."

I blabber on about my relationship with Will, his wife's accident, and Rourke blackmailing me. When I finish talking, I apologize. "I don't know why I told you all that. It has nothing to do with The Six."

"I'm an investigative journalist, Julia. I report on all types of cases, not just The Six. Although this is complicated. I need to give it some thought." Delilah massages her chin. "What is it you want, Julia? A future with Will? Or are you hoping to start over somewhere new? Somewhere safe?"

"I'm tired of living in fear, Delilah. I want my life back. I want the chance to find out if I even have a future with Will."

"Then let's get it for you." She tugs an ink pen from the messy bun atop her head. "Do you know Will's in-laws' names?"

"Clarence and Loretta Beaumont."

Delilah goes rigid as the color drains from her face. "I don't believe this."

I sit up straight, moving to the edge of my seat. "Believe what?"

"Clarence Beaumont is one of the two I suspect of being members of The Six."

THIRTY-EIGHT
WILL

I anxiously await Maurice's return from his trip to Sandy Island. When he appears in my office doorway, I jump up from my chair and come from behind my desk. Pulling him into my office, I close the door. "Well? How is she? Is she safe?"

"She's great, boss. A real lovely lady."

I let out a sigh of relief. "Did you give her the phone?"

"Yes! With all our contact information stored in it. I also made sure the Internet is working. I can vouch for the computers being clean. I installed them myself. She's hunkered down for the day. I can think of worse places to hide out."

"Me too." I squeeze his shoulder. "Thank you, Maurice. Keep your phone close today in case I need you to go back out there."

"You've got it, boss."

I wait for Maurice to exit my office before sending a text to Carter. *We need to talk. Can you meet me in Waterfront Park in twenty minutes?*

He responds right away. *Of course.*

I'm gonna grab a coffee. Can I get something for you? I ask and chuckle at the frou-frou drink he requests.

After stopping in at Corner Coffee for our drinks, I head over to the waterfront and sit down on a park bench overlooking Catawba Sound. When Carter arrives a few minutes later, I hand him his drink.

"Here's your soy vanilla Frappuccino with caramel drizzle. Sounds more like an after-dinner drink than coffee."

He takes a sip. "Ahh. But it's so delicious. I don't splurge on them often." He takes longer sip. "Are you ready to tell me about last night?"

"Yes. But this discussion doesn't leave this park bench." Carter listens with a pinched expression as I tell him about Julia's house getting ransacked. "We need to find a way to protect her. How much does Marlowe know about The Six?"

"About as much as anyone. Which isn't much."

"Do you think he can help us?" I ask in a tone of desperation.

"I'm not sure. I spoke with him for a long time last night. He's hit a roadblock on your case. While Marlowe is certain your father-in-law's business dealings are far more nefarious than we imagined, he's been unable to get evidence to use against him."

"I don't understand. Marlowe is the best."

"Apparently, Beaumont has a private security army protecting him."

My pulse quickens. "That's impossible. I was married to Tracy for ten years. I never saw any bodyguards."

"Because Beaumont prides himself on being a law-abiding, upstanding citizen. He's the president of Beaumont Brick Company, a multigenerational family business. Surrounding himself with bodyguards would pose too many questions."

"I guess you're right." Getting to my feet, I walk in small circles to loosen my muscles. "Tracy often talked about how strict her parents were. Maybe they feared for her safety. Which makes me wonder why they want custody of my children."

"To a man like Beaumont, children and grandchildren are possessions. Trophies for them to display to all their wealthy friends. They also make excellent cover-ups for his underhanded dealings."

"That's a good point," I say. "And explains a lot about Tracy's relationship with her parents."

"We don't have the resources to take down a cartel. Our best bet would be to get Rourke to back off. Then we could get Julia and the kid safely out of town and help them start a new life somewhere else."

"I don't want Julia to start a new life somewhere else. I want her to continue the life she started here."

Carter's eyes narrow. "Speaking of the devil. There's Rourke."

I turn to see a black sedan parking nearby in the waterfront's community lot. Rourke is getting out of the car and heading our way when my cell rings with a call from Julia's prepaid phone. I accept the call. "Are you okay?"

"I'm fine," she says in a lowered voice. "But you won't believe what I just found out."

"Whatever it is will have to wait. I'm at the waterfront with one of my investigators. Rourke has just arrived, and he's headed our way. I'll call you back in a minute." I end the call and stuff the phone in my pocket.

Rourke marches up to me. "Where's Julia?"

I yearn to strangle him with my bare hands, but I force myself to remain calm. I don't need any more trouble. "How would I know? You're the one who's been following her. Did you lose her?"

"This is serious, you jackass. I'm surprised you're not more concerned about your missing girlfriend."

I get up close to Rourke's face. "You don't care about Julia's well-being. You're worried about her because she's your witness. Without her you have no case against me."

The skin stretches taut across Rourke's face, and I worry he might burst some blood vessels. "I know you were at her cottage last night. What time did you last see her?"

"Hmm." I stare up at the gray sky. "Around seven thirty, I guess. When I left, she was cleaning up the mess you made. Or was it the cartel who ransacked her house? Maybe the cartel came back and kidnapped her."

Rourke stares down his nose at me. "How do I know you're not hiding her somewhere?"

"You don't. But I'm not." Tormenting him is so much more fulfilling than fighting him. "I enjoy Julia's company. But I'm not in love with her. Despite the lies you and Striker have been spreading, I didn't meet Julia until after Labor Day."

"Maybe you murdered her, like you murdered your wife, to prevent her from testifying against you."

I cross my arms over my chest. "She was never going to testify against me. She's too principled to lie under oath." I jab a finger at his chest. "If anything happens to her, Rourke, it's all your fault. You put an innocent woman in harm's way."

Rourke's left eye twitches. I'm getting under his skin. "You haven't heard the last from me, Darby," he says and storms off.

Carter waits until he's out of earshot to burst out laughing. "You get a gold medal for that performance, Will. Poor man doesn't know what to think."

"Good. I hope he's sufficiently confused," I say as I click on Julia's number and bring the phone to my ear.

She answers right away. "What did Rourke want?"

"He's looking for you. But he won't find you. Sorry I had to hang up. What were you going to tell me?"

"You're not going to believe this, Will. My friend at WITSEC gave me the name of an independent investigative journalist who has done extensive research on The Six. I reached out to her through social media. To make a long story short, we put two and two together, and she's pretty sure your father-in-law is a member of The Six."

My jaw hits the ground. "No way."

"It makes perfect sense, Will. Remember, I told you about my visit from Beaumont's attorney, Landon Whitfield. He knew every-thing about me, and he threatened to turn me over to The Six. I didn't realize it at the time, but he said it like he knows The Six personally."

"Hang on a second while I tell Carter." Lowering the phone to my chest, I repeat what Julia said.

Carter's blue eyes bug out. "Put her on speaker."

We sit down together on the bench, and I click the speaker button on my phone. "Julia, meet Carter."

Carter says, "Hello, Julia. Your journalist has made an inter-esting accusation. Who is he? Is he reputable?"

"You tell me. *Her* name is Delilah Hart."

Carter falls back against the bench. "Whoa. I know her work well. Of all people, Delilah would know. Can you give me her number?"

"Yes! I'll text it to you. She's waiting to hear from you. Or someone. She has a thick file on Clarence Beaumont she's eager to share. Please keep me in the loop."

When we get Delilah on the phone, she informs us she's on the way to Water's Edge from Tennessee. "I should be there around six o'clock."

"We'll meet at Marsh Point," I say. "I'll text you the address."

Marlowe lets out a loud whoop when he hears the news. "Finally! This is the break in the case we've been waiting for. If I leave now, I should make it by six."

I SEND Ashton and the girls to town for dinner, and I have Mia's casserole warming in the oven when my guests arrive promptly at six. Delilah is a beautiful woman with sparkling green eyes that seem to look everywhere at once, as though afraid she'll miss some-thing. Over cocktails on the veranda, she fills us in on all she knows about my father-in-law.

Marlowe admits, "I knew Beaumont was involved in some heavy-duty criminal activities. But it never crossed my mind he might be one of The Six."

"Do you think Beaumont knew Julia's identity from the start?" I ask, taking a long pull off my beer bottle.

Marlowe nods. "I'm certain of it. He pays his people a fortune to find out everything about everyone. And Julia played nicely into his scheme."

Carter adds, "When she refused to perjure herself, he sent his attorney to offer her a deal, a new life in exchange for her testimony against him. When that didn't work, he sent the cartel to scare her."

We move inside to the dining room where we discuss our options for dealing with Beaumont over spaghetti casserole, Caesar salad, and homemade yeast rolls.

"We need to hit Beaumont in his weak spot," Marlowe says, sloshing red wine around his glass.

Delilah looks up from forking her salad. "What weak spot? I wasn't aware he had one."

Marlowe raises his glass to her. "Everyone has a weak spot, Delilah. And Max Rourke is Clarence Beaumont's."

Delilah sets down her fork and wipes her mouth. "Please explain."

"Beaumont likes to hire people who are down on their luck. He offers them a chance in life, which makes them forever indebted to him. Rourke was addicted to heroin and facing prison time for drug-related charges. Beaumont sent him to rehab and set him on his way to becoming a police officer."

"A pretty smart system when you think about it," Marlowe says and sips his wine.

"So how do you suggest we go after Rourke?" I ask, twirling spaghetti noodles around my fork.

The table listens with rapt attention as Marlowe outlines his plan. I'm against it at first, as his scheme places Julia in danger. But with further discussion, I realize it's the only way.

As the red wine flows, the conversation turns to more pleasant topics. Delilah, in her southern drawl with her dry sense of humor, charms us with escapades from her illustrious career. Marlowe appears quite taken with her, and more than once she flashes him a dazzling smile. Neither have ever been married. These two would make an impressive match—the detective and the investigative journalist.

Over apple crumble and coffee, we return our attention to the situation at hand.

"Time is of the essence," Marlowe says. "We need to speak with Julia as soon as possible. Since meeting with her in person isn't an option, we should set up a video conference."

"No time like the present," Carter says. "I have a clean laptop with me."

Marlowe looks over at me. "Text her, please. See if she's available."

"Sure." I thumb off the text, informing her of the Zoom call and warning her not to agree to their scheme if she has any reservations.

THIRTY-NINE
JULIA

Four sets of eyes stare out at me from the desktop computer. Their gazes are intense. They are committed to helping me. But when they lay out their plan, my gut turns to stone, and rivulets of sweat trail down my back.

"What about my son? I won't put Conrad's life in danger."

"I'm going to ask Ashton and Sully to take all three kids to Charleston for the weekend. They can stay in Sully's apartment," Will says.

"What if they're not available?" I ask.

"I'll think of something else. But you have my word, Conrad will be out of harm's way." Will's genuine smile offers the reassurance I need.

"How will you lure Rourke here?"

"That part's easy," Marlowe says. "Rourke has given explicit instructions that he is to be notified *if* and *when* you resurface. Delilah, pretending to be a concerned neighbor, will notify the police of suspicious activity at the Mathesons' house, a possible intruder who matches your description."

I consider this strategy. "That could work. I wasn't aware you can use evidence obtained via a wire in court."

"If we get a judge to issue a warrant, we can," Marlowe says. "I've been texting with Jimmy Riley, the detective who lost his promotion to Rourke. He's eager to get involved in the case. He's also willing to recruit some officers as backup while the operation is going down."

The hair on the back of my neck bristles. "Operation? As in a sting operation? This all sounds too risky for me."

Marlowe lets out a sigh. "I won't lie to you, Julia. It *is* risky. But you won't be alone. I'll be hidden inside the house within earshot. If anything goes wrong, I'll intervene."

My throat tightens. "But what if I freak out and give myself away?"

Delilah chimes in, "We'll draft a script, and I'll coach you. We'll keep it simple, so you won't mess up."

"Take some time to think about it," Marlowe says. "But not too long. The clock is ticking."

Will winks at me. "Hang in there. I'll call you back after everyone leaves, and we'll talk some more," he says, and the foursome vanishes from the computer screen.

I pace a hole in the hardwood and chew two fingernails down to the quick while I wait for Will to call me back. When my phone finally rings at almost ten o'clock, I snatch it up and accept the call.

"What do you think, Will? Should I do this? It seems so dangerous."

"I can't answer that. This has to be your decision. *If* you decide to go through with it, Ashton has agreed to take the kids to Charleston. I had a long talk with her just now. That's why it took me so long to call you back. She and Sully want to help. Carter and a team of his best investigators will provide protection for them for the entire weekend, from the moment they leave Water's Edge."

"That makes me feel a little better, I guess."

"I've been racking my brain, Julia. I can't think of another way."

"There's always another way, Will. I feel like everyone is relying on me. I hope I don't let them down. But it's worth a try. Tell Marlowe I'm in."

His sigh of relief is audible. "You're gonna do great. We won't let anything happen to you."

"You can't guarantee that. But if something *does* happen to me, can I count on you to take Conrad to my parents in Texas?"

"You have my word. I will personally hand deliver him to them." He fingers an *x* over his heart before signing off the call.

Too keyed up to sleep, I access my novel document and pore my heart out to my characters until the wee hours. I fall asleep with my head on the desk. I'm still there when Conrad wakes me at seven thirty Thursday morning.

I spend the morning with my son playing games, working on puzzles, and reading books. My heart aches, thinking I may never see him again. But the idea of him growing up without either parent gives me determination to proceed with my mission.

For lunch, I heat up the homemade Brunswick stew Maurice brought. After we finish eating, I turn on a movie for Conrad and sit down at the computer for my scheduled video call with Delilah. We discuss my talking points and devise a script for my confrontation with Rourke.

While Conrad naps on the sofa, I pack his clothes for his trip to Charleston. I list the contact information for my family members on a sheet of computer paper, seal it in an envelope, and hide it in the side-zippered pouch of his suitcase.

Around three o'clock, Will texts me the schedule of events for the afternoon. Ashton will pick Conrad up at five. An hour later, Marlowe will arrive with Detective Riley, who will position his team of officers at strategic locations around the property. Once the wire is in place, Delilah will call the police and report the sighting of an intruder on the Matheson property. How long it takes Rourke to respond is anyone's guess. Could be minutes. Could take hours.

When Conrad wakes from his nap, he's overjoyed to learn of

his weekend trip to Charleston. Keeping him calm until Ashton arrives is a challenge. I choke back tears as I bid him goodbye.

"Have a wonderful time and mind your manners. Who knows? Maybe by the time you get home on Sunday, I'll have moved back to the cottage."

His face lights up. "Really?"

I hold up my hands, showing fingers crossed.

Tears stream down my face as they drive away in Ashton's convertible. Swiping at my tears, I draw in a deep breath and head back inside to await my fate. I can't screw this up. Too much depends on it.

Marlowe shows up promptly at six. I don't spot any members of his army, but I sense their presence. He hands me a nondescript black leather belt. "You'll need to wear this. Your listening device is concealed inside."

Taking the belt from him, I slide it through the loops in my jeans.

"One more piece." He shows me a tiny clear object. "I'll place this inside your ear canal so we can communicate with you."

Once everything is in place, he tests the equipment to make certain it's working.

"Are you ready?" he asks, and I bob my head, too afraid to speak.

"Delilah, you may place the call to 9-1-1 now," Marlowe says into his Bluetooth headset. "And the countdown begins."

"What do I do while we wait?" I ask.

"You need to be visible from the outside but not standing in front of the windows. Putz around in the kitchen. Make tea. Pretend to be working on dinner. Riley is positioned near the driveway. He will notify me when Rourke arrives, and I will let you know."

"What if police officers come instead of Rourke?"

"That's highly unlikely, but I will handle it if they do." Marlowe gives my shoulder a squeeze. "You've got this, Julia.

Remember you're in hiding. When Rourke does arrive, don't rush to the door. Pretend to be afraid."

"Trust me, I won't be pretending." I hold my chin high, portraying confidence I don't feel.

Marlow gestures at the adjacent hallway. "I'll be right down the hall in the laundry room. I can hear everything you say. If you get into trouble, I will come to your rescue." He gives my shoulder another squeeze before disappearing down the hall.

I turn on the Keurig to heat while I search the kitchen for tea bags. When I don't find any, I brew a cup of decaf coffee instead. Some fifteen minutes later, I'm heating up the remainder of the Brunswick stew when Marlowe says in my ear, "Showtime! Rourke is pulling into the driveway now."

Listening carefully, I hear the sound of his engine followed by his footfalls on the stone steps outside. The doorbell rings, the knocker clangs, and Rourke barks, "Open up, Julia! I know you're in there."

I close my eyes and grip the counter, willing myself to wait.

He pounds loudly on the door. "I'm not joking, Julia. I know you're here. I'll break this door down if I have to."

Crossing the living room, I crack open the door and peek out at him. "Go away. Whatever you're selling, I don't want any."

He forces the door open and brushes past me into the house. "You're a difficult woman to track down."

I close the door behind him. "By design, Detective. I've been in hiding since someone ransacked my house on Tuesday."

He feigns surprise. "Who would do such a thing?"

I glare at him. "We both know who."

Rourke spreads his arms wide. "Pretty swanky hideout you've got here. I don't imagine the owners will be too keen to learn they have a squatter in their new billion-dollar home."

"I have permission to be here, thank you very much."

He narrows his beady black eyes. "Oh really. Who granted this permission?"

"None of your business." Despite my racing heart, I manage to appear bored. "What do you want, Detective?"

"To make a deal. We both know you're in over your head with The Six. But I can guarantee your safety in exchange for your testimony against Will Darby."

"And how do you plan on keeping me safe?" I ask in a sarcastic tone.

"The usual way," he says. "New identity. Fresh start in a location of your choice."

"Who's making this deal? Surely you don't expect me to believe you have the resources to make me disappear."

"I have more clout than you think."

"Right. I forgot. You have The Six on speed dial."

A wounded expression crosses his face. "You don't believe me?"

I shake my head. "Not hardly."

"Your boyfriend's father-in-law is making the deal. He's a member of The Six."

I roll my eyes. "And I'm the Easter Bunny."

"I'm being serious, Julia. Clarence Beaumont is a member of The Six."

I drop my smile. "Then I'm definitely not taking the deal. As soon as he helps me find this fresh start, he'll exterminate me."

"No, he won't. You have his word."

"There's no way I'm trusting *you* with my life. Let alone my son's life. I'll need to hear that word from your boss."

Rourke hesitates.

I chuckle. "Just as I suspected. You're bluffing. Furthering your career is the only thing on your agenda. You want bragging rights for solving Tracy Darby's murder case. Even though she wasn't murdered. Her death was a tragic accident."

"You're a dead woman if you turn down this deal."

"I'll take the deal if you can prove it's legit."

"Fine." Rourke taps on his phone and presses it to his ear.

I'm standing close enough to hear Beaumont's disgruntled voice. "What do you want, Rourke? I told you never to call me on this line."

"I realize that, sir, but this is an emergency. Julia Becker needs your reassurance that your people will not harm her once she's established her new life. She's standing right here. Will you speak with her?"

Beaumont lets out a low rumbling groan. "You idiot! She's wearing a wire."

Rourke's face goes deathly pale. "I'll call you back," he says to Beaumont and ends the call.

I shoot Rourke with my finger gun. "Gotcha."

Rourke's face turns beet red. "Why you little bitch!" He comes after me, clawing at my clothes. "Where's the device?" He wrestles me to the ground and straddles me. His hands are all over my body. Buttons fly as he tears open my shirt. He's tugging at my jeans when Marlowe appears in my line of sight.

With pistol aimed at Rourke's head, Marlowe yells, "Freeze! Get off her, you punk." With his left hand, Marlowe hauls Rourke to his feet and shoves him face-first against the wall. "You're under arrest."

I'm scrambling to my feet when the front door bangs open, and the room fills with officers.

A female officer shields me from the others while I pull my blouse tight around me. "Are you okay? Do you need medical attention?"

"No. I'm fine. I just need a minute." Over her shoulder, I spot Cody Porter, the baby-faced officer who accompanied Rourke the two times he interrogated me. When Cody winks at me, I pretend not to see him. I want to believe he's one of the good guys. But the list of people I currently trust is short.

As soon as Marlowe turns his new prisoner over to Riley who handcuffs Rourke, he comes to check on me. "Excellent job. You deserve an Academy Award for that performance. Did he hurt you?"

"No. But I'm glad you came when you did."

Feeling weak-kneed and overcome with relief, I'm grateful when Will shows up.

Engulfing me in a hug, he says, "You did it, Julia. You were brilliant."

I rest my head against his chest. "I'm just glad it's over. What happens now? Can I go home?"

Marlowe shakes his head. "Not yet. There may be fallout. The next couple of days will be crucial."

"Will Beaumont be arrested?" I ask.

"I certainly hope so," Marlowe says. "Although maybe not until tomorrow. We're working with law enforcement in Savannah. They'll keep us informed as events happen."

"Delilah just left town," Will says. "She's headed down there now. After working on this case for over a decade, she wants to be present for the action." He kisses the top of my head. "She said to tell you, bravo, Julia. You did an excellent job."

Marlow pats my back. "You certainly did. You have nothing to worry about. The hard part is over. I'll make certain you have round-the-clock security until we're sure you're out of danger."

Will tightens his arms around me. "Can she stay with me at Marsh Point?"

Marlowe's face softens. "I don't see why not."

My eyes well with tears, and I bury my face in Will's shirt, so the others don't see me cry. It's over. I'll soon be getting back my freedom.

FORTY
WILL

I straighten up the sitting room while I wait for Julia to gather her belongings. I fold blankets, brush crumbs off the coffee table, and raise the blackout shades. When I jiggle the computer's mouse, the screen lights up and a Word document appears. Upon closer inspection, I realize the document is a chapter from the novel Julia is working on.

When I hear the shower turn on across the hall, I sit down at the computer and begin to read. I'm immediately engrossed in a love scene. I'm pretty sure the couple isn't married. I can't tell how long they've been together, but it appears they are breaking up. I'm not an avid reader, but I know enough about fiction to assess Julia's writing. Her words flow smoothly, the dialogue is realistic, and the plot holds me captive. Something about Anna's heartfelt sentiments as she expresses her undying love to Jason touches me deeply. Is it because the emotions feel so familiar?

Julia clears her throat from the doorway, bringing me to my feet. "I'm sorry. I was being nosy. But I couldn't help myself. You're very talented." I point at the computer. "Are you writing about us?"

Dropping her backpack on the floor, Julia enters the room,

closes the document, and powers off the computer. "I admit our relationship has provided inspiration for these particular characters." She turns to face me. "Are you upset?"

Julia's creamy skin glows, and her hair is still damp from the shower. I want to take her in my arms and have my way with her right there on the sitting room floor. "Upset? No way. I'm enormously flattered. Do you feel about me the way Anna feels about Jason?"

"After what happened here today, I'm not in the mood to play games. Yes, Will, I'm crazy about you. I was devastated when we broke up. We've only known each other for a few weeks, but it feels like a lifetime. I'm throwing caution to the wind by saying I'm falling in love with you. I'll survive if you don't feel the same way. But please don't lie to me."

"Oh, I feel it all right." I pull her into my arms. "I fell in love with you the first time we met. I think it's soon for both of us. But that doesn't deter me." I kiss her lightly on the lips. "With Ashton and the kids in Charleston, we'll have the Marsh Point house to ourselves. Would you be okay with me seducing you later?"

The yellow flecks in her brown eyes are aglow as she looks up at me. "Provided you meet my requirements. A moonlit view of the sound, a bottle of red wine, and romantic music."

"Done. Let's go. Our security detail awaits."

AFTER A NIGHT OF INTENSE LOVEMAKING, Julia and I sleep until nine o'clock on Friday morning. We're standing at the stove together—both of us wearing my boxers and undershirts, as she scrambles eggs and I fry bacon—when Marlowe stops by with updates.

"You two look refreshed. You're practically glowing," he says with a mischievous glint in his eye.

Julia and I exchange a look. We know what he's thinking, but we don't care.

I glance back at Marlowe. His clothes are rumpled, and dark circles rim his eyes. "I wish I could say the same about you. Did you get any sleep?"

"Not a wink. The station is in chaos."

I fork bacon out of the pan onto paper towel to drain. "Can I offer you some breakfast?"

Marlowe shakes his head. "Thanks. I already ate." He eyes the Keurig. "I'd love some coffee though."

"Help yourself. There's an assortment of pods and some mugs in the upper cabinet."

Once his coffee has brewed, Marlowe sits down opposite Julia and me at the breakfast table. "There's so much to tell you, I'm not sure where to start."

"Start with Beaumont," I say shoveling a forkful of eggs into my mouth.

"He was arrested overnight, and he's singing like a canary. His wife too. Apparently, she was heavily involved in his business dealings."

"Humph. That doesn't surprise me. She's an old battle-ax."

Marlowe chuckles. "According to Delilah's source, Beaumont is whining about being too old to go to prison. He's expected to turn state's witness against his cohorts in The Six in exchange for a plea deal. That could happen at any minute."

"What about Rourke?" Julia asks as she crunches on a slice of bacon.

"There will be no plea deal for him. Thanks to you, the prosecutor has a rock-solid case against him. He's taking others down with him. Chief Dorsey has been relieved of his duties. One of our senior officers, Wayne Romero, will take over as chief until a replacement can be found."

"What about the dirty cops you mentioned?" I ask.

"Those two have also been fired," Marlowe says. "The two who arrested you for the Striker incident."

"Chrome Dome and Four Eyes. Good riddance. I'm surprised there weren't more."

Marlowe lifts a shoulder. "Only takes a few to rot the core of an organization."

"What about Rourke's sidekick, Cody Porter? What side of the fence was he on?" Julia asks.

A warm smile spreads across Marlowe's lips at the mention of the young officer. "Cody is definitely one of the good guys. He's been my informant these past few weeks."

I nod. "He was kind to me when I was in jail. What about you, Brice? Did they offer you your job back?"

"They did. But I'm not sure I'm going to take it. When I leave here, I'm headed to Savannah to meet up with Delilah. I may try my hand at investigative journalism for a change."

I offer him a high five across the table. "Good for you!"

Julia grins. "I thought I sensed some chemistry between you and Delilah."

Marlowe blushes. "We'll see. Truth be told, I've been itching for a change for some time. Jimmy Riley has certainly proven his worth. He deserves the promotion."

Julia pushes her empty plate away and sits back in her seat. "Does this mean I can finally return to my cottage?"

Marlowe gets up from the table and rinses his mug in the sink. "I would feel better if you remained here with your security detail through the weekend. Until Beaumont makes his next move and the rest of The Six are apprehended."

Disappointment crosses Julia's face. "Can I at least get some more clothes and begin the process of restoring order to my cottage? My landlord has a habit of showing up unannounced. If he sees the mess, he's liable to evict me."

Placing his mug in the dishwasher, Marlowe turns back to face us. "You're free to go wherever you'd like, Julia. I just ask that you communicate with your security team."

Julia visibly relaxes. "I can do that."

"Okay, then. I'll leave you two lovebirds to do your thing." Marlowe heads for the door. "I'll be in touch as soon as I know more."

I wait for him to leave before pulling Julia close to me on the banquette. "Looks like you're stuck with me for the weekend. We can spend two glorious days in bed together." I try to kiss her, but she pushes me away. "Not until I get some clean clothes."

I nuzzle her neck. "Fine. I'll go with you. We'll whip the cottage back into shape in no time. And since Conrad's gone, we can christen your bed."

Julia gestures at my phone on the table. "Speaking of my son, let's call Ashton to check on the kids."

"Good idea!" I say and call Ashton on speaker. When she answers, we can hear our kids squealing in the background. "What on earth is going on? Are you torturing the children?"

Ashton chuckles. "Sully's playing pirate with them."

Julia gives me a curious look. "How do you play pirate?"

"Don't ask. Hang on a second. Let me get away from the commotion." The squealing fades as Ashton goes into another room. "What's going on? Beaumont's arrest made national news, but they haven't said a word about you and Julia."

For the next few minutes, Julia and I recount last night's events and pass on the updates Marlowe just shared.

"We're waiting to hear more about the other members of The Six," I say.

Julia leans closer to the phone. "Marlowe wants us to keep the security detail through the weekend. I don't want to impose, but are you okay with keeping the kids in Charleston until Sunday?"

"No imposition at all," Ashton says in a cheerful voice that sets Julia at ease. "Those three are having so much fun, they'd be crushed if I told them we had to cut our trip short."

"Thank you so much, Ashton. I feel better knowing Conrad is safe with you."

"You're more than welcome, Julia. You two have fun. And don't worry about a thing."

"Bye, sis," I say, and end the call.

I'm scrolling through emails on my phone when Julia gets up to turn on the television. "I'm curious about what they're saying on the news."

Ellie's face fills the screen. "I always knew Will Darby was innocent. As much as he loved his wife, he would never have cheated on her."

Julia stares dumbfounded at the screen. "Can you believe her? What a two-faced liar."

I burst out laughing. "She's an opportunist. I'm just glad she's out of our lives for good."

Julia powers off the television. "That's enough news for one day. Let's get dressed and go to my cottage."

FORTY-ONE
JULIA

We spend much of the day at the cottage. After giving all the rooms a thorough cleaning, we take a long walk on the beach, eat a picnic lunch on the porch, and have crazy sex in my bed. My love for this man continues to grow, surpassing anything I've ever imagined one person could feel about another.

When we return to Marsh Point around four o'clock, Ethan Striker is waiting for us on the front stoop. I fully expect Will to lose his temper.

"I'll have the security team deal with him." Will rolls down the window and motions for the patrol car behind us to pull up alongside us. "Do you mind getting rid of that reporter?" he says to Officer Johnson in the passenger seat. "We're not in the mood for company."

Officer Johnson salutes him. "Yes, sir. I'm on it."

The patrol car continues up to the house, and Johnson gets out to speak with Striker.

Will notices me staring at him. "What? Did I do something wrong?"

I reach for his hand. "Not at all. I'm proud of you for not losing your temper."

"I haven't lost it *yet*," he says, returning his attention to the front porch.

After a brief word with Striker, Officer Johnson pats him down and walks back towards us.

"Striker would like a word with you both. He wants to apologize for the way he treated you. I searched him. He's unarmed. My guess is he's harmless. I can make him leave if you prefer."

Will looks over at me and I shrug. "I guess it won't hurt to hear him out."

We get out of my truck and tentatively approach the front porch.

"I owe you both an apology," Striker says. "My behavior is unforgivable. Rourke offered me a large amount of money to report his lies. I didn't care whether you were innocent. My greed got the best of me. I crossed several ethical boundaries, and I may lose my job for it. But I'd like to make it up to you."

"Do you have any idea the damage you've caused?" Will says with feet apart and arms folded over his chest.

"I do." Striker turns his attention to me. "I put your life in danger. And I'm so sorry for that. I'd like to hear your story. Our entire community *needs* to hear your story."

Will's face reddens. "I figured you had an ulterior motive. If I weren't learning to control my anger, I'd punch you in the nose. Again."

My hand shoots out to Will. "Hold on a second, Will. I want to hear him out. Why do you think anyone cares about my story?"

"I painted an unsavory image of you. Because of me, everyone in this town thinks you're a marriage wrecker. They should hear how you sacrificed your safety to protect Will. If you agree, we'll have a sit-down interview and a one-on-one conversation. I'll let you take the lead. I have a camera crew on standby. They can be here in a matter of minutes."

I'm torn. Part of me wants Will to kick him off his property, but the other part very much wants to clear the air. If Water's Edge is going to be my home, I want its citizens to know the truth about me. Especially now that I no longer have anything to hide.

"I'll do it."

Will narrows his eyes. "Are you sure?"

I nod. "Positive. As long as I can edit out anything I don't like."

Striker grins. "Done. I'd like to do the interview here. The late afternoon lighting is perfect." He looks at Will. "You can choose the location."

Will expels a reluctant sigh. "The veranda would probably be best. I'll show you, and you can decide."

"I need to freshen up. I'll be back down in a minute." I grab my overnight bag out of the car and hurry inside. I change into jeans and a fresh white blouse and smear on a little makeup. When I return to the veranda, two chairs are set up in front of a waiting camera crew.

Ethan and I sit down together, the camera rolls, and I start talking, the words flowing smoothly. Ethan says little during the interview except to prompt me when I get sidetracked. I tell my story from the beginning, from the time I realized my husband was a criminal to Rourke forcing me to testify against Will.

I look straight into the camera. "I'd like to set the record straight once and for all. I didn't meet Will Darby until after Labor Day. I did not know him at the time of his wife's accident. Her tragic death was a devastating loss for him. We were two lost souls who developed an unlikely friendship. Will is a good man, and I have always believed in his innocence. And you should too."

The cameraman says, "Cut! That's a wrap."

Ethan jumps up and pulls me to my feet. "That was lovely, Julia. Very compelling. If we hurry, we can lead with it on the six o'clock news. But I won't have time to send it to you for approval. We could wait until tomorrow night, but with tonight being Friday, we'll have a better audience. You have no reason to trust me, but I promise I won't let you down this time."

I look over at Will, who is rubbing his eyes. I can't tell. Is he crying? "What do you think?" I ask him.

"I say go with it. There's no way he can mess that up."

At five minutes before six, Will opens a bottle of red wine, and we sit down together on the sofa in the family room to watch the news.

Ethan leads the story with a heartfelt apology to the community. "I betrayed your trust, and I am truly sorry. This story has taught me many valuable lessons." Striker swipes at his wet eyes. "I had a chance to sit down with Julia Becker earlier today. I think you'll find her story as compelling as I did."

Pride bursts inside me as I watch the footage. In hindsight, it took a lot of courage for me to tell my story. Living under an assumed name made me feel guilty, like I was a criminal keeping a dirty secret. But it was my husband's dirty secret, not mine. I've done nothing wrong. I have nothing to be ashamed of. I needed to admit that to myself as much as to the world.

When the segment is over, Will takes my wine glass from me and sets it down on the coffee table. He places his hands on my face. "You're an amazing woman, Julia Becker or Casey Bishop. Your name matters not to me. I only care about what's inside. You have the most beautiful heart of anyone I've ever met. I don't know how it's possible when I've only known you a short time, but I love you with every fiber of my being."

"And I love you, Will Darby, with every fiber of my being."

FORTY-TWO

WILL AND JULIA

Conrad returns from Charleston a changed child. He's more carefree and less tense. I never realized how anxious he's been. Learning the boogeyman chapter of our lives is over and that we no longer have to live in fear has given him a more hopeful outlook for the future.

The first days of the following week pass in peaceful bliss. After dropping our children at school, Will and I spend our mornings in my bed, making love and getting to know each other better. On the days he doesn't have to rush off to work, we bundle up against the October chill and go for long strolls on the beach.

Twice during the week, Conrad invites a new friend to come home with him after school. Jamie is well-mannered and they are content to play in the sand at the edge of the yard while I work on the porch. On Thursday afternoon, I finish the last draft of my novel and send the manuscript off to my editor. The cover draft is stunning, although I haven't yet decided which name to use. I have a large following as Casey Bishop, but I'm not sure my cozy mystery readers will be interested in romantic suspense. Perhaps I'll use Julia Becker as my pen name and write in both genres going forward. Now that I no longer have to hide my identity, I have direct access to my royalties, and I can continue to promote my backlist.

As for real life, I've grown accustomed to my new name, and everyone in Water's Edge knows me as Julia Becker. Julia feels right to me. She's the young woman who took on a corrupt organization and won. Maybe one day soon, I'll trade Becker for Darby. Julia Darby has a nice ring to it, don't you think?

———

I'VE TAKEN over morning carpool duty from Mia. I enjoy listening to the girls chatter during the drive. I'm leaving school after dropping them off on Friday morning when my real estate agent calls with a full-price offer on my house.

Sadie pushes back when I tell her to accept the offer. "Are you sure about this Will? Are you ready to give up the memories of the life you spent there with Tracy?"

"I'm positive, Sadie. My memories of Tracy are in my heart. And I'm ready for a fresh start." My future is with Julia, and since she's become as one with the ocean, I wouldn't dare ask her to live inland. "I'm ready to get serious about finding something on Catawba Sound."

"Coincidentally, I'm working with a couple to put their home on the market. It's a fabulous property but needs a lot of work."

My hopes soar. "Sounds ideal. Tell me more."

"Brace yourself. The location might be a deal-breaker for you. It's the Sullivan's property on Pelican's way. How do you feel about living across the street from your sister?"

I smile to myself imagining how excited my girls would be to live in such close proximity to Marsh Point. "A year ago, I wouldn't have considered it. But now, I'd love nothing more than to live across from Ashton. Besides, I've always admired the Sullivan house. When can I see it?"

"The Sullivans are out of town for the weekend. I mentioned

you might be interested, and they've agreed to let me show it to you. As you know, they are older, and they'd prefer not to go through the turmoil of showing the house to dozens of people who aren't serious buyers. I'm in the area. Any chance you're available now?"

I glance down at the dashboard clock. Julia is expecting me. "Now is fine. Can I bring a friend?"

Sadie snickers. "Only if the friend is Julia Becker. I'm dying to meet our town's newest celebrity."

"Ha. You mean our town's *only* celebrity. I'll see you in a few."

I wait until I'm stopped at a red light to send Julia a text with the address. *Short notice. Sorry. I'm looking at a house and would love your opinion.*

She texts back right away. *Be there soon.*

I arrive at the property ahead of Julia, and Sadie suggests we wait inside out of the morning chill.

I knew the Sullivan kids growing up, and I visited the house many times as a child. I remember well the feeling of grandeur created by the curving staircase, wide center hallway, and vast rooms.

"It's stunning," I say to Sadie. "More impressive even than Marsh Point."

Sadie elbows me in the ribs. "I wouldn't go that far."

When Julia arrives, I make the introductions, and Sadie takes us on a tour. Other than updating the kitchen and baths, the house is in relatively good shape. The twelve-foot ceilings, detailed woodwork, and random-width oak floors captivate me. The waterfront location lends a casual air to a house that would otherwise be formal.

Upstairs in the primary bedroom, Sadie excuses herself to take a call. I throw open the French doors, and we step outside to the second-floor veranda. We mosey over to the railing and look out across the sound.

"What do you think?" I ask Julia.

She inhales a deep breath of salt air. "I think it's positively scrumptious. It's just what you've been looking for."

I turn to face her. "Can you see yourself living here? Because once the dust settles, I aim to make you my wife."

"I—"

I press my finger to her lips. "Let me finish. I'm a broken man, Julia. But I'm feeling stronger every day. I'm hopeful I will eventually beat my battle with anger. I may not be perfect, but I can offer you my whole heart."

"You're perfect for me, Will Darby. And I will love you with my whole heart as well. And yes, I can totally see myself living here. Are you ready to be a father to my son?"

"Are you kidding me? I'm crazy about Conrad, and I can hardly wait. Tracy always said I was meant to be a boy dad. What about you? Are you ready to be a mother to my girls?"

"I can hardly wait. I already love them like my own." Her soft words and delicate smile transform her into the most exquisite creature I've ever seen.

I take her in my arms. "Maybe one day, we'll have a son or daughter of our own."

———

I HOPE you've enjoyed *Echoes of the Past*. Are you ready for more from the Darby family? In the next installment, *Songbird's Second Chance*, Savannah Darby returns home to South Carolina to search for the child who was abducted from her thirty years ago.